John Harris was born in 1916. He authored the best-selling *The Sea Shall Not Have Them* and wrote under the pen names of Mark Hebden and Max Hennessy. He was a sailor, airman, journalist, travel courier, cartoonist and history teacher. During the Second World War he served with two air forces and two navies. After turning to full-time writing, Harris wrote adventure stories and created a sequence of crime novels around the quirky fictional character Chief Inspector Pel. A master of war and crime fiction, his enduring fictions are versatile and entertaining.

BY THE SAME AUTHOR
ALL PUBLISHED BY HOUSE OF STRATUS

JOHN HARRIS

SUNSET
AT SHEBA

HOUSE OF
STRATUS

This edition published in 2001 by House of Stratus, an imprint of
House of Stratus Ltd, Thirsk Industrial Park, York Road, Thirsk,
North Yorkshire, YO7 3BX, UK.
Also at: House of Stratus Inc., 2 Neptune Road, Poughkeepsie, NY 12601, USA.

www.houseofstratus.com

Typeset, printed and bound by House of Stratus.

A catalogue record for this book is available from the British Library
and the Library of Congress.

ISBN 0-7551-0224-X

Author's Note

When the Great War broke out in Europe on 4 August, 1914, the new Union of South Africa, formed out of the old defeated Boer Republics of the Orange Free State and the Transvaal, and the English colonies of Cape Province and Natal, found itself threatened in the West by the enemy colony of German South-West Africa.

To many of the Boer South Africans, many of them leaders of great distinction in the war of 1899-1902, this immediately seemed an opportunity to recoup their losses and regain a free and independent country. Men like Generals Beyers, De la Rey and Christian de Wet, leaders of great skill in the earlier war, were vigorous and still active, but thrust by defeat and the passing of years among their memories.

Like Napoleon and his marshals before the Hundred Days, they were still smarting under the not-far-distant collapse of their armies; and though many of them had tried to settle in peace, they had too recently been in arms against Britain and the transition in 1914 from the role of enemy to that of champion was too violent. Egged on by the young and the hotheads, they felt they could cleanse their hearts of the corroding bitterness.

De la Rey was very soon removed from the scene. Driving through Johannesburg on 15 September, with Beyers, his car was shot at in mistake for that of a gang of bank-robber-murderers, for whom, by sheer coincidence, the police had thrown a cordon round the city, and De la Rey was killed instantly.

Beyers and De Wet managed eventually to get the rebellion going in the Western Transvaal and the Northern Free State; and Jan Smuts and Botha, the Prime Minister of the Union, former Boer leaders who had remained loyal to the new state, were obliged to take the field against their old comrades.

This is not a story about De Wet or Beyers, or about Smuts or Botha. With the exception of an obvious few, the characters are all imaginary. The military units – apart from those of Botha and his commanders – are also imaginary.

It is a story about minor ficticious events after the beginning of the rebellion and before its collapse, which culminated in an incident that became known as the Battle at Sheba.

PART ONE

one

It began in Plummerton West, a thriving little town set in the wide hot plain in the south-western corner of the Transvaal, not far from the borders of the Orange Free State, an ugly little place which up to then had always been too busy with gold to bother about beauty.

In spite of the few imposing buildings which had sprung up, many of the streets were still, in 1914, unpaved and edged with board walks and not far behind busy Theophilus Street, the main thoroughfare, sparse faded grass still grew in front of most of the houses. For Plummerton West, less than thirty years before, had been nothing more than a sleepy supply depot for the farms of the scattered Boers who scratched a meagre living from the thin soil of the veld, a huddle of mud and stone buildings which overnight had become a jumping-off spot for the gold fields of the district.

But from the day the first bright stone had been kicked by accident through the grass, men had come in their hundreds – on foot and on mules, in carts and in coaches, even on bicycles and in hansom cabs, from Johannesburg and Kimberley and the Cape – Dutch Boers who'd abandoned their farms at the prospect of quick money, sugar planters from Natal, ex-officers from the Cape garrison who'd resigned their commissions in the hope of a fortune, Germans from the South-West, Portuguese from Delagoa Bay, Americans from the Rocky Mountains, French, Spanish, Dutch, Australians, Canadians and Englishmen. The sun-scorched veld round the tiny dorp had become crowded first with tents and wagons and then with flat-faced wooden buildings whose iron-roofed verandas stretched over the board walk.

The place had been called originally Madurodorp, after some dusty Boer farmer who had halted his wagon there on the way north, then in the hectic days of the gold find, when it had been populated by a flamboyant crowd of enthusiastic men, it had gloried briefly in the name of Shotgun Camp. In the 'nineties, when you could no longer drop a springbok just off the end of the main street, the bank had arrived, and an hotel or two had sprung up, and its name had been taken from that of Theophilus Plummer, the man who had done most to make it respectable, the man who had changed it from a camp to a town and given it some vestige of law and order; and just before the Boer War, when it had gloried in a brief but unsuccessful siege, it had begun for all time to be known by the prosaic and ugly name of Plummerton West.

The name was there on the front of the biggest hotel the place could boast, a brick and stone building with a new rococo Victorian façade – *Plummerton Hotel,* the first thing you saw. It seemed, in fact, to be on every alternate building in the town – *Plummer's Livery Stable, Plummer's Store,* the bank, the offices of the *Plummerton Building Company,* the imposing edifice of the *Plummerton and District Estate and Mining Corporation,* the newspaper, everything – for its owner had contrived to make a fortune for himself also in the building of the crude and ugly parody of a town that had spread, raucous and noisy, farther out into the veld than its original dusty founder ever dreamed about.

Now, in 1914, though the market-place had been paved and a branch line ran from the railway junction at Plummerton Sidings, its twin town to the south, the place had still not quite made the transition from brick and tin, and the ugly little dwellings of the last century were still there among the neo-Gothic edifices which the business houses were beginning to thrust up. And in the same way, the primitive emotions which had been there when the first brick was laid on the bare veld were still not far below the surface.

In the essentials, Plummerton West was still the same raucous little town it had been twenty years before. The land was the same land and the air still had the same heady atmosphere of adventure.

t w o

The sun climbed higher, grew fiercer and seemed to glow in the brassy sky; and the land lay boldly bright and blistering in the sun. The red dust was deep in the roadway for there were still long spans of oxen in the town heading through from Plummerton Sidings, shuffling up the suffocating clouds that powdered black men and white alike to a bright yellow-red.

The road was shimmering and the heat intense. The dust seemed to edge along with a man as he walked so that he drew it in with every breath he took, and the oxen, the horses and the mules that still outnumbered the motor vehicles in the streets had rings and lines on their faces where the moisture from their eyes, nostrils and mouths had caught the dust and turned it to mud. The heat was above, below, around, and a thousand glistening surfaces mirrored back the intensity of the sun's merciless rays. The air above the town moved in wavering lines, and the new concrete of the Standard Bank of South Africa stood out gleaming white like old bones in the sun.

In spite of the early hour, the streets were already crowded when the little cavalcade came in from the north-east. Everybody seemed to be busy arguing about the war in Europe and the news of the rebellion in the North, and nobody noticed them arrive at first. There were five of them in two cars – a white man and two Kaffir servants in a battered Vauxhall with a shining brass bonnet, and two more white men setting the pace in a big yellow Daimler.

They came into Plummerton at a rush, not slowing down, confidently expecting the passers-by to look after themselves as they hurried down Theophilus Street, the new pneumatic tyres humming over the wooden blocks of the newly-paved main thoroughfare. The crowd scattered and shouted good-natured imprecations after them as they roared in, pumping the rubber bulbs of their horns; and a small black piccaninny was snatched just in time from under the wheels of the Vauxhall by a white man in a straw boater and guillotining collar, and sent screaming to its mother with the palm of his horny hand at its bare behind.

The little cavalcade slid to a stop with locked rear wheels in a whirl of dust in front of the Plummerton Hotel, and a crowd began to gather immediately, their eyes on the fancy Daimler with its brass-edged mudguards, for it was a vehicle which had never been seen in Plummerton West before. Its yellow spokes, brass lamps and bright tan leatherwork put it in a class by itself, and the word sped up and down Theophilus Street that someone important had arrived.

At once, heads appeared in the windows of the offices on either side of the hotel. The manager of the branch office of the Standard Bank of South Africa, with its green-glazed windows and brass plate, appeared at his door and started talking to the lawyer from the adjacent office, which bore his name in blue and white enamel over the list of insurance and mining implement manufacturing companies he represented. Then people began to emerge in ones and twos and groups from the store, the mining consultant's rooms and the newspaper office, which huddled together, flat-faced and dusty, round the hotel, indicating by clear inference where the first, the very first, business of the town had always been done.

There was a pause while the dust settled, then the party from the cars began to descend to the sidewalk, the white man in the Vauxhall first, stiff-legged from too much sitting.

He was greeted from the steps of the hotel by a man in military uniform who had obviously been waiting for them, a handsome man in his fifties, with thick black hair and moustache just turning grey, his keen brown eyes staring out of a sharp military face, a dark fierce soldier whose restlessness sat on him with the same easy distinction as his uniform.

The man from the Vauxhall, plump and spectacled and awesomely respectable in the noisy crowd which was gathering, nodded and lit a cigar, slapping from his clothes the dust which had insinuated itself into the tonneau of the car round the square, upright windscreen, and the isinglass side curtains. The driver of the Daimler – a tall slender boy with a high aristocratic nose – waited for one of the Africans to open the door before he climbed out, rubbing and flexing his stiff fingers and shaking the leather coat he wore. The circular motoring goggles on his forehead, which rested on a narrow cap worn horizontally over his eyes, gave him the look of some strange monster with a flat head and great round eyes.

His passenger was the last to step on to the sidewalk and all the rest of them waited respectfully for him as the African removed the rug from his knees, all of them hanging back from the steps of the hotel to let him pass up them first.

As he stood knocking the dust from the folds of his clothes, he seemed bigger than all the rest of them together, not only because of his bulk which was considerable but because of his confidence, his obvious wealth, his clear expectation of respect. He was tall as well as broad and still not old, with a florid face and a yellow moustache just beginning to turn grey. His light grey suit had never been created within miles of Plummerton West or even Johannesburg, and a few idlers moved up the street eyeing him curiously as he stretched himself, staring with pale pop eyes at a faded notice set behind glass by the steps of the hotel, a relic of the days when the town had been responsible for its own destiny during the long-forgotten Kaffir wars.

It was in gaudy red and black, the ink still smudged where clumsy fingers had first set it up on a wall in the urgency of a crisis thirty years before.

Wanted, it read, *Volunteers for the Front, and for Colonel Makepeace's Grand Attack on Chief Jeremiah's Town. Loot and Booty Money. Better Prospects than the Diggings. Same Rations as a General. Enrol now at the Plummerton Hotel, before it is too late.*

It was dated 1884 and signed *Hector Stark Kitto* in a bold flourishing hand that seemed to indicate that the owner of such a resounding name felt inevitably destined for immortality.

The big man stared at it, still dusting his clothes, watched all the time by the others.

'Not seen one of those for a long time,' he said shortly to the soldier on the steps, jerking a plump white hand at the notice.

'Turned up a few weeks ago,' he was told. 'They thought it ought to be displayed. Bit of history.'

The big man nodded. 'Makes you feel old suddenly,' he said.

For a moment nobody spoke, then the big man slapped his leg with his gloves and headed up the steps, trudging heavily as though his weight were just beginning to be a burden. As he climbed, the auctioneer from the office down the street, called by an excited clerk, put his head out of the doorway, stared at the crowd, then emerged in his entirety, followed by an arguing client whom he was obviously brushing aside in search of more important business, and as the big man and his followers vanished from sight, he broke into a run, still followed by his client, and headed for the hotel bar.

The bar of the Plummerton Hotel was one of the biggest single rooms in the town, stretching as it did the full length of the building, from the entrance hall to the dining-room where, in the old days, a man could always sleep on the floor at night when rooms were in short supply.

At one end of it a card game was in progress, the chatter of the excited players cutting through the small talk at the zinc-topped counter. The shelves of bottles along the mirrored wall were punctuated here and there with the skulls of springbok, eland and the magnificent kudu with its ponderous spiral armament, relics of the days when they could be shot almost in Theophilus Street. They were set in pairs flanking the picture of the gentle, bearded man who was King of England, screwed directly to the bare wall which here in the bar had been kept untouched by the heavy red and gold paper that graced the rest of the hotel.

The four newcomers paused in the entrance, staring round them, then they pushed through the crowd unnoticed towards the billiard-room door, a hotch-potch of glass like the porch of a chapel in coloured cubes and lozenges. The Portuguese, newly up from Delagoa Bay who was acting as reception clerk, looked up as the door clashed behind them, every scrap of glass chattering in its leaden socket, then he threw down his pen and hurried after them.

The big man with the yellow moustache was standing by the billiard table glancing round him, tapping the dusty green baize with restless white fingers. For a long time he said nothing, then he swung round, smacking the flat of his hand down on the table.

'Where's Winter?' he snapped. 'He's supposed to be meeting me here.'

The other three – the soldier, the tall high-nosed boy and the plump spectacled legal-looking man – watched him silently, saying nothing, and he swung round, staring irritably about the room, as though searching the sparse furnishings.

'This is a damn' fine time to go and hide himself,' he growled. 'Go and get him, somebody, and let's have something to drink. How about a glass of cham' with a lump of ice for a cooler? I *need* something to take the taste of dust away.'

As the boy moved to the door, the Portuguese clerk appeared, proud of his English and eager to please.

'Good morning, gentlemen,' he said. 'If you're wanting rooms, I'm sorry we're full up.'

The big man stared at him down his long nose. 'Don't talk damn' nonsense,' he said shortly.

'Sir?' The clerk's jaw dropped.

'I don't want a room,' the big man said. 'I'm here to talk business.'

The clerk glanced round dubiously for a moment, startled by the big man's reaction, then he licked his lips and tried again.

'We have an excellent lounge,' he said. 'Perhaps I might suggest...'

'No, you mightn't,' the big man said fiercely. 'I know you've got a lounge. *And* a writing room. *And* a coffee room. But I *like* this room. We used to hold smoking concerts in here in the old days. *Let me like a soldier fall* and *Champagne Charlie* and *The Queen, God bless her*. It was in here we decided to put a stop to Chief Jeremiah's damn' nonsense and bring Dhanziland into the Empire. It was here I always did business with Rhodes and Barney Barnato and Beit. I started doing business in this room thirty years ago, and I've used it ever since. I've got used to it now. I've hired it – as from this minute and for as long as I want it.'

The clerk hesitated by the door, scared a little by the big man's manner and uncertain what his next move should be.

The big man picked up a cue and, bending over the table, poked listlessly at the scattered balls. From the bar the muffled sound of argument found its way through the door, then the high-pitched voices of a group of Kaffirs quarrelling in the street outside the window broke into the room.

'Stop those boys making that damn' row,' the big man said; and the glass door clashed as the spectacled man stepped outside. The racket of voices ceased abruptly.

The Portuguese clerk, still uncertain what to do, was watching cautiously, awed by the big man, who leaned over the table and sent one of the balls spinning down its length with a twist of his thick fingers. At last he seemed to realise the clerk was still there waiting alongside him, and he stared down at him with pale watery eyes.

'Winter been here?' he demanded.

'Winter, sir?'

'Francis Winter, from the newspaper. Where is he? He knew what time I'd arrive.'

There was something about the peremptory tone he employed that indicated he was used to being obeyed, and expected to be obeyed, and the clerk put on a show of eager servitude.

'I'll send a boy for him, sir,' he said. 'At once.'

'Better go yourself. I don't trust those damn' boys.'

'But sir...'

'Get going, man! For God's sake!'

The clerk was halfway out of the door and into the bar before he realised that he was being propelled by the big man's hand on his elbow.

'Yes, sir – of course! But who shall I say wants him?'

He was outside now, gazing back into the billiard room, baffled, a little scared, but eager to please still.

The big man stared at him, then at his three companions, and finally back at the clerk.

'I'm Plummer, you damn' fool,' he said in a loud voice. 'I started this place. Offy Plummer.'

three

Plummer was still pottering round the billiard table when Winter arrived, apparently absorbed but arguing all the time with the various minor politicians, agents and hangers-on who had made their way into the room as soon as the word had got round that he was in town. He gave his instructions and offered his opinions, laying his hands on every facet of the complicated machinery of his professional and political organisation, without once stopping his slow trudge round the billiard table and his unskilful poking at the yellowing balls.

But, in spite of his absorption, there was a fretful agitation behind his expression that kept breaking out in angry exclamations, a petulant anxiety that showed his attention was not wholly on the men who had gathered there to receive his decisions. The plump spectacled man who had arrived with him squatted, straddle-legged, across a chair by the door, his elbows resting on its back. The youngster with the high nose was stretched at full length on the horse-hair bench that ran round two sides of the room, his leather coat on the floor beside him, his eyes fixed on the noisome fly-papers on the brasswork fitted over the table to hold the lights. The soldier who had met them stood wide-legged at the window, his hot eyes on the street, his thin face alert, his body tensed, a taut handsome figure with his bright rows of medal ribbons, his mouth grim as he held his obvious impatience in check with difficulty.

The sycophantic group of hangers-on by the door were talking quietly, all of them with drinks in their hands, paid for by Plummer, waiting their turn while a man wearing the black armbands of a printer followed the great man backwards and forwards round the table, juggling a glass of whisky as he tried to listen to him over his broad shoulder.

Plummer seemed at last to have dispensed with his business and the agitation in his manner had come out into the open now.

'Keep it out of the paper, Hazell,' he was saying urgently in a soft voice that didn't carry beyond the table. 'Not a word, for God's sake!'

'Not a word, Mr Plummer.'

Three years before they had given Plummer a belated and somewhat reluctant knighthood for his services to the Empire but no one had ever got into the habit of calling him anything else but 'Mister'.

'Where's my brother now?' he was asking angrily. 'Is he still in town?'

'I heard so.' The reply was given cautiously. 'But I don't know.'

'Dammit – ' Plummer struck the white ball and watched it glance off the red into a pocket. The soldier by the window retrieved it silently and sent it down the table to him ' – dammit, Winter was supposed to keep an eye on him. *All the time!* We all knew the old fool hadn't much sense. Good God, guns and ammunition at a time like this!'

He placed the ball on the spot at the head of the table and nodded to the soldier who had returned it. 'Thanks, Kitto,' he said. He glanced round him before leaning across the table again. 'Where the hell is that damn' Winter?' he asked.

'They're looking for him now,' the boy stretched on the settee said languidly.

'Well, get him!' Plummer looked up in the middle of his stroke and barked the order. 'Get him, Romanis! Don't just loaf about like that.'

The boy on the bench rose quickly, his face sulky, and crossed to the door, trailing his leather coat. Plummer finished his stroke, reaching across the table with a grunt, then as Romanis pushed through the group at the door, he lifted his head again. 'Don't come back without him,' he called. 'He should be here. What the hell was Willie thinking about?' he went on bitterly, talking to himself, almost as though he were alone. 'Selling weapons to the bloody Boers!'

'I heard he was just hoping for a bit of quick profit, Mr Plummer,' Hazell said helpfully. 'Just some old Army stores. Coffee. Tea. Sugar et cetera. He didn't bother to inquire where the stuff was going, that's all. Nobody objected. Nobody stopped him, so he just went on. After all, there've been a lot of funny things happening lately, so he wasn't alone. Rifles have been disappearing in towns loyal to the Government, and they've been making biltong and Boer biscuits for De Wet as fast as they can go up round Rustenburg and Marico. There's plenty of talk of sedition.'

Kitto, the soldier, gave a quick restless terrier-like movement. 'Wish I'd known about it,' he said. 'He deserves to be shot. Might be *my* people who'll be on the wrong end of those damned guns.'

'Take it easy, Kitto,' Plummer said heavily. 'Nobody'll ever get the chance to use 'em. Botha and Smuts'll have De Wet in the bag before they get that far.'

He slammed hard at the balls and watched them as they clicked together and rolled to a stop in the centre of the green baize. 'This damn' table's out of true,' he observed bitterly, then he swung round on the others, his face puzzled and angry at the same time.

'Willie must have been mad,' he said. 'They tell me he was using the home of some damn' fancy woman. By Snuff, I ought to let him face it.'

'You ought to have thrown him over years ago,' Kitto said scornfully. 'He was never much of an asset.'

Plummer dug at his boot with the heel of the billiard cue. 'If it had been something else – another of his damned swindles,' he said, 'I'd have let him go hang. By Ginger,' he ended with a despairing goaded fury, 'why did it have to happen *now,* of all times?'

'He was always the same,' Kitto said from the window. 'Even when he first came out here twenty-odd years ago.' He turned, his narrow honest face indignant. 'Fights,' he said contemptuously. 'Gambling. Those damned coloured bits from the Bree Street shebeens who used to come up here to try for white and make their fortunes.'

Plummer made a despairing gesture, ignoring Kitto.

'I'd managed to build up a reputation here for integrity,' he said bitterly. 'I had 'em almost eating out of my hand. And then this, *this!*' He fought to control the anger that blazed in his face for a second, the muscles at his jaw line working, then he turned to the newspaperman again.

'What's the feeling round here anyway?' he demanded sharply. 'Whose side are they all on?'

The newspaperman was rubbing his chin, picking his words carefully, anxious not to offend.

'Hard to say, Mr Plummer,' he said slowly. 'I don't think there'll be any striking, as there was on the Rand, no burning the *Examiner* Office like they did with the Jo'burg *Star.* But what with Grant smashed by the Germans at Sandfontein, and Maritz turning traitor and selling out to them from Upington, they're beginning to wonder what the hell's going to happen. What can you expect, with Beyers loose in the north with fifteen thousand men, and De Wet running riot in the Free State? It isn't so very long since the Boer War, and feelings still run a bit high.'

'Don't worry about De Wet and Beyers,' Plummer said confidently. 'Botha and Smuts'll settle *them*. They've got the money and its money that wins wars. Botha's already forced De Wet into Bechuanaland. He's got cars, fast cars, and De Wet's only got horses and no supplies. I'm raising men and arms as fast as I can to help. They've only got to pin him down.'

The newspaperman shrugged. 'Well, someone had better pin someone down soon, Mr Plummer.'

Plummer bent over the table again. 'Where the hell's Winter got to?' he said gloomily. 'By the time he arrives, it'll be all over town.' He looked up at the printer. 'Go on, what else do you know? About Willie, I mean.'

'Everybody's talking about the affair, of course,' Hazell said. 'The police were on to it like a ton of bricks. They're naturally red hot on any sign of disaffection just now, and that damn' fire-eating lawyer, Fabricius, who leads the Afrikaners here – naturally he's got his ears pricked well up.'

Plummer nodded, gave the white ball a vicious bang, missed badly and flung down the cue with an angry gesture. It rolled off the table and clattered to the floor, and Kitto, by the window, stooped and, picking it up, handed it back to him silently, his dark handsome face faintly touched by scorn.

'God damn Willie!' Plummer said bitterly.

It was at that moment that Romanis returned, almost falling into the room. He slammed the door behind him, setting all the cubes and lozenges of coloured glass rattling in their sockets.

Plummer winced at the crash and looked up. 'Go on,' he commanded sharply.

'Winter's here,' Romanis said, his lanky frame disjointed with excitement. 'I just saw him coming into the hotel.'

Immediately, the buzz of conversation in the corner of the room stopped. Plummer paused with the cue in his hand, then he laid it down on the table with a clatter. The newspaperman moved away and Plummer waved an irritable hand at the group by the door. They nodded and backed out quickly so that only the intimates were left. Romanis, Kitto, Hoole and the newspaperman.

Plummer stood facing the door, and the man who came in.

'Well, Frank,' he said with brusque immediacy. 'Let's have it. Where's Willie?'

four

Winter didn't answer for a moment and Plummer thought he was worried by the heat and the dust outside. He was staring at him, his expression a mixture of anger, anxiety and concern, then he turned his head to Hoole and spoke peremptorily.

'Get him a drink,' he said over his shoulder, and Hoole sloshed Rhynbende gin into a glass and, filling it with soda, passed it silently to Winter, a supercilious expression on his face.

Winter nodded his thanks. His lined face and bright tired eyes stood out in direct contrast to Plummer's pouchy plethoric countenance. The flannel suit he wore, long since pulled out of shape and size, clung to his thin legs, crumpled and startlingly slovenly alongside the groomed smartness of the others.

He had watched them arrive from his room over the *Plummerton Examiner* office across the street, a bare shoddy room with a roll-top desk, and rows of dog-eared books on dusty planking shelves. The air had been thick with flying grit as he had crossed Theophilus Street, the hot wind from the veld whirling it in little spirals between the mimosa shrubs and the thin pepper trees with their speckled trunks and sparse shade, and even here in the hotel you could still smell it and taste it in your throat.

He leaned on the table, smiled round at them all, undisturbed by the hostility, and swallowed his drink.

19

Plummer's anger seemed to be rising again as he watched Winter, still fidgety with impatience.

'Where's Willie?' he repeated.

Winter smiled and, pulling up a wickerwork chair, stretched himself out in it, his long legs folded, one hand in his pocket, his eyes half-closed so that he looked a little like a seedy setter with his untidy colourless hair and shabby clothes.

'Keep your hair on, Offy,' he said gently. 'He's all right. He'll be halfway to Durban by now.'

'He'll *what?*' Plummer's jaw dropped and his eyes glowed with sudden pleasure.

Winter smiled again, a faint disturbing smile that lit up his tired eyes. 'Half-way to Durban,' he repeated. 'He can get a ship from there to the Cape. He'll be in Cape Town before the week's out.'

He saw Plummer's big frame relax and the breath come out of his lungs in a gusty sigh.

'Thank God,' he said. 'I knew there was *someone* I could rely on in a pinch.' He stared round at the others, accusing them, as though he suffered wretchedly from ineptitude in his subordinates. 'You worked fast. I expect you've been up all night.'

Winter shook his head. 'Only part of it. It's the brandy makes me look like this.'

Plummer offered a crocodile leather pouch, the irritation gone from his face at last. 'Ceegar?' he asked. Winter nodded, and Plummer struck a match quickly.

'You know everybody here, of course? Captain Romanis, Hoole.' He nodded at the uniformed man. 'Kitto and you are old friends, of course.'

Kitto stared at Winter without any marked enthusiasm, his taut, efficient body angular by the window – almost as though he were deliberately trying to throw up Winter's drooping languor into contrast. Winter smiled with the same lack of enthusiasm and Plummer hurried on, not noticing their indifference.

'How was he?' he asked.

Winter's smile disappeared. 'Scared,' he said shortly. 'Scared as only an old man can be.'

Plummer frowned. 'The damned old fool!' he said. 'Why did he do it?'

'I didn't stop to ask. I just got rid of him as fast as I could.'

Romanis recharged Winter's glass from the bottle of Rhynbende and filled it with soda. Winter nodded his thanks.

'I didn't even let him go back to his hotel,' he went on. 'I just drove him over to Plummerton Sidings to catch the night train. We made it by the skin of our teeth. Nobody saw him leave.'

Plummer nodded approvingly.

Winter swallowed the contents of his glass again and looked up. 'I went to his hotel then,' he said. 'I took everything that belonged to him and burned it. Then I wrote a story for the personal column, saying he'd left town. I back-dated it for safety, in case questions are asked.'

Plummer smiled admiringly. 'That was a good idea. Hoole' – he swung round – 'pick up the next train to the Cape. Find Willie. Tell him to draw on my account.' He turned back to Winter. 'It's a good job you were tipped off,' he said, walking slowly down the room. At the bottom, he turned and jabbed a white episcopal finger at them. 'I know these people here,' he said. 'I've seen 'em toasting the Kaiser's birthday and hoping we'll be defeated in France. There's nothing they'd like better than to get something like this on me. They always hated us – all of us, Rhodes, Robinson, Barnato, me.'

He paused, puffing at his cigar and blowing out smoke in little blue clouds. He stared at it for a moment and waved it into disintegrating wisps with a plump hand.

'This damn' war's a calamity for us out here in South Africa,' he went on. 'It comes too close on the heels of the other one, and there are too many people regarding it as a heaven-sent opportunity to reassert themselves. And if the police find out about Willie – '

'Or Fabricius does,' Kitto interrupted.

Plummer halted, and put his hands in his pockets. 'Or Fabricius does,' he agreed. 'With feelings as high as they are at the moment, I wouldn't get around to explanations. They've been looting in Jo'burg – German shops and shops belonging to Beyers' supporters – and round Marico and Rustenburg, Britishers who refuse to make biltong and Boer biscuits for De Wet are being set about. Dammit, he's been *flogging* people in the Free State who refused to support him. The beginning of a war isn't the time to be caught out in something like this.'

He turned to Winter, suddenly looking tired. 'What about this damn' woman?' he said. 'This woman whose house he'd been using.'

'Polly Bolt's the name,' Winter said. 'Parasol Poll, they call her in the Theophilus Street bars.' He stared at the ceiling, recounting the facts from a retentive mind almost as though he were reading from notes. 'They say she's the daughter of an Irish trooper from the Imperial Light Horse. Nobody knows her mother – same as her, I imagine. She dances a bit at the Theatre Royal and earns a little on the side between engagements in an establishment in Buiderkant Street.'

Romanis sneered. 'A tart?'

Winter looked up sharply, his face ironic. 'You talk as though you'd run the whole gamut of impropriety, Romanis! Polly's good-hearted and kind and there's many a man in this town would fight *you* to the last breath to defend her.'

Romanis blushed. 'I don't see – '

'For God's sake, stop being romantic, Winter,' Plummer cut in realistically. 'Let's get down to brass tacks. Do you know her?'

Winter smiled. 'Only professionally,' he said.

Plummer frowned. 'Will she keep her mouth shut?'

Winter stared gravely at him. 'As it happens, she's a patriot, bless her, and she agreed for the sake of England, home and beauty to put Plummerton behind her for a bit.'

Hoole interrupted incisively, a faint edge of impatience in his voice, as though he were anxious to get back to his office. 'Well,' he said, 'with Willie out of the way and the woman taken care of, we've nothing to worry about. We're clear.' Plummer nodded, reached over and picked up the cue again. But Winter smiled and shook his head.

'Not quite.'

They all looked at Winter.

'Not quite?' Plummer turned round slowly. 'What do you mean?'

'There's *one other.*'

'What?' They were all on their feet again now, staring at him.

'Who, man?' Plummer demanded. 'Who?'

Winter grinned. 'Polly's beau,' he said.

five

Winter rose and walked across the room to the gin bottle.
Filling his glass again, he sat down by the window. A fly,
caught on the sticky paper hanging from the light fitting,
buzzed noisily in the silence.

Plummer put the cue down again and, sticking his hands
in his pockets, walked to the window and stared out at the
street.

'This boy friend,' he said after a while. 'Think we can do
anything about him, Frank? Is he another of your
disreputable friends?'

'Our paths have crossed,' Winter replied cautiously.

'How?'

'At Polly's.'

'I've told you before about your blasted womanising,'
Plummer complained. 'What's he like?'

'Rum cove. Doesn't talk much. Not much education. Just
the man to carry goods for Willie without asking questions.'

Plummer's shoulders seemed to sag as his anger subsided.
He stood silently, his hands in his pockets, staring blank-eyed
at the window.

'Will he sweeten?' he asked suddenly.

'Try offering him one of your directorships,' Kitto said
contemptuously, the uninspired incorruptibility that enabled
him always to face up to Plummer without fear shining out
of his lined face. 'It always used to work.'

24

Plummer frowned. 'Everybody's not like you, Kitto,' he said. 'Most men have their price. And if I've wanted to get things done and the process could be facilitated by making people company directors I've never seen why people should complain. I haven't tried sweetening anybody for years but now isn't the time to worry about consciences. Will he play, Frank?'

'He *is* doing.' Winter smiled at the incredulous delight on Plummer's face. 'It'll cost a bit,' he added.

'That doesn't matter a damn! You know that.'

Hoole smiled and Romanis laughed outright. Even Kitto's dark angry face relaxed. For the first time they were all of them looking more cheerful. Plummer indicated the door.

'Don't let anybody in, Hoole,' he said, and the plump man crossed the room and put his back against the door, his hands in his pockets, the light that came through the glass chips glinting in flecks of colour on the lenses of his spectacles.

'What did you say his name was?' Plummer asked gaily.

'I didn't, but it's Schuter. Sammy Schuter.'

Plummer looked up sharply. 'That's not an English name,' he said. 'Sounds more like Dutch.'

'It's neither as a matter of fact,' Winter said. 'It's Jewish. Nobody knows where his relations are but he's a Jew all right. Whitechapel Jew.'

'A damned Jehoodah!' Romanis stared, his face indignant. 'Trust the Sheenies to have a hand in the game!'

'– A game that Willie started,' Winter reminded him placidly. 'I don't suppose he's been near a synagogue in his life anyway. Judging by the way he lives, he's more a Boer than the Boers themselves. He lost his parents during the war, I gather. Polly's father brought them up together.'

'But dammit' – Plummer gestured – 'he's British! You said he was. Whitechapel, you said. You don't have to bribe Britishers at a time like this. Didn't you tell him what was at stake?'

'He was in need of the money.' Winter gulped at his drink and grinned. 'Still, he didn't waste time,' he explained. 'He's on his way already by wagon. He's taken Polly with him. He's dropping her at Plummerton Sidings to pick up a train, and then he's going on alone.'

'Where to?'

'I told him to head for Oliphants River.'

Plummer's head jerked up. 'But that's several hundred miles!'

'Take him a long time to get there,' Winter said blandly.

'There's no one out there, there's nothing.'

'Less people to talk to.'

Romanis grinned and they all seemed to slip into more relaxed attitudes again. Plummer shifted his position from one foot to the other, pleased but a little uneasy.

'But good God – how'll he live?'

'He'll live all right,' Winter said calmly. 'He's spent half his adult life out there, shooting for the market.'

Plummer waved a hand half-heartedly. 'Couldn't you have sent him anywhere else?' he asked.

Winter gestured deprecatingly with his glass. 'Where, Offy? South Africa hasn't many places these days where people can't be found and where it's hard to get back from.'

'He sounds as though you don't trust him,' Romanis grinned.

'I don't.'

'What?' They all stared at Winter, and in a moment the cheerfulness had gone again.

Winter smiled, sliding farther down on the horsehair bench, his hands in his pockets. 'I told you he was in need of money,' he said. 'He had all his equipment pinched a few months back. He's been having to use hired horses and a condemned police Martini with a kick like a mule.' He paused and smiled again. 'He could thread a needle with it, mind,' he added.

'He needs cash to build up his outfit again,' he went on. 'Even shooting costs money and he's a bit desperate. He's just come out of jail. A slight fracas with the man who robbed him. Suppose Fabricius thinks of offering him a bigger bribe *not* to go away, how are we to know he won't be tempted to change course or even turn round and come back?'

Romanis straightened his back with a jerk. 'Anybody but a Yid wouldn't need bribing,' he said loudly. 'He'd have done it for the Old Country.'

'Needs must when the Devil drives,' Winter said cheerfully.

Romanis was sitting on the edge of the horsehair bench now, his blank youthful face indignant. Kitto was standing with his hands in his pockets, his eyes contemptuous, as though he were disgusted with all their machinations, and Hoole was by the table, the door forgotten. Hazell stood alone in the background, still holding a sheet of paper as though he were there only to take notes.

They were still like that, grouped round one corner of the billiard table, when a fist clattered on the coloured lozenges in the door. Guiltily almost, they started apart.

'Who the hell's that?' Kitto demanded sharply.

Only Winter remained where he was, stretched out on the bench near the window, his hands in his pockets, his glass on the floor beside him.

'See who it is,' Plummer said.

Hazell crossed to the door and opened it. The little Portuguese clerk was there, trying to see past him, trying to find Plummer.

'What is it?' Hazell demanded, and the clerk leaned forward, muttering something softly.

Hazell turned, his eyes a little scared. 'It's Fabricius,' he said. 'He's in the hotel. He's asking to see you, Mr Plummer.'

Plummer glanced quickly at the others.

'Better see him,' Hoole advised. 'He's only fishing. He doesn't know anything. Give us a minute, though. Just give us a minute.'

Plummer nodded and Hazell muttered something to the clerk and closed the door softly.

'Blasted treacherous bung-nosed Boer,' Kitto said. 'He's one of De Wet's men. What's *he* want?'

'Information, I suppose,' Hoole pointed out. 'About Schuter. But we can stand him off all right. We've nothing to worry about. Not yet. Not with Willie out of the way. We've only to decide what to do about this Schuter chap. That's all.'

Plummer was studying the floor and he looked up quickly. 'Can't we make certain he *doesn't* change his mind?' he asked.

'What?' Romanis looked startled. 'Kill him?'

Plummer swung round. 'For God's sake, Romanis!' he said. 'Will you never learn? You've been reading too much Henty and Marryat. This is the Twentieth Century. There musn't be any violence.'

Romanis looked sulky. 'What's a Sheeny or two?' he said.

Hoole took off his glasses and started to polish them. 'You said he shot for a living?' he asked, peering shortsightedly at Winter.

Winter nodded. 'For the Kimberley and Jo'burg markets. You can get a pound a carcass even here in Plummerton. That's why he was so perfect as Willie's middleman. Few friends. No questions asked. He's not the type to ask questions. Keeps himself to himself. More used to the veld than the town. Quiet chap with a habit of sitting still and looking harmless. But don't be taken in by *that,*' he ended. 'It's an old hunter's trick.'

Romanis leaned across the billiard table to where Plummer was sullenly poking at the balls again.

'I'm damned if I'd have too many scruples in dealing with a bloody Sheeny,' he said. 'Especially one with a criminal record.'

'When you've a few more years on your back, Romanis,' Plummer said with insulting calmness, 'I'll start listening to you. Barnato was a Jew. So were plenty of others. For the time being there'll be no violence.'

Kitto snorted. 'Rhodes would have said "Clap him in irons and say he was drunk",' he muttered over his shoulder.

'This is the Twentieth Century,' Plummer persisted.

'And there's a war on. And a lot at stake.'

'Perhaps a *slight* show of force,' Winter suggested quietly. 'To encourage him on his way. What's wrong with Kitto seeing him clear of the town, seeing he goes where he promised to go? Why not a few men between him and Plummerton so he can't come back even if he *does* change his mind?'

Plummer turned. 'Kitto's no longer employed by me,' he pointed out. 'He doesn't lead company police these days. He leads Government troops. He's a soldier and he volunteered. He's in charge of a military area now with orders to look out for De Wet. I wouldn't ask him to get himself mixed up in any of your crazy wild west schemes.'

Romanis looked up. 'Besides,' he said, 'what about the woman?'

Winter laughed. 'Where did you learn your gallantry, Romanis? The Trocadero? The Criterion bar? Polly would probably welcome the company. She's a warm-hearted soul and likes a man about the house.'

'Suppose he got awkward?'

'With Kitto and his armed might just behind?'

'This is a company matter,' Plummer persisted. 'And Kitto's interests in my affairs are subordinated to the nation's now – with my complete approval.'

Winter looked up at Plummer from the corner of his eye, then glanced at Kitto who had taken no part in the discussion.

'Don't rush it, Offy,' he said. 'I think I see a Homeric craving for martial valour brewing up.'

Kitto was flicking at his boots with his crop, the everlasting soldier, enduring and honest to the point of embarrassment. He was watching them with a faint hard scorn in his eyes and as Winter spoke, he clasped his hands behind his back and stalked down the room before turning to face them. 'None of you've noticed that the country's interests are marching side by side with Offy's for the moment,' he said brusquely, with a suggestion of contempt for the narrowness of their vision.

'What do you mean?' Plummer laid down the cue and looked up.

Kitto's face was twisted disdainfully. 'What could bring down Offy could bring down the Government,' he pointed out. 'If Fabricius picks this boy up, all this about Willie'll be worth a thousand men to De Wet – a thousand of those damn' Dutch – Huguenot farmers who were born with a rifle in their hands and a horse between their legs. Any hint of British sympathy with them could mean the end of Botha, *and* the Union – the end of South Africa, the end of England. I only came here today for old time's sake, but looked at that way this affair comes within my sphere. What's to stop me taking an armed patrol into Dhanziland, ostensibly to search for De Wet, and sitting on this merchant's tail? I'd not be transgressing from my orders, and at the same time I might do a lot of good.'

'That's the answer, Offy,' Romanis said enthusiastically, the everlasting schoolboy with a head full of easy solutions. 'That's just the thing you want.'

'I'm not doing it for Offy,' Kitto snapped immediately, incensed by the suggestion that he was caught up in their intrigue. 'I'm doing it because it's obviously my duty.'

Plummer was thinking deeply, studying the cigar he was smoking, his pale blue eyes expressionless.

'It'd have to be a large patrol,' Kitto went on slowly. 'I couldn't risk being caught out there by De Wet with just a few men – but if I took the cars I'd be good and mobile and I could get back easily if I'm needed. I can pick up a detachment from the Sidings and wait for him there. But he'll shift all right when he sees us coming. He might even lead us to De Wet. *That'd* be a feather in my cap after all these years.'

'You might even save Britain the year of grace and the series of defeats she seems to need to set about fighting a war,' Winter grinned.

Hoole moved forward, uneasily. 'I don't like it,' he said. 'It sounds risky and I feel we oughtn't to go *too* far, Offy. The whole thing's too trivial. Fabricius could never make his accusations stick.'

'Mud will *always* stick,' Plummer growled. 'Willie holds several of my directorships, and in politics that makes us the same person.'

Kitto had been standing by the door, his honest none-too-clever face calm and self-assured, his stance Napoleonic, waiting for Plummer's approval.

Now he half-turned, eager to get on with the job. 'Don't worry,' he said. 'I'll see this damn' Yid off the premises for you.'

Plummer nodded. 'Thanks, Kitto. I'll see a word's put in the right ear for you. You've been neglected too long.'

Kitto's expression didn't change. 'I don't need bribing,' he said. 'I'll do the job properly without that.'

'Perhaps a little chivvying now and again might even encourage them,' Romanis suggested enthusiastically.

'Don't be so confounded bloodthirsty!' Plummer snapped. 'There'll be no violence.'

'Sammy Schuter's not the sort to ask for kid-glove treatment,' Winter pointed out. 'He'd understand perfectly well what you meant if you rode his camp down in the darkness. He's done it himself when he's found people poaching on his hunting grounds.'

'There'll be *no violence*,' Plummer insisted. 'Understand, Kitto? *No violence.* Just see he leaves, that's all.'

'If he's only got a horse, I'll run rings round him,' Kitto said confidently. 'I'll go and organise it now.'

'I'll come with you,' Romanis said. 'I'd like to be in on the fun.'

Plummer winced as the door slammed behind them, and Winter sighed.

'I thought people like Kitto went out of date when the last Spartan fell dead at Thermopylae,' he said.

Plummer looked weary, unmoved by humour. 'He's too damned honest,' he said. 'That's the trouble with Kitto.' He turned to the newspaperman. 'That'll be all, Hazell,' he concluded flatly. 'Thanks for your help.'

Hazell nodded, accepting his dismissal, and the door clashed behind him.

'Better have Fabricius in now, Hoole,' Plummer said, and Hoole stopped polishing his spectacles and went to the door. 'And don't go away. Stay with me. I'll need you.'

Hoole nodded and as he disappeared, Plummer turned to Winter.

'Frank,' he said. 'Go with Kitto.'

Winter sat up abruptly. *'Go with him?'*

'Keep an eye on things for me.'

'Offy, I'm no soldier!'

'I can have you accepted as an accredited correspondent any time. Only requires a telephone call. Kitto'd be glad to have his name in the paper. Many a soldier's reputation's been made by having a newspaperman handy.'

Winter considered for a moment. 'I thought my job was digging up other people's dead dogs for you, Offy. Digging 'em up and nailing 'em to the wall where everybody could see 'em. Or keeping your own well buried and stamped down.'

Plummer frowned. 'Kitto's hotheaded,' he said. 'I need someone with him to keep an eye on things. And Romanis is no damn' good. I've never been lucky with my subordinates.' He looked up, smiling faintly. 'Still, neither was Rhodes. Look at the people who surrounded *him*.' He gazed at Winter appealingly. 'There's a lot at stake, Frank.'

Winter looked puzzled. 'Surely Kitto can be relied on to do his job?' he said. 'You ought to know that. You were there in Dhanziland when he sat on that damned hill thirty years ago with ten mounted policemen, blowing bugles and waving and pretending to twelve thousand Dhanzis spread all over the plain in front that Makepeace's column was just behind – not twenty miles away, as it was. *He* got you Dhanziland, Offy.'

Plummer nodded, his eyes distant at the memory. 'Yes,' he agreed. 'He got the bit between his teeth all right that day.' He puffed at his cigar, a shadow of doubt on his face, then he smiled, reminiscing, warmed momentarily by the recollection of shared glory. 'He stood out there in front of me – just a slip of a boy he was, in those days – holding his carbine, his sabre stuck in the ground in front of him in case they rushed him. It even got in the papers back home. He became a legend. All the same' – he paused – 'you heard him just now. He feels he owes no allegiance to me and I'd like someone around I could trust.'

Winter stared at his glass. 'Seems to me it'd be less complicated if you brought Willie back,' he pointed out. 'And let him face the music.'

'I'd rather do it my way, Frank.' Plummer seemed to be searching his soul, and he looked older suddenly.

Winter shrugged. 'As you wish. But if this comes out, you'll be hard put to keep your seat in the Cape Parliament. And then the financial wizards'll be after you. They'll drag *everything* up – even your lady friends.'

Plummer smiled faintly. 'They're after me *now,*' he said. 'They're after you from the day you make your first thousand.'

Winter opened his mouth to protest again, but the loose glassware in the door clashed as the marble handle moved.

Plummer turned. Hoole stood in the doorway ushering in another man – a tall man with a blond beard and a broad suspicious face.

Winter saw Plummer smother a sigh and advance towards him, his hand held out.

'Dr Fabricius,' he said. 'Come in.'

Fabricius stood still, not attempting to shake hands, and Plummer's arm dropped to his side. Winter saw the weariness in his face as he gathered his mental and spiritual resources, and he emptied his glass quickly and touched Plummer on the shoulder.

'All right, Offy,' he said. '*Tot siens.* I'll go. I'll get a drink or two first. I'll be thirsty work round Plummerton Sidings.'

six

A line of ragged trees marks the first sight of Plummerton Sidings as you approach it from Plummerton West. To this day, they stand out of a fold in the flat rocky surface of the veld, monumentally startling in the vast undulation of a plain markedly bare of vegetation.

Beyond, far beyond, wrapped in the pearly haze of distance, lies the stump of Sheba, sticking out like a stub of broken tooth against the sky. Originally, Sheba had been called Bokskop, after the little klipspringers which had once lived on its slope, but the idea that it had once been the city of the fabulous Queen of Sheba, a story put out by some wandering Englishman with an imagination and a carpet bag full of classics, and had been petrified into stone for all its wickedness, had appealed to the superstitious Dutch and the name had stuck.

The man on the little cart which was rolling with squeaking wheels towards the Sidings behind an old shaft-worn grey mare, stared across at its hazy shape as he reached the top of the rise, then his eyes fell into the shallow valley between and he leaned back on the seat and tautened his hand on the reins.

The little mare between the shafts shuffled to a halt, bored and dispirited, the chink of her harness loud in the stillness, and for a moment, the man sat staring at the line of trees before he was able to pick out the liquid shimmer among them that indicated the first sight of corrugated iron roofs.

It was only a small cart he drove. Its wooden body – almost like a shallow coffin with hoops of iron for the canvas cover it sometimes wore – contained only a few odds and ends, a horse blanket, an old rust-scarred rifle and a rope; a sack of provisions and a trunk tied with stout string, which belonged to the woman who half-dozed beside him on the seat, her head on his shoulder nodding to every jolt of the cart.

For a long time he sat motionless, almost as though he were part of the cart, chewing a piece of grass, his restless gaze quartering the distance. His Semitic long-nosed face was thin and smooth, and his eyes under the battered felt hat he wore were so pale they seemed like spots of white in the shadow. His skin was dark, touched with the suggestion of a beard, and his forelock fell over his eyes like the broken wing of a raven.

In front of him a group of eucalyptus trees gave a scrap of sparse speckled shade to the crown of the ridge, white and bleached-looking against the sharp metallic blue of the sky like some pagan monument, and he sat staring beyond them, his washed blue eyes distant as though they were looking over the curve of the next slope. His rumpled trousers were coated with the reddish dust of the road and he wore an old salt-and-pepper jacket that looked like someone else's cast-off. His face was young and largely unlined, the face of a boy who had grown into a man too soon, but there was something in the unquiet blue eyes that was very adult and experienced.

The sun seemed to boil in the diamond-bright sky, making the shadows harsh and mirror-clear, so that every single pebble on the dusty track had its own oasis of sharp shade, its own shimmering lines of heat. Beyond the eucalyptuses the flat roofs of Plummerton Sidings glinted like fragments of bright glass among the trees that fringed the railway yards and the shining ribbon of metal that ran to the north and south until it disappeared from sight. Along its track, the wide rolling land stretched unbroken almost from sea to sea, from the south where its tip broke the streams of the Atlantic and Indian Oceans, separating the waters like the blunt prow of a ship, away to the north beyond the Vaal and the Limpopo, onwards and upwards to Rhodesia and even farther.

They had been moving quietly, indifferent to any need to hurry, and the man had been content to let the old horse in the shafts set its own pace. He turned his head slowly to look at the woman who was sleeping against his shoulder, her mouth open, her hat pushed sideways over her face. She was a good-looking woman with clear plump features, which the over-generous make-up that was rubbing off on his sleeve couldn't disguise. Her feet were braced against the foot-board, and her skirt was above her knees in a froth of dusty muslin and pink ribbon, pulled up for coolness, showing long well-shaped legs in black silk stockings and pink shoes.

He nudged her sharply and she woke quickly, reaching for her hat. She sat up, blinking rapidly and grabbing for a hold as he flicked the reins and set the horse in motion again with a jerk.

'We home yet, Sammy?' she asked.

He answered without turning his head, in a soft voice that had the same smooth gentleness as his movements. 'We aren't going home, Polly,' he pointed out. 'Remember? We're going to Plummerton Sidings.'

He pointed with a jerk of his thumb and the woman nodded and disconsolately straightened her hat, a small straw affair decorated with cherries and flowers and what appeared to be a spreadeagled bird, then she rubbed her hand across her face and stretched, the cotton blouse she wore taut across her breasts and showing the strength and roundness of her body.

She looked round her, still blinking, drowsy and beautiful with sleep and dizzy with the sunshine, then she nodded. 'I remember now,' she said slowly, 'I fell asleep.' She studied the little town rising out of the dip with disapproval. 'It looks worse than Plummerton West,' she commented heavily. She stared ahead again for a moment then she yawned in a tear-starting jaw-cracking way and licked her lips distastefully. 'Lor',' she said, 'I feel as old as the hills. It's the brandy, I suppose.'

Sammy indicated her uncovered knees.

'Better fix your clothes, Polly,' he said. 'They aren't going to like seeing you like that.'

Polly looked at him placidly. 'Aren't they?' she said. 'Well, it's cooler this way, and if people don't like me with my skirts above my knees, there's not much point in my being here, is there? They're nice legs anyway,' she added with a warm luxurious pride.

Sammy said nothing, and went on whittling at a piece of stick. He had been whittling all afternoon without speaking while she slept, letting the little mare find her own way, picking up a fresh chip of wood out of the back of the cart whenever he needed one. Polly had turned her eyes towards the Sidings again and now, as she woke completely, her countenance brightened hopefully. 'I bet a girl could get a job here,' she said with growing enthusiasm. 'Lots of railwaymen. They're well paid and they like to spend. Bound to be plenty of work for a girl in the bars round the station. Probably plenty of fun too. Maybe I'll stop off for a bit.'

Sammy sliced off a sliver of wood from the stick he was cutting, and watched it spin to the ground. 'You promised Plummer's man you'd clear off,' he pointed out. 'You said you'd go. I heard you.'

'I've changed me mind,' she said comfortably. 'I needn't stay long. Just till I earn the fare south.'

'You should have taken the money they offered you. Then you wouldn't have to earn it. Why didn't you?'

She looked wistful, puzzled at her own impulsive patriotism. 'I dunno,' she said. 'They could have afforded it. Anyway, I didn't. But I can earn some here – enough to get to Kimberley anyway. That's a real place. Easy to get a job *there*. Plenty of bars – bigger bars than Plummerton West. I can save up the fare to the Cape even. I'll earn it quick in Kimberley.'

He was looking up at her and she faced him calmly, her large clear eyes devoid of secrets. 'Go on, look,' she said without anger. 'You know damn' well how I'll earn it. Same as always. The only way I've ever known. That's how.'

Sammy flicked a shaving of wood from his trousers, his face inscrutable, and Polly turned her head away, studying the landscape, calm again.

'You're a fine one to have fancy ideas,' she said, once more without rancour, her soft fine eyes on the horizon. 'Your record's not exactly unblemished. It's easy to criticise a fancy girl and plenty of people do, but it's not so hard to become one if you've no Ma and no birth certificate and your Pa does nothing but booze. You get stinking with some bloke in a bar because you've no one to tell you better, and before you know where you are you find yourself in bed with him and it becomes a habit. The way *you* talk, anybody'd think I was like them Bree Street coloured gals who used to auction themselves off to the highest bidder. Now *that's* what I call brassy.' She paused and glanced round at him. 'Men never understand,' she announced maternally. 'Especially young 'uns like you, still wet behind the ears.'

He lowered the knife and the piece of wood. 'I'm as old as you,' he said.

'You're three years younger. I ought to know. I had to look after you.'

'What's three years?'

39

'Enough.' She faced him again. 'I don't know what *you've* got to grumble about,' she said. '*You* never encouraged me to stay home before. Dashing off shooting. You think a girl wants to sit around a place like that rotten old farm we had with only Pa drinking hisself silly all the time to keep her company? It's no wonder I got lonely and went looking for a bit of fun.'

She stopped dead, her voice wistful. 'And now I've had enough fun,' she said slowly. 'I want to go to Kimberley.' Her voice rose on a plaintive note, her eyes gentle and pleading with him. 'I'm sick of dust. I'm sick of men. I'm sick of the only shops being the ones that sell saddles and mining machinery. I want some pretty clothes. I've never had any pretty clothes. Not real ones – from a smart shop like the ones they have in Commissioner Street and Adderley Street in Cape Town. Clothes that make me look nice. I've got a good start and it's a pity to waste it.' She smoothed her blouse across her breast. 'That's real, y'know,' she pointed out. 'Not whalebone, like some folks'.'

She stared at him for a moment, as if she expected him to dispute it, then her eyes became wistful again. 'All I've ever had,' she said, 'is just a lot of rough blokes, who think they're gents, all staring at me when I danced and pawing me when I didn't. And dust. All the time, just dust and sunshine. That's all you get round here. No wonder I've got a skin like old boots.'

'Your skin's all right,' Sammy said quietly.

She looked at him with an oddly tender expression on her face for a moment. 'Thanks, Sammy boy. Nice of you to say so. Only I know it isn't true. I read a book once,' she went on. 'Women in Cape Town and Durban, they've got parasols. They use 'em all the time. Yet they laugh themselves sick up here when I use one to keep from getting all burned up. They've got pretty clothes, too – and nice gardens, with flowers in – and trees. I wouldn't mind having a garden with flowers and trees.'

'Who's going to look after you down there?'

She looked up accusingly. 'Who's going to look after me *up here*?' she asked calmly.

'I would.'

'You never shaped much as if you wanted to,' she pointed out calmly. 'Riding round enjoying yourself, bangin' off your gun like billy-o all over the veld, killing things, when you should have been home.'

Sammy started whittling again. It was an old dispute which had been going on between them for years and it would never be settled.

'I'll drop you at the Sidings as we go through,' he said flatly.

He was watching her out of the corner of his eye, with a trace of caution, as though he expected her to develop her theme but she was regarding him anxiously now, seeming younger and less certain of herself and of him.

'Where are you going, Sammy?' she asked.

'South-west,' he said. 'Out Namaqualand way.'

'That's close by them Germans. They've been having fighting that way. They nobbled Grant out that way.' She paused, her kind heart awed by the thought of war and wounds and pain. 'Besides' – she studied him, concern in her eyes – 'there's *nothing* out there, Sammy. There's nothing west of the railway track at Plummerton Sidings – only the Wilderness. Nothing till you get to Upington. And then not much. It's bare out there. I've heard Pa say so, when he had the cart and used to sell things. No people. He'd never go there.'

'Your Pa was after trade.' He grinned. 'It's not for trade they're sending me there.'

She was silent and he gestured with his knife towards the railway track.

'It's Plummer country over there,' he went on shrewdly. 'It has been ever since he annexed Dhanziland. He's always had the say-so round here and west of the track. Besides, there's nobody to talk to. Nobody to know I ever knew Willie Plummer. No Fabricius to find me and get me to spin the sort of yarn they don't want me to spin. Nice safe country.'

Her eyes were worried now. 'You must have been barmy,' she said glumly.

'I didn't know a lot of silly fatheads would take it into their heads to start a rebellion,' he defended himself. 'I only did a carrying job for Willie Plummer. That's what I did. I took his money and carried what he gave me without asking questions. I didn't know who was getting them.'

'That old fool,' Polly said heavily. 'Doing this to a girl. He must have been crackers, using my place. And so must we, not to keep an eye on him, letting ourselves get mixed up with money. You get out of your depth.' She turned to him again, her face softened into anxiety once more, clearly unable to concentrate on her own worries for her thoughts of him. 'What'll you live on, Sammy?'

He grinned. 'That's the least of my troubles,' he said. 'There's plenty of game. That's one thing. No need to worry about food so long as you've got a gun.'

'A gun's not enough. You'll need a horse.'

'I've got this one. I'll pick up another in the Sidings for riding. Or mebbe a mule. A mule can work a hoss into the ground. I've got plenty of money. Winter gave me plenty.'

She shrugged. 'Suits me,' she said, unconvinced. 'Sooner it was you than me, though.'

By the time they had reached the outskirts of the town, she had forgotten her worries and had picked up a concertina from the back of the cart and was singing softly to herself in a detached way, as though she knew no one was listening to her.

Then she paused, staring at the little town ahead again with an expression of alarm on her face.

'It's not my idea of a big city,' she observed. She studied it for a moment, then shrugged and went on singing, unable to be unhappy for long.

After a while, however, she turned her attention to Plummerton Sidings again, sitting uncomfortably on the seat beside Sammy, the concertina limp in her hands, staring ahead with an expression of marked distaste.

It was only a small place, set solidly athwart the old missionary road opened by Moffat and Livingstone and finally Rhodes, its chief reason for existence being the shimmering steel lines that had been run there from Kimberley in 1894, and onwards in the following years to Bulawayo. Its spreading mass of sidings and engine sheds had made it invaluable to the British in the Boer War.

It had a few hangdog streets, most of them still unpaved, and in the broad dusty area of its square a brand-new garage backed up by the still-necessary livery stables where the rigs stood outside in the sunshine.

The whole place looked as though it had been scattered carelessly across the veld, for in that vast expanse of land no one had been concerned with saving space when the town grew up, and only near the railway track was there any suggestion of neighbourliness. Beyond the railway line, the dun veld stretched desolately towards the river, a muddy trickle under the iron bridge, the rocks smooth and black in the river bed.

Sammy let the horse move at its own pace through the streets into the outskirts of the town. Behind the solitary hotel, among the pomegranates and the brick-edged flower-beds, and the fallen twisted leaves, a dove was moaning heartbrokenly.

The area round the station seemed emptied of white men in the hot silence of the afternoon. A group of Kaffirs and yellow-faced Hottentots with their peppercorn hair dozed in the shade like bundles of old rags, their heads down on their knees, their dogs as though dead in the dust. A few Indians trying to sell chickens as skinny as themselves stood thin-legged as storks in the sunshine.

There were soldiers billeted near the station water towers in a shabby warehouse just off the splintery platform, volunteers in raspy grey-back shirts, Bedford cords and spurred brown boots – Dutch and native-born South Africans mostly, with a sprinkling of British and other nationalities – farmers, clerks, diggers and railwaymen, the men Botha was trying to use against De Wet's rebels instead of Imperial troops in the hope of keeping the uprising a private quarrel; deeply-burned men, hard-bitten and fined down by hard living to a curious uniformity of countenance. Their horses were huddled together round a hitching post, flapping at the afternoon flies with their tails, while in the shade a couple of seconded Army Service Corps mechanics tinkered with the engine of a big Rolls-Royce, a lean-looking vehicle, painted brown and stripped of unnecessary fittings to make room for racks for petrol cans.

For the rest, the street was empty, silent and still in the afternoon sun, only the long-drawn-out hiss of a standing engine beyond the sheds disturbing the silence.

Polly stared at the flat-fronted shabby buildings in dismay. 'I didn't know it was like this,' she said. 'A girl couldn't pick up much here.'

She was caught by a sudden resentment, and went on in a beaten disconsolate tone. 'Why we've got to get out of Plummerton just because *they* want us out, I dunno,' she said bitterly, feeling rootless and adrift suddenly as she thought of the sparse comfort of the rooms behind Buiderkant Street she had left behind and the few belongings she had given up because she couldn't pack them. There hadn't been much, just a roomy bedchamber with red curtains and cheap gaudy wallpaper fly-spotted round the light, a chest of drawers, some without knobs, a greenish looking-glass and a brass-knobbed iron bedstead with a turkey twill cover – and an American-cloth armchair set by the window where you could watch the traffic and the people. But outside there was a white-painted fence which made it look like home and a couple of white-washed drainpipes overflowing with Indian cress, set on either side of the gate under the dusty pepper trees.

Not much, she thought again, but there must have been *something* about it to attract people because they always came – and not always because she had the sort of figure that whetted their appetites. Sometimes they came – Winter among them, she thought bitterly, as she considered how he had ranged himself against her now – merely to sit and drink with her, satisfied simply to be with a woman who was kind and thought about their comfort without making demands on them.

As she sank into her own private reverie, Sammy said nothing, and the cart rattled slowly past the crates of machinery, the sacks of flour stacked outside the office of the forwarding agents bearing the inevitable name of Plummer, a musty place with an odour that was a strange compound of tea and green coffee, of ropes and saddles and sides of leather, the saltiness of bacon and the sharp metallic tang of hardware, all larded with the strong chemical odour of sheep-dip.

'We're getting out because they've got all the money, Poll,' Sammy said slowly at last. 'This is *all* theirs – every last bit of it. They've got the power and the say-so. People like you and me have to do as we're told.' He became silent again, not resentful in spite of his words, as though in his world the weakest had always gone to the wall without complaining.

They were moving up the main street now, past a waiting tram, whose horses dozed in the sun, its coloured driver silent and huddled in one of the seats. The sun was past its zenith but fiercer than ever, so that the sky paled and the dust hung motionless in the air, and the heat drew all the vitality out of the land, squeezing out the marrow from the bones of the earth and leaving behind only the vast empty husk of the African afternoon.

Polly stared about her and at the men lounging along the front of the hotel.

'Sammy,' she said, a doubtful worried note in her voice, 'I don't like the look of this place. I want to go to Kimberley.'

He turned to her, his face blank, his flat light eyes unemotional. 'There's no train for a while,' he said.

She smiled at him, wheedling, her mercurial Irish good humour returning. '*You* could take me, Sammy.'

'Me?' He stared at her, his eyes wide at last in the shadow of his hat.

'Why not?'

He scowled, resisting her blandishments. 'Because I'm not going to Kimberley – that's why not.'

Polly put on an act of scorn for his benefit. 'Lor', aren't you slow?' she said. 'What's to *stop* you?'

Sammy avoided her eyes, knowing her ability to coax blood from a stone. 'I promised,' he said evenly. 'I promised Plummer's man I'd keep away from towns for a bit.'

'Never knew you worry about promises before,' Polly said quickly, seeing a chink in his defences that she could exploit. 'You've broken plenty to me in your time. Standing a girl up like she was an umbrella in dry weather. You particularly anxious to go to Namaqualand or something?'

'You know I'm not.'

'Well, who's to know you *didn't*.'

He flicked the mare's back with the whip. 'We've got no supplies,' he said.

'You've got the gun.' She indicated the ancient Martini Henry in the back of the cart. 'I never knew you be stuck. You said yourself you'd manage.'

He eyed her without speaking, and she went on hurriedly. 'I've got all my clothes with me,' she persisted. 'There's a blanket in the cart. We can get another. We can stop here and get anything we want. It's only four days' journey.'

Sammy grinned. *'And* a bit more,' he said. 'And there's no hotels in the Wilderness.'

'We don't need hotels.'

'*I* don't.'

'Neither do I then!'

'You ever tried it?'

She gave him an encouraging jab with her elbow. 'Go on, Sammy,' she encouraged, smiling. 'There's plenty of game. You were going to buy flour and coffee and such here in the Sidings anyway before you crossed the line. Well, now you can buy twice as much. You've got the spondulics.'

He paused, studying her silently. 'Another hoss is the first thing,' he said and she smiled secretly to herself, knowing already that she'd persuaded him and that he was only putting on a show of resistance to prove his manhood to himself. 'It's easier to stalk game with a hoss, and an old nag like this isn't much good for riding. And another gun I'd need – a shotgun.'

'You've got the money. Frank Winter gave it you.'

'Not to go to Kimberley, he didn't.'

'Sammy Schuter' – she brought up her heavy artillery – 'if it was *me*, I wouldn't let 'em sit on me. I'd go where I wanted. I'd have a shy at it, I would.'

He looked at her soberly. 'It's a long way, Polly,' he said slowly. 'You don't know. It'd take several days. Longer than you think. We'd have to sweep out wide a bit to find the game. They don't run close to the railway these days.'

'What's it matter? I'm not afraid.' She smiled up at him again, warm-hearted, bright-eyed, irresistible. 'Let's give it a whirl! Go on, Sammy. You've talked me into it.'

'It'll be rough.'

'I'm not scared of that, not me. It's not as though I've been used to eating off gold plate. It won't hurt us. Or are you worried you'll lose your way or something?'

Sammy grinned and looked at her with those opaque eyes of his, knowing she knew his pride in his skill as well as he did himself.

'Poll,' he said, 'I know the country up here like I know my own face. I've spent weeks round the salt pans out in the Kalahari. Good country for game. I know it all – from the Orange River up to Khama's country. I've killed for the markets in Windhoek and Keetmanshoop and Port Nolluth. There's not an inch I haven't crossed again and again.'

'Well then – ?' She stared at him, daring him, and he began to fold the leather of the reins in his hand.

For a long time he sat shaping and reshaping it, his face thoughtful, then at last he flipped the reins along the grey mare's back.

'Let's go and buy them victuals,' he said with a grin.

seven

The night grey sky was changing to green and orange and the last violent red in the west where the sun had set. A few clouds striped with black the bowl of the heavens as it slowly began to take on the luminous light of night.

Plummerton Sidings was silent and still and dead but for the few yellow lights in the windows of the shabby houses. Over by the railway sidings on the soft breeze whispering from the Kalahari came the lowing of oxen from where the wagoners waited for the morning, rising over the gentle hiss of steam from a locomotive, and the clank of wagons being shifted from the points.

From the direction of the soldiers' billets the sound of crunching boots was followed by the roar of a motorcar engine being revved, harsh like the tearing of calico, drowning the witless chatter of the frogs and crickets, then falling rapidly to a sewing-machine murmur behind all the other sounds of the town.

Winter shifted uneasily in the chair he had placed on the stoep of the hotel and reached for his glass. At the other side of the square there was a low store with the single yellow glare of a gas jet beyond its glass door. For a while, a few Kaffirs had sat on the stoep in the lowering sunshine, chattering noisily in the still warm air, then even they had vanished and the place lay in silence.

In front of him the veld stretched out in a great sweep of earth, impressive in the prodigality of its space, while overhead the tall African stars, steady and unwinking, picked out the scattered gum trees beyond the town, and the few sparse peppers along the square. The fan of a dwarf palm nearby rusted into thin whiskers, its spikes reflected in the glassy water of a horse trough where grass grew round a dripping tap.

Winter sipped slowly at the brandy in his hand and stretched his legs. Behind him in the hotel he could hear an argument going on, over the soft batting of moths against the lighted screen door.

'The bloody Boers ought to be all shot,' someone was saying loudly. 'Starting a civil war. Setting about us when they've been beat once.'

The argument was drowned abruptly as someone started playing a concertina, and a husky male voice, rich with drink, began to sing –

> *'There was Brown upside down,*
> *Mopping up the whisky off the floor –*
> *Booze, booze, the firemen cried*
> *As they came knocking at the door –'*

Winter put down his glass and lit a cigarette. In front of him the horse tethered to the hitching post out in the dusty road shook its head suddenly with a jingle of its bit, then dropped back into a silent somnolence. Suddenly the night seemed stiflingly hot and airless.

There was still no sign of Sammy Schuter's dusty cart and Winter began to wonder if the boy had been lying when he had promised to head to Upington and the west. He had seemed willing enough to go but there had been the same sort of contempt for politicians in his face that Kitto always showed, a derisive condescension that was probably powerful enough to make him susceptible to any offer Fabricius might conceivably have made to him.

He could still remember the shrewd, youthful face, watching him with strange steely eyes as he had made his own offer, and he remembered that the sly humour behind it had brought into his mind all the doubtful things he had ever done for Offy in the name of business, all the crafty deals he had worked out in that shabby office over the newspaper, all the bribings with shares of intractable opponents, the small positions of trust that had been discreetly put forward, the pensions, the directorships, even the blackmail when nothing else had worked – the dead dogs he'd dug up, trying to ignore the fact that it wasn't entirely honest by persuading himself that it was necessary, and that circumstances demanded a loosening of the bounds of moral obligation.

He shrugged, smiling at his own unexpected flash of conscience, and it was while he was still stretching and yawning, stiff with sitting and bored with waiting, that he heard the throb of an engine and saw the yellow glow of a motorcar's lamps as it swung into the square. It moved slowly down the eastern side of the dusty patch of ground, away from the faint light of the stars, then it came round in a big sweep that sent the dust flying, and stopped sharply in front of the hotel, sliding on the loose surface and quivering as the driver raced the engine. Winter recognised the long square snout and studded bonnet of Kitto's Rolls-Royce scout car, and a few Africans, attracted by the noise and the lights, gathered immediately from nowhere and stood in the glow that came from the bar, grinning with a child-like appreciation.

The door slammed and Kitto jumped out of the car, stamping on to the stoep where Winter sat. He had changed the smart uniform he had worn to meet Plummer and wore drill trousers now and boots and a wide-awake hat decorated with blue goggles, his Sam Browne and revolver strapped over a navy jersey, his body literally draped with the straps of his compass, binoculars, map case and other equipment.

Romanis was with him, also in some sort of uniform, but still wearing his leather coat and cap.

'Look slippy,' Kitto said quickly, indicating the car. 'Jump in!'

Romanis grabbed his arm, but Winter backed away, still holding his glass. 'Steady on,' he said. 'Where are we going?'

'Out there,' Kitto said, indicating the broad sweep of land beyond the railway track. 'Look slippy, they've dodged us. They've got clean away.'

Winter got his back against the veranda, refusing to be hurried. 'All right, all right,' he soothed. 'But for God's sake just tell me what's happening.'

'They've been here already,' Romanis said. 'We found they bought stores. At a place near the station. They're on the way to Kimberley.'

'Kimberley! How do you know?'

'Something they let drop in the store.' Kitto flicked impatiently at his boot with his crop. 'You were right. The bastard's not to be trusted.' His thin cheeks were sucked in with irritation. 'He's got a damn' good start too,' he concluded.

'How good?'

'Ten-twelve hours.' Kitto grinned suddenly, his sharp fierce face lighting up. 'But we'll pick 'em up all right,' he said. 'These vehicles of mine move amazin' quick.'

'It's a good job they do,' Romanis said. 'There are a lot of Fabricius' friends in Kimberley.'

'And a lot of Offy's enemies,' Winter added.

Kitto turned with a faint ring of triumph in his voice. 'Don't worry,' he said confidently. 'I'll get south of 'em in no time and set 'em on their road again.'

Winter stretched and yawned. 'Offy'll like your loyalty,' he said.

'It's not a question of loyalty to Offy.' Kitto was on his dignity at once, opaque in intellect and unyielding in his honesty. His face, yellowish in the light that came from the screen door, was frosty in his humourless disapproval of Winter.

'We'd better get this straight here and now,' he suggested. 'To me, this is a military operation and nothing more. Politics don't come into it. You can act as Offy's jackal if you like, Winter. *I* don't.'

'I wish I'd got your principles, Kitto,' Winter smiled. ' "*What stronger breastplate than a heart untainted?*" '

'I'm concerned with only one thing,' Kitto went on. 'And that's my country. I was one of the men who helped pull down the Transvaal flag and I had to watch the bloody politicians in Whitehall give it all back to them. You don't think I'm going to let a few hotheads like De Wet drag apart all we've built up, do you? Now let's get going.'

Winter shrugged, humbled by Kitto's obsessed pride. 'Have it your own way,' he said, 'but we can't follow their tracks till daylight, surely?'

'I think we can.' Kitto sounded cheerful again. 'I've got an ex-scout with my mob. Chap called Le Roux. He could follow the spoor with his nose. He can smell it in the dark. He's out there now. And these damn' people can't ride a horse at sixty miles an hour.'

'Good God,' Romanis added, 'this Schuter's only a Sheeny backvelder! He can't read or write. He's never been to school. Surely some bloody ignoramus of an old clo' merchant's son isn't going to put it across *us.*'

Between them they swept the unwilling Winter into the box-like rear of the car and slammed the doors. The engine howled metallically.

'Hold tight,' Romanis shouted. 'This driver's hell-bent for glory.'

The clutch was let in with a jerk that flung their heads back and as they roared out of the square, Winter realised he still held his empty glass in his hand. He shrugged and tossed it over his shoulder into the cloud of dust they trailed behind them, and concentrated on keeping his eyes closed against the flying particles of grit that washed against his face like spray.

'Where do you hope to pick 'em up?' he shouted.

Kitto raised his voice above the roar of the engine. 'Sheba,' he yelled gaily. 'Somewhere south of Sheba. They can't have got far beyond there.'

e i g h t

Sheba. Rising out of the limitless veld as though it had no connection with the flat unturned earth around it, it stood in an eerie stillness, precipitous to the south, east and west, and sloping sharply towards the north. Its summit and sides were covered with unscaleable rocks that looked like the broken parapets of giant castles, time-smoothed ramparts like minarets flecked with colouring that gave it the appearance of some towering eastern city.

Every variety of colour blended on its sides, grey, black, yellow, red, brown and purple, all harmonising, all weather-worn and softened, its only inhabitants the few remaining klipspringers and dassies, the little rock rabbits who lived in the crevasses between the vast stone spires.

In front, beyond the sloping side to the north, lay a smaller pile of stones thrown up in the same vast prehistoric upheaval, a bare heap of sandy-coloured rocks which had become known, by the same token as its bigger neighbour, as Babylon; standing alone like Sheba, a miniature kopje, its southern end finishing in a pile of loose boulders tumbled haphazardly across the dusty plain.

Here, in front of Babylon, Sammy Schuter and Polly Bolt had camped for the night.

The day started in a spot of pink beyond the bleak enigmatic plain and spread slowly, washing the eastern skyline. The brick red earth turned lighter as the purple grey of the night faded and the outlines of the distant folds of land became visible in the first pale glow of day.

The fire had burned down to a hot incandescent heap of charcoal and the smoke that spiralled upwards had thinned to a single twisting pencil line. The light night winds had died and the whole enormous landscape of short dry grass and far distant purple slopes was utterly motionless in the first hint of the sun's glow.

Polly was standing by the fire scrubbing out the cooking pot with gritty dust, her eyes smarting from the milk-blue wood smoke that had rolled across the little camp. Her cheeks, dusty from travel, were stained where she had rubbed the tears away. They had breakfasted on buck liver and fat cookies prepared by Sammy, and strips of meat crozzled on sharpened sticks, eating them Boer fashion, crossed-legged round the fire, their backs against the cart. The heat of the food was penetrating now through her body and the chills and discomfort and all the myriad fears of the unfamiliar and unfriendly night she had spent out there on the veld were slowly disappearing from her mind.

She watched Sammy for a while as he worked, steadily and efficiently by the back of the cart, flaying the body of a dead duiker he had shot the previous night as it went plunging in its curious diving motion for the scrub. He had brought it up all-standing with a sharp shrill whistle, its head up, its ears pricked, its tail flapping, and dropped it quickly with a bullet through the brain that had flung it end over end and left it sprawled on the grass, its head thrown back. They had covered it with a frame of grass and sticks to keep away the night-prowling animals and before she was awake he had cleared the obstruction and, cutting a stick, had braced the hind legs apart, piercing the shanks with its pointed tips. Then he had hung the carcass from the tailgate of the cart with a length of hide he had stripped from the body, and he was now engaged in cutting slices of flesh down the centre of the back, in deft swinging strokes, and rolling them in salt spread on a board in the cart. The prepared strips of meat lay in a row on a rock beside him, ready for drying in the fierce heat of the sun when it rose in the heavens.

She watched him as she moved about the fire, rinsing out the gritty greasy cooking pot with a cupful of boiled water. She stared dolefully at the scum the operation left on her fingers, then she tossed the pot into the back of the cart and, wiping her hands on the limp print frock she'd changed into, lashed out at the flies with a cheerful violence.

'This is a fine old way to wash things,' she said. 'Sammy, can't we get any water? That stream's more mud than anything else.'

'You ought to know by now,' Sammy replied calmly, 'that when you fall into a South African stream you get suffocated by the dust. We can pick up water tonight,' he added. 'I know a sure place. Plenty of time. Got to learn to make do.'

'Sammy Schuter, we've been making do ever since we left Plummerton! I've got dust in my eyes, in my nose, in my mouth. My hair's full of it. I haven't looked in a mirror since we left. How's a girl to take a proper pride in herself?' It was less of a complaint than the mourning cry of a town dweller whose personal appearance was part of her life.

'It won't take long,' he consoled her. 'Then you'll be able to comb it all out.'

She looked at him candidly, demanding the truth. 'Sammy, when are we going to find a decent-sized town again? These flies fair take the flesh off you.'

'I told you,' he said patiently. 'Four-five days. A bit longer perhaps.'

'A bit longer's right,' she said ruefully. 'I didn't think it'd be like this.'

'I warned you.'

'No, you didn't. You just said there'd be no hotels. You didn't say there'd be no water either, and all this dust.'

She picked up the concertina and stretched out on the ground, idly squeezing a tune out of the instrument. Her face felt like leather and she was uncomfortably aware of the grease that still lay between her fingers from the rudimentary cooking and cleaning.

For a while she studied the veld, gently undulating, wide and empty and featureless to the distant horizon, and the immeasurable saffron dome of the sky. The land lay very still in the first streaks of light, and the faded green patched with reddish-brown stony earth looked like a desert. The Wilderness. It was well named. With its scant vegetation and wide patches of coarse grass alternating with slopes of thorny scrub, it looked like the bleak landscape of another planet, for trees were rare enough to be a landmark beyond the patch of mimosa along the deep dry bed of the stream.

Polly stared at it, comparing it with the single bedroom which had been her home in Plummerton. Used as she was to the sound of a piano somewhere in the background, the chatter of voices, the rumble of traffic outside, she was still unable to accept the tremendous silences that made her feel as though she were suspended in space.

'Sammy,' she said uncertainly.

'Yep?'

'How much longer will it *really* take?'

He glanced down at her, busy with his task. 'We've hardly started yet!' he said, avoiding an answer.

She looked up at him, slashing at the flies again. 'I didn't get any sleep last night,' she pointed out. 'I was cold. I had a stone in my back. And, Sammy, I could imagine creepy-crawly things all the time. I heard 'em once. I heard something howling.'

'Wild dog mebbe,' he said, unmoved. 'Nothing to worry about.'

She regarded him with a wry expression on her face. 'I bet you knew it'd be like this,' she accused.

'Course I knew.'

'Sammy, why didn't you tell me?'

'I tried to, but you wouldn't listen.'

'Did you have a bad night?'

'No. Slept like a log.'

'Anybody'd think you were enjoying it.'

He grinned at her. 'I am. I like it best out here. Better than towns.' He looked up at the horizon and wiped his hands on the grass. 'Better be making a move,' he said. 'We're not here for pleasure.'

Polly jumped to her feet and began to load pans into the back of the cart.

'What are we going to do?' she asked, eager for anything that would take her mind off their discomfort.

'A bit o' shootin',' he said.

She stood with an armful of their belongings, watching him over the top of them as he lowered the carcass of the buck to the ground.

'Sammy' – her eyes shone suddenly as excitement caught hold of her – 'shoot me a springbok! I've never seen a springbok shot, only that measly little thing you got last night!'

He glanced at her, enjoying the gaiety in her face. She hadn't bothered to put make-up on and instead of doing her hair in elaborate rolls, as she usually did, she had tied it simply behind her head with a ribbon she had unthreaded from her petticoat, so that she looked softer, fresher and curiously younger in the old print frock and with the coils of her hair free about her neck and throat.

Sammy was staring at her, his eyes steady on her face, approving and warm. 'Don't know why you ever put all that muck on your face,' he said, apropos of nothing.

Polly frowned, but it was a half-hearted gesture, spoiled by the look of pleasure in her eyes. 'A girl don't look her best less she titivates herself up a bit.' She stared at him primly, nearer to blushing than she'd been for years. 'We going to stand here all day?' she demanded loudly.

He grinned. 'I'll get the hosses.'

He loped off to where the horses were grazing – the old mare that they used in the shafts and the one-eyed Argentino police horse that they'd bought for ten pounds in Plummerton Sidings, a bad-tempered animal which shied every time they approached it from its right hand side. They were both of them knee-haltered a short distance away, cropping at the grass.

'We'll pick up meat for a few days,' he said as he returned. 'Then we'll get moving. When we get nearer Kimberley, we'll fill the cart. It'll fetch a pound or two in the market. Get that fire out, Poll.'

Polly was already kicking dust over the remains of the fire as Sammy harnessed the bony grey mare into the shafts, but the smell of coffee and fried meat still hung faintly round the small encampment.

Sammy swung himself into the saddle of the little Argentino with its age-whitened muzzle, fighting it as it moodily protested against his mounting on the wrong side. For a while, it jerked its hindquarters, lifting its legs with hints of kicking, a tough little animal which for all its age and lightweight had already proved its stamina, then he mastered it and waited until Polly had swung herself up on to the seat of the cart and adjusted the folds of her skirt. He passed her the old shotgun they'd bought with the horse and she sat holding it gingerly.

'Don't blow your head off,' he warned.

He pulled the Martini Henry from the scabbard and laid it across his saddle, holding the reins with one hand and the rifle with the other.

'Let's go,' he said. 'Now's the time to pick up the buck. They're kind of slow before the sun warms 'em up. We'll find 'em in the hollows licking the salt off the dried water holes.'

The day was still only a faint promise of gold in the east and it was a pure morning, with all the world still and the air invigorating. Even Polly was aware of its clarity.

'Kind of cleans out your lungs and brain,' she admitted, gesturing vaguely at the space around them.

Sammy nodded silently. There was a quiet, unhesitating sureness about him, a definiteness of purpose in his movements that inspired confidence. Taking out a yellow bandanna handkerchief, he removed his hat and passed the handkerchief round the brim, not looking at it, his eyes moving down the valley.

The land seemed empty, bare and rolling, covered with thin brown grass dried through the summer by the shimmering heat of the sun. The ridge beyond them rose slantwise, rough-edged like a saw where small outcrops of rocks broke through the surface and edged the skyline.

The Argentino stood in silence, snorting softly through its nostrils, nuzzling at the dried blood on its foreleg where it had cut it climbing out of a donga the night before, and Sammy's hand moved gently along its neck, soothingly, feeling the greasy sweat where the reins lay. Then he licked a finger and held it up thoughtfully.

'What wind there is, is coming from the west,' he said quietly. 'That's good. We can keep the sun behind us and stay downwind at the same time. Won't affect the shooting neither.'

Polly stared around her at the endless horizons. The exhilarating climate lifted her heart and for the first time in her life she knew the pull of a different existence from the one she had lived in the saloons and bars of Plummerton with their smell of stale smoke and spilt liquor, and the dusty plush and gilt furnishings.

'You know,' she said grudgingly, 'this place's maybe got something after all. I'm beginning to see why we could never get you home, Sammy.'

He nodded. 'Some men's for towns,' he said shortly, 'and some's for the veld.'

She sniffed the air, noticing in it a freshness she had not caught during the heat of the previous day. 'It's sort of clean-smelling in the morning before the dust gets up, isn't it?' she said. 'You've got to get up early to get a proper whiff of it.'

He nodded again.

'What's the matter?' she demanded. 'Cat got your tongue?'

He grinned. 'Nobody ever shot anything who told it he was coming first. They've got ears like you. Keep your eyes open and your mouth shut. That's the way to pick up a buck.'

He grinned at the startled indignation on her face.

'You've got to learn,' he said. 'Only born fools stay fools all their lives.'

She shut her mouth with a click at the implied rebuke and he nudged the Argentino ahead of the cart. She flicked the reins across the grey mare's back and followed him, her lips clamped, trying hard to behave with his taciturnity and finding it, with her normal capacity for endless chatter, difficult to the point of being exhausting. Fully awake now though, her nose in the air and sniffing, she felt keenly the space around her, and for the first time was curiously content simply to be there.

As they reached the top of a fold in the ground, he reined in – not sharply, but gently, with an instinctive movement as though he never moved awkwardly or in any abrupt way that might break the rhythm of his movements.

'Springbok down there,' he said softly. 'Moving slow. They like to loiter when they're undisturbed.'

She stared into the floor of a shallow valley, a vast basin with sloping sides, the purple hills like clouds beyond it. Other folds opened out from the main valley, some veiled in this mist, others just touched by light, and all filled with a curious blue glow that came from the milky vapours, so that they seemed to be looking into the depths of clear water. The ground before them was studded with ant heaps and a few karroo flowers, their foliage grey-green against the red soil.

Polly strained her eyes, trying to see what Sammy saw. 'How do you know there's springbok?' she asked.

'I can see 'em,' he said, a hint of surprise in his voice.

Polly stared again. 'You got damn' good eyes!' she retorted, unbelieving.

'Practice,' he said. 'I can see things because I'm looking for 'em. They're scattered now. They're always like that till the sun gets up. You can see their heads out of the mist if you look careful.'

He was glancing round him, moving slowly and deliberately in the saddle.

'Stay here,' he said. 'Come on down when you hear me shoot.'

'Will that mean you've got one?'

'Usually does. I don't miss often. You can get down in the valley with the cart, but keep upwind of 'em, if you can. Then if they whiff you they'll scatter towards me. Give me a chance to get across the other side first though. That's all.'

For a moment, as he sat with one leg cocked over the saddle he seemed almost statuesque on the little knoll, sharp against the brightening sky, then he kicked the horse into a gallop and a bunched flock of guinea-fowl in the distance, black-barred and grey, and squat and round as barrels, scattered quickly along the edge of the dusty track, moving like shining beads of lead, 'chinking' excitedly as their turkey heads disappeared into the stubby grass.

He had been gone some time and she was feeling incredibly alone when at last she caught a glimpse of a group of animals at the far side of the valley above the milkiness of the mist, moving rapidly along the sloping bowl of the land. With a spasm of excitement she knew at once they were springbok from the speed with which they moved. With their bright lithe bodies they seemed like a stream of water rippling in the growing daylight, almost as though their bodies reflected the glowing sky.

For a moment, she was puzzled, for these couldn't have been the herd that Sammy had seen, and she moved slowly farther into the valley, among the ghostly tops of the thorn trees. Her first glimpse of the nearer buck was of one or two dim ghostly shapes suspended against an invisible background, bodies without legs, heads without bodies. She had stumbled on them unexpectedly and she halted the cart, not quite sure what to do, and while she was still debating with herself, two shots rang out on her right.

Twenty or thirty horned heads shot up immediately out of the mist where before she had only seen two or three. Then they began to move towards her and she saw the whole herd as the mist shifted. Like drops of bright water flung against a stone they broke apart abruptly at the alarm, then they swung together again like metal filings under the influence of a magnet. They were racing across the veld now in a straight line diagonally across her front and disappearing behind the fold of the next slope. Excitedly, she realised they would cross her path, and the next second the buck, sweeping up the slope in a strung-out cloud, rolled over the curve of the hill towards her, swinging past her almost as though they were all attached to the same string.

Then they were spraying outwards round her, a whirlpool of racing animals in a cloud of dust to right and left of her, in full flight, dozens and dozens and dozens of them, springing and jinking as they passed her at top speed, giving little sneezy snorts as they leapt over each other in graceful nine-foot curves in their efforts to escape. She found herself screaming with excitement as the brown and black and white striped bodies shot past her, and almost too late she remembered the shotgun. Dragging it out of the cart, she blasted into the tail-end of the herd as it swept past, and to her delight, a big ram stumbled and fell.

Before she knew what was happening, the rest had swept on up the slope, the sound of their feet dying through the drifting dust, bright shifting motes now where they had once been animals, disappearing over the top of the slope where the sun was already touching the curve of the earth, only tiny stirrings of movement, more like changes of light than the manoeuvres of a herd of antelope swinging out of danger and melting into the far pathway of the horizon.

She laughed, her heart still thumping with excitement, and turned to where she could see the body of the buck sprawled in the dust forty yards away.

'Well, that's not bad for the first go at it,' she said gaily, pleased with herself.

She whacked the horse into a shambling gallop and rattled across to where the buck lay, the cart jerking and rolling over the uneven track, the hubs screeching on the axles, small stones flying out from under the iron rims of the wheels. Gradually, with the help of the slope, the old horse moved faster and she suddenly found herself bouncing about on the seat, struggling to keep her balance.

'God's truth,' she cried out, in sudden alarm as she realised the horse was enjoying itself also and had broken into a furious gallop; and she began heaving on the reins, sawing with them at its mouth so that it swung off the track and across the rough ground.

She reached the buck with the horse weaving in a staggering gallop as it tried to dodge the ant heaps and the small dry karroo bushes that disappeared beneath the wheels in an explosive shower of twigs, and as she pulled up, her box bounced clean out over the tailboard and went rolling across the ground, bursting open to scatter her belongings on the grass, her underclothes flying through the air like great white birds. Then the back end of the cart hit a rock, bounced off in a whipping turn and almost rolled over.

Polly sat up, panting and scared, as they came to a stop and stared back at her scattered clothes. 'Lor',' she said aloud, 'there's more to this lark than meets the eye.'

She climbed down and moved towards the buck, cautious at first, afraid and excited at the same time, and then faster as her curiosity caught hold of her. Stopping alongside the slim body, she was consumed with disappointment and despair at the sight of the staring velvety eyes. The hide, which had seemed so smooth at a distance, now seemed shabby and rough and the long frail legs ending in the sharply pointed hooves worried her that she had stilled them for ever. Then, while she was still staring, she saw the hindquarters heave in a spasmodic movement and the head lifted, the jaw working, curious formless sounds coming from the throat.

A scream was jerked out of her and she began to run, stopping only when she realised she wasn't being followed by the crippled buck. For a second she stared back then, her legs still unsteady, she began to collect her clothes with nervous haste, stuffing them anyhow into the box. Bundling it into the cart, she climbed on to the seat and sent the old horse shambling into the wreaths of mist, suddenly wanting to be nearer to Sammy, more than ever aware of loneliness in the vastness of the plain.

Sammy was bending over the carcass of a buck on the floor of the valley, his knife slitting it up the belly, gutting it, until it was no longer a lovely living thing but a small faded heap of hide and flesh and bone. He looked up as she approached and saw her face.

'What's the matter?' he asked.

'It just don't seem right,' she said, in a small voice.

'What don't?'

'When they look like they do,' she explained inadequately. 'They're pretty for wild animals.'

He nodded. 'Often think that meself,' he said.

He removed the liver and set it aside, then he wiped the blood from his fingers with a handful of sparse grass and stood up.

'There's another across there,' he said.

'I shot one too, Sammy,' she said, unable to restrain the pride in her voice.

He looked up and grinned, surprised, and her face fell again.

'It's up there,' she went on, her voice trembling. 'It's not properly dead. For God's sake, come and put it out of its misery. I'm not so sure I like shooting.'

He straightened up in a loose, smooth movement and slung the carcass of the buck across the back of the cart. 'You get used to it,' he said. 'Let's go and get it.'

He searched round quietly in the mist for a moment and stooped. When he returned, she saw he had the body of another buck across his shoulders, slung on his rifle like a pack, the front legs through the slit tendons of the hind legs. He gutted it quickly and laid it with the other in the back of the cart, then he swung into the saddle and indicated the slope of the hill with the Henry.

'With two of us shooting,' he grinned, 'we'll have so much meat to eat, we won't be able to move. I'll go and fetch it. You wait here.'

He glanced upwards and jerked his thumb. The vultures were above them already, black ragged dots circling directly overhead with unmoving wings. He grinned again, and kicked the mare into a gallop and she saw him scrambling up the slope, growing smaller as he climbed into the sunshine.

As he reached the top he stopped, looking for the buck, and she saw him sit there for a moment, huge against the sky-line, his rifle like a lance across his body, then he jammed the weapon into the scabbard and swung the horse round abruptly. She saw the puff of dust as he moved farther back down the slope, and slipped from the saddle again.

For a second, thinking he had found the buck, she was puzzled, feeling she had been lower down the slope when she had shot it. But he didn't stoop. He remained standing, staring over the top of the fold of ground towards the south, then he took his hat off and held it low over his eyes, still staring into the sun.

For a moment, she thought he hadn't been able to see the buck and was on the point of whipping the old horse up the hill towards him, when he swung into the saddle again, and dragged the Argentino swiftly round and came down towards her at a flat gallop. To her surprise, he hadn't got the buck.

He pulled up alongside the cart and pointed with his hand.

'Soldiers,' he said. 'Right in front of us.'

'Right in front of us?' She glanced towards the hill, startled to find they were sharing the vast expanse of the veld with someone else. 'Who are they, Sammy? De Wet?'

He shook his head. 'Kitto's crowd,' he said. 'The soldiers from the Sidings. In front and to the east a bit. I saw 'em from the top of the hill. They've got two motorcars out there, and a lorry.'

'How do you know they're Kitto's crowd?'

'Well, they're not Germans,' he explained. 'Not this far east. Besides, they're going the wrong way for Germans. And it's not De Wet. *He's* got no motors.'

She stared at him, beginning to be a little afraid. 'Sammy, are they following us? Have they found out we're not going where they said we'd got to go?'

He shook his head. 'I dunno. Maybe not. They're soldiers, after all, not Plummer's men. Maybe it's just a patrol looking for De Wet, but they're there right enough. Must be a couple of dozen horses too, spread out in a big line either side of the motors, looking for a trail most like.'

He turned in the saddle and gazed up the slope. 'At least they can't see us here,' he went on. 'And we'll always be able to see them first. Motors make so much dust you can see 'em miles away. Let's get going, Poll. Whatever they're up to, we don't want to get mixed up in it. I don't want to find myself in the middle of a war. We'll head more west round the curve of the valley. They'll most likely miss us then. They're heading south.'

She shot a glance towards the crest of the hill, puzzled and uneasy, then turned again to Sammy, who sat staring back over the hill, his eyes narrowed, mere ice-blue slits in the shadow of his hat, his whole body still with the stillness only an experienced hunter could manage. She'd seen him sitting like that many times back near her father's farm as a boy, his eyes on something he was watching, motionless as a tree, knowing that it wasn't his shape that startled a buck so much as his movement. He seemed almost as though he weren't breathing, stilled by an instinct for danger that had become developed in him by all the hunting he'd done.

Then he pulled the Henry out of its scabbard and slid a cartridge into the breech with a click. As he did so, he looked up and caught her eyes on him. The significance of the action had not escaped her.

'Sammy,' she said quietly, 'I'm scared. Are *you* scared?'

He shook his head, forcing a smile.

'Not yet, Poll,' he said cheerfully, 'but if that lot *should* be follering us for some reason, I'll soon start to get scared.'

She slapped the reins across the back of the mare and the cart started to move.

'That's it. Keep her going, Poll,' he encouraged. 'Perhaps if we can get round them hills, they'll miss us.'

He nudged the Argentino into motion and dropped into position behind the cart, glancing back continually over his shoulder.

As they moved, the vultures were drifting towards the shining heaps of entrails, dropping lower as the cart moved away, not circling any longer. Then they came down in a long slanting dive that carried them low over the cart, ugly heads out, wings all but shut against their bodies, right over Polly's head with breathy 'whoosh'.

nine

The little sand-covered heap of ashes stood out in the inhospitable earth of the veld like a sore, clear even in the fading light. Low down over the horizon, the long bars of cloud were purple and grey and the lavender-coloured hills had changed to blue.

The motorcars had stopped, the Rolls first, the Napier just behind, with the lorry with the supplies farther astern still, their engines throbbing and harsh in the silence, the faint scar their wheels had made stretching behind them into infinity across the veld. The cavalrymen, who had bunched together in a half circle near the Rolls-Royce, had dismounted, easing their behinds, walking their horses to cool them down. They were adjusting girths now, swilling their mouths from their canteens and slapping the dust from their clothes, weary after a day-long ride south until they had realised they had lost the track.

They had turned north again during the afternoon, pushing ahead to meet Le Roux and the group of Kaffir scouts who were working beyond the horizon, the cars smashing across country to keep in front of the horsemen and sending the squadrons of buck and zebra that they disturbed with the popple of their exhausts sprinting for miles into the folds of the plain.

The faces of the crews were masked now with a layer of dust which clung to eyebrows and moustaches, and their lips were cracked with the dryness of the air. Galled by the grit which had found its way down shirts and into eyes, nostrils and ears, their bodies ached with hanging on to the high swaying vehicles as they swung on two wheels like ships in a heavy swell every time they turned on the steep slopes. Their nerves were drawn taut as bowstrings with watching the patchy earth over the bonnets as they had ground through the hollows where the dust was deep and rushed along with wide-open throttles where the surface was firm.

Kitto stood by the running board of the Rolls, his blue goggles on his forehead, his eyes, inflamed by the flying particles, ringed with white dustless patches where his goggles had been. The binoculars on his chest had swept a clean swathe in the grime where they had swung across his clothes.

The Army Service Corps driver lovingly brushed the grit from the pasted-up magazine picture of a Kirchner girl on the dashboard who winked archly at them from a froth of inadequate lace lingerie, then climbed stiffly out to ease his legs, knocking the dirt from his face with an oily hand. For a while, he stamped his feet in the soft, heat-powdered ground whose carpeted dust waited for the low west wind from the Kalahari to sweep it across the plain in a blinding storm, then he stretched, reaching upwards to beg a drink from a cavalryman's canteen.

'Gawd, this dust,' he said, licking his dry dirt-caked lips. 'Give us a wet, man!'

Winter sat in the box body of the Rolls smoking, his face tired, his eyes gritty and burning, staring up at the spires of Sheba, that clawed at the sky like the atrophied fingers of a giant dead hand, dwarfing them all. After a while, he rose, stretched, and climbed down from the car. But his legs, numbed with sitting, gave way and he flopped down abruptly on the running board and reached into his pocket for a flask of Cape brandy. Romanis approached him from the tender, his face aged with the dust on it, his leather coat flapping as he walked, and offered him a cigarette.

'Rum go, this,' he said, like the rest of them jaded with the dust and the rough travelling.

Winter nodded heavily, holding out the flask.

'Try it,' he croaked. 'It'll help. It's the stuff that kicks the boards loose and gives you room to move.'

He watched Romanis put the flask to his lips, his eyes smarting from the sunshine, his body feeling as though he had just come swimming up from the bottom of a muddy sleep in which he had endured a nightmare of violent movement.

He lit the cigarette Romanis had given him and watched the smoke unreeling upwards in the still air, dragging it down to his lungs in grateful gasps.

Romanis stared down at him, grinning and rubbing his stiff legs: 'You're always sitting or lying, Winter,' he observed. 'Don't you ever get tired of it?'

'I'm a tired man,' Winter replied. 'This sort of travel doesn't go with dopper brandy. What's the situation?'

'We'll know in a minute.'

Le Roux, Kitto's scout, was kneeling by the little pile of ashes. His horse, its chestnut flanks and neck smeared with dirty white lather, was held by one of the other men while he peered at the remains of the fire, his broad Dutch face keen and suspicious.

Kitto, his maps and compass in his hand, moved forward to stand by him as he stirred the grey-blue ashes with his foot. Finding them cold, Le Roux prodded them with his fingers, feeling deep into the heart where the last hot cinders had been, then he rose and moved around, staring at footprints and hoof marks, and the place where the horses had been standing for the night. The dark stain on the stones where the blood of the duiker had dripped and the scattered remains of its innards were covered by swarming battalions of black flies, and on the ground all round were the sharp claw marks of the mice and the field rats which had come nosing out of the donga for food.

Le Roux glanced around him, at the indentations in the grass and the blackened splashes of blood, then he walked away slowly until he found the bones of the buck lying bare, dragged behind the rocks and picked clean already by the vultures.

'This morning,' he said in his thick South African tongue as he looked up at Kitto, 'he killed and cut up a buck here. A duiker by the look of it. They slept the night here. Good place for a camp.' He grinned, his flat expressionless face suddenly lit with evil. 'Especially with a woman!' he added. 'Nice and cosy.'

Kitto seemed impatient to move on. 'How far ahead are they?' he asked.

'Eight-ten hours. *Ek weet nie.* Hard to say.'

Kitto stared towards the west and the last bright line of yellow sunshine.

'We'll push on,' he said. 'We'll push on till it's too dark to go any farther. Which way would they go?'

'They'd maybe turn south here,' Le Roux said. 'Unless they were going over the plateau.' He indicated the low ridge of hills in the distance. 'But they wouldn't go that way. There's only the salt flats that way.'

'Where *are* they going then? Not *east,* for God's sake!'

Le Roux pointed. '*Nee.* They swung out to the west. I found a dead buck. Hadn't stopped to gut it even. Must have seen us. It's up on the hill. The vultures took me to it.' He swung an arm up to the sky where they could still see the black ragged shapes wheeling in the south. 'If we go out that way, we're bound to come up with their spoor somewhere.'

'Let's get going then. We've wasted enough time.' Kitto turned to the men behind him, their horses grouped round the cars, and waved his arms. Winter almost expected him to call for a bugler.

'Do we *have* to push on?' Romanis was demanding in a whine, still rubbing his legs. 'There's always tomorrow.'

Kitto looked at him contemptuously. 'Better get back in the Napier,' he said quietly, and Romanis moved away sullenly, his feet kicking the sand in little puffs as he walked.

The horsemen were edging forward now, the iron-shod hooves of their mounts clicking against the pebbles between the sparse grass. Behind them the two or three Kaffirs huddled on their Basuto ponies were staring backwards longingly in the direction of the lorry on the rise of the ground in the last of the light.

Something in Kitto's keenness made Winter uneasy at being there. Suddenly Kitto seemed to have forgotten that ostensibly he was supposed to be searching for De Wet as he became absorbed with the task of finding Sammy Schuter. There was an urgency about him that seemed to suggest he needed and expected a success to set against thirty years of indifferent plodding which, after the beginning in Dhanziland, should have reaped him glittering rewards instead of a third-rate job with Offy Plummer and a lowly volunteer's rank in the army.

He was standing now by the open door of the Rolls, waiting for Winter, his expression keen and optimistic.

'Are we *really* in such a hurry?' Winter protested weakly.

'You want to look after Offy, don't you?'

Winter shrugged at the sarcasm. 'I don't want to look after *Offy*,' he said. 'I want to look after my salary, that's all.'

He stared round at the scattered remains of the camp, feeling vaguely like an intruder, then up at Sheba, seeing nothing but rock, spire on spire of it, valleys and slabs and grottoes of rock, between which the steep stony sides of the kopje slid upwards through patches of cactus and sparse shrub.

He shuddered, awed by the fierce silence of it, and turned towards the car. One or two tired men were trying to pad the dusty box behind the driver's seat with blankets and they looked up and grinned as he approached.

'Ready?' Kitto asked.

'It's all yours,' Winter replied. 'Don't ask me to make a decision. I haven't the initiative of a wet dishrag. All I ask is that you come up on 'em soon and get it over with, so we can go home.'

He knew he was turning his back on the unethicalness of Kitto's behaviour – as he had turned his back on unpleasant things before – because he didn't wish to see it. He climbed into the car, telling himself, as he had so often in the past, that Offy represented civilisation and progress in a still primitive country, and that civilisation and progress demanded their victims; but faced with Kitto's growing enthusiasm for the chase he began to wonder if all they were doing and had done was right.

Kitto was climbing into the car now behind him and slamming the door. He signed to the driver and the engine roared as the wire-spoked double wheels thrashed at the deep sand. As he waved he got an answering wave from Romanis in the Napier, then the car jerked forward and ground ahead, whining and shaking in low gear.

What they drove over now was not a road but a set of dim tracks with deep beds of dust sucking at the wheels, and patches of stone, shingle and potholes, hiding fangs of rock, ready to break a spring or bend a back axle.

'Rough country,' Kitto said enthusiastically, his face full of fierce pleasure. He was standing up in the front seat, clinging on beside the driver, his body swinging to the roll of the vehicle. 'But it's quicker this way,' he said. 'And war's an impatient thing. We'd better start asking them to hurry.'

t e n

They were moving more slowly now along the raw red wound of an old hunting route, the horses sleepy in the sunshine – over wretched ground covered with nothing much more than hundreds of anthills, stones and dwarf karroo bushes and the eternal white camel thorn which, though sparse, seemed with the illusion of distance to crowd together into bushland, so that they seemed to be travelling in a perpetual clearing. The boiling power of the molten sun poured down from an immense empty sky, metallic as a brass gong, and as the shade grew smaller, the thunder began to growl and rumble in the curve of distance beyond the flat-topped mimosas with their scanty foliage. It was so hot now even the birds and the insects seemed to be still among the shrivelled flowers, and the meerkats prowling between the brick-hard anthills and the tail-trailing widow birds had vanished. For hours they had seen no sign of game – not even a solitary duiker plunging for cover, or a scattered squadron of springbok in the distance – and the dried leaves were silent, for the air seemed like a scorching breath. There was no wind, but little dust devils kept whirling around them, so that there seemed to be a warning in the atmosphere, probing through the fine impalpable smell of dust that permeated the whole countryside, a stillness, a heaviness that caught the breath.

Sammy seemed impatient and was watching the sky, sniffing the air from time to time, turning his head this way and that like a dog which has picked up a scent, sitting with one leg over the saddle as usual, letting the tired old Argentino choose its own pace. Away in the east, across the flat solitude, the thunder rumbled and the roof of the sky seemed to have come down to meet the earth, grey and purple and sullen-looking.

'Storm blowing up,' he said, indicating the clouds building up behind them.

Polly stared round her with aching eyes at the endless veld, and the steel-blue stillness of the sky. 'That's hard luck on us,' she commented shakily. 'There's not much shelter, as I can see.'

Everywhere about her the view seemed the same and every mile looked exactly like the last mile. The land seemed to her like a brazen oven, the karroo bushes mere withered sticks with twisted fingers. Only the marching ants and the basking lizards moved before their wheels and, caught by the immensity of it and the silence, she was suffering from the nameless horror of being lost.

She stared round her uneasily, lacking Sammy's confidence and knowledge of the countryside, doubtful of their route and uncertain of her courage.

'It's flat as a billiard table here,' she said. She indicated the growing sombre mass of cloud. 'Nowhere to hide when it comes down.'

Sammy grinned. 'You've got the cart,' he said. He indicated the canvas cover they had dragged out and fitted over the iron hoops when the first big drops had fallen and vanished again half an hour before, disappearing at once into the dry, greedy earth.

Polly stared at the threadbare sheet. 'That'll keep a lot out,' she said.

She glanced behind her anxiously. She knew something of veld storms. They could come with sufficient power to destroy all movement, flooding the dongas in a matter of minutes, drowning sheltering cattle, even men and horses. There was sometimes even hail that could kill small buck and reduce birds as big as quail to pitiful heaps of wet feathers in the flattened dust. Back in Plummerton she had seen them stop the traffic and drive the people off the streets, smashing the leaves from the pepper trees and scattering them across the square, coming down with the sudden stunning force of a hammer blow.

Sammy saw her agitation. 'It's not going to be much,' he said reassuringly. 'Rain, that's all. We'll keep going.'

She stared at him, a driven feeling inside her. 'Sammy, I'm getting sick of keeping going,' she said, pleading with him to show mercy. 'We're not even heading in the right direction now.'

'We will. When we get away from that lot in the motors.'

'Are they *still* following?'

Sammy nodded. 'They're right there.'

Polly found herself staring backwards again, touched with a feeling of uneasiness once more. She herself had still seen no signs of their pursuers, but she knew Sammy well enough to know he was making no mistake. It was an eerie sensation to be travelling in that vast wide void of sun and dust and to know that every step was being watched, every twist in the track followed by people who were making no attempt to pass them.

'You're certain they're the same bunch,' she asked.

Sammy nodded. 'Same bunch all right,' he said. 'Kitto I've seen once. And Le Roux's there. He's casting big circles on that chestnut of his, looking for our tracks. I've seen him several times. I dunno what they're up to, Poll. Can't see why they don't bother to come up with us. They're faster than us and they've got no reason to sit behind us, just watching us and pressing us. They sure as hell aren't after De Wet, not the way they're hanging on to *our* trail. All I can think is that they're seeing us off the premises and they want us to go west.'

Polly stared back again over the uninhabited veld. 'You're sure they're there?' she asked.

Sammy nodded and indicated the fold in the distance they had just crossed. 'Saw 'em when we crossed the bit of higher ground there an hour or two back,' he said.

'I didn't see anything.'

'You don't look right. You get used to seeing. Just a speck or two that shouldn't be there. Then you can see it's moving, and if you hang on to it hard, you can make out what it is.'

She stared at him curiously. 'You're not natural,' she commented.

Sammy glanced up at the sky then, he grinned at her. 'I'm going to fool 'em,' he said. 'This is just what I've been waiting for. When this lot comes down, Poll, it'll wipe out all our tracks. Every bit. If we can keep goin', we can maybe throw 'em off the scent. I'm going to turn north.'

She stared, twisting on the seat of the cart. 'North?' she said. 'That's back where we came from?'

He nodded. 'That's right. They're shoving us out west all the time at the moment, and we're gettin' no nearer where we want to go anyway, so we might as well make a proper job of it and go north for a bit.'

'But that's going to put days on the journey.' She gaped at him, sick with disappointment.

Sammy shrugged. 'Maybe,' he said. 'Maybe not. What's the odds? We're getting nowhere going in this direction. When they've got west of us, I'll double back behind 'em and head south. They'll lose us altogether then. The rain'll cover our tracks. I don't like people sitting on my tail all the time, do you?'

'No,' she admitted, 'I don't. Especially when I don't know why. All the same, I don't want to go back where I come from, Sammy.' There was an appeal in her voice, a plea to him not to let her down. 'I'd got myself all worked up about Kimberley, Sammy. I've been looking forward to something a bit different, where a girl's got a bit of pride, a bit of dignity.'

Sammy looked up at her suddenly, his pale eyes bright. 'You going to do the same in Kimberley as you did in Plummerton, Poll?' he asked cautiously.

She shook her head. She had long since made up her mind about that. She had no intention after enduring all this just to go back to where she had started.

'A girl needs to think of the future,' she said. 'You can't look far ahead with that kind of life. A girl sometimes thinks she'd like to get married. Have a man about the house.'

Sammy said nothing for a while, his eyes still quartering the horizon.

'It was no job for a decent woman, anyway,' he pointed out.

'Men have got to have women,' she said, not excusing herself, and he became silent again.

After a while, he nudged the Argentino ahead of the cart, studying the ground, and as he drew away there was a tremendous unheralded crash followed by a flash of lightning, and drops of rain as big as half-crowns began to pit the dusty track, rustling the dry tufts of grass. She saw him glance upwards, then he swung his horse back towards her as the drops began to fall more heavily and the sudden smell of rain-rinsed air came to her nostrils. As he reached the cart he leaned across, took the bridle of the bony old mare, and swung her round towards the north, while Polly scrambled into the back of the cart and dragged out the rubber ground-sheet they carried. Then, as he wheeled the horse round in a big curve, leaving the vanishing sun behind them, she began to jerk the canvas cover forward. Picking up the reins again, she cowered back underneath it in the well of the cart on their few belongings, staring out at the transformed veld, her mind too tired, her emotions too flattened, to care.

It arrived like an explosion and for an hour or more it came down on them, blotting out immediately all their tracks and blurring the veld to a grey blank wall. Sammy, an indistinct, rain-faded shape just ahead, seemed to ignore it, hunching lower in the saddle, the battered old hat low over his face, his collar turned up, ignoring the deluge and the weird frightening roar that seemed to strip the earth to its very bones.

There was a two-foot screen of spray over the ground now as mingled dust and splashes leapt up and long spears of rain dashed themselves to atoms, each one bursting with a little puff of dust from the powdery earth. Then the distinct puff and patter, as the rain struck the dried grass, sweeping aside the twigs and stalks, began to give way to a steady sweep and hiss, the trickling hurrying sound of water finding its lowest level, filling the folds and dongas to the height of a man's head. The hoof prints and the wheel tracks filled with rain, became puddles, then their shallow crusts broke under the downpour and they joined each other and spread until the whole surface of the veld was a fine thin sheet which the greedy earth couldn't soak up fast enough.

The smell of baked soil gave way to a purifying scent that was full of dust and damp, and the rain-scoured atmosphere seemed fresh suddenly, a new gloriously clarified air that gave a sense of rinsed earth in a newly-washed world.

With the whole veld asheen beneath their plodding hooves, Polly sat in oppressed silence, her hair in damp rats' tails, the rain running down her back, awed by the fury of the storm, her head low on her shoulders to dodge the spray forced through the cover into the cart. Already little pools were forming alongside her on their belongings and the water ran in steady streams down the inside of the canvas.

The old grey horse between the shafts kept stopping and trying to turn aside, but she kept its head to the north, following the blurred shape of Sammy, who plodded doggedly ahead just in front.

Then, within an hour, the rain had stopped and the water was running off the land into the dongas and the ground was already drying again, steaming heavily in veils of mist with the damp scent of a hothouse, the sun greedily swallowing the moisture out of the earth, while the black column of rain moved ahead of them to the horizon.

Sammy swung his horse round as it slackened off and rode in a large circle round behind the cart, coming up on the other side, his clothes steaming.

'Washed our tracks out clean, Poll,' he called gaily. 'Not a sign of 'em. That'll fool 'em! We'll head north a bit longer, then I'll scout west and south and see if we can turn towards Kimberley again.'

eleven

Kitto's column had started to straggle away from the cars in the blinding rain, losing touch with each other as they held their heads down to escape the lash of the weather. One or two of them had even swung round and turned from the storm, so that when it passed on, rolling in great iron-grey clouds to the south, they were scattered far across the veld in ones and twos and groups like the fragments of a broken necklace.

As the sun came out once more, they began to join up again, picking their way through the rivulets that were running in every hollow, making their way back towards the cars which were struggling across the muddy, uneven earth, their engines screaming, their wheels scattering sprays of red mud as they spun uselessly in the watery hollows.

Irritated by the delays the cars were causing, Kitto had exchanged seats with one of the troopers and was now mounted on a horse, scouring the ground with Le Roux, and cursing the rain which had obliterated the tracks. Behind the lorry the remains of the column rode in silence, strung out and weary, the steam rising from their clothes as the fury of the sun came on again.

Then the Napier, rolling into a hollow in the ground, up to its hubs in a pothole, came to an abrupt stop, its double rear tyres hissing on the shifting ground in a spray of flying mud. As Romanis sounded the klaxon in warning, the Rolls just ahead of it stopped, swung round and turned back, rocking over the stony ground. A rope was attached and for a while they struggled, the Rolls trying with a screaming engine to tow out the Napier, then Kitto galloped up, the flanks of his horse slashed with red mud. Sending Le Roux to bring in half a dozen of the stragglers, he began to curse Romanis for his carelessness.

As they harnessed horses to the front of the Napier, an aeroplane floated past overhead, a Union Defence Force Maurice Farman sent north to look for signs of De Wet, its open fuselage of struts and wire frail against the sun. Kitto stared at it as it banked and swung down to look at them, the goggled leather head of the pilot distinct above them. Several of the men waved and cheered as the machine roared overhead, then someone flapped a Union flag, and the machine turned away, the sun shining on the varnished surfaces of its wings.

'By God,' Kitto said. 'I wish we'd got one of those gadgets.'

Winter, sitting on a boulder, watching the efforts of the cavalrymen to free the Napier, looked up at Kitto as he walked up and down, restless and fidgeting to be on the move. His anger seemed to be growing with each delay, and Winter sensed that, taking the place of his original enthusiasm for the chase, there was now a frustrated bitterness that he was being kept from what he conceived to be his duty. He had clearly hoped and intended that this, his first action of the new war – a war in which he had promised himself he wouldn't put a foot wrong and so recoup all the lost years in the wilderness – was to be a quick neat affair, as smooth and surgical as an operation, which could be recommended to his superiors for the skill with which it had been completed, a reminder to them of all of their years of neglect of him.

But, thwarted by the rain and by Sammy Schuter's plainsman's skill, bogged down, his quarry lost, his men growing resentful at the pace he was forcing, he was beginning to behave like an angry animal goaded by tormentors, his anger taking control of his good sense.

He came up to Winter, his clothes splashed and muddy, and stood in front of him, slashing at his boots with his crop. 'They must have turned north somewhere during the storm to throw us off,' he said bitterly. 'They can't be more than very far in front but they must have seen us somewhere and guessed we were following. It probably means they're trying to contact De Wet, or why else would they dodge?'

'Probably they dislike being dogged,' Winter suggested.

'Dirty little traitor,' Romanis growled.

There was fury in his boy's face, the disappointed fury of an angry schoolboy cheated of a win at games, and Winter shifted uneasily on his seat on the running board, disquieted again by his part in the affair, feeling he should protest, yet fully aware that the first germ of the idea had been put into Kitto's mind by himself. Finally, he shrugged, trying to put it out of his head as something which concerned only Kitto and Offy Plummer. But it persisted in coming back to him, nagging at him, reminding him all the time of his own procrastination over the years and the protests he ought to have made ages before, not now when it was almost too late. Somewhere in the lifetime since he'd jolted up from the Cape in a dusty railway carriage, fresh out from England and with nothing to his name but his ability and a lot of hope, something had got lost, he realised, idealism perhaps, honesty even, for inevitably there had been a certain smothering of his conscience at times in his dealings with Offy's affairs.

He rose and walked up and down for a while, pretending to stretch his legs, but in reality trying to hide from himself. The man who cheated always had a pigeon hole in his mind he could never quite close, and when it suddenly burst open, as it had a habit of doing, it had an unsettling effect that threw him out of gear for a while.

He threw away the cigarette and stood with his hands in his pockets, conscious of the grit down the collar of his shirt and at the corners of his eyes, then Romanis and Kitto moved towards him again, talking.

'Olfy's damn' lucky,' Romanis was saying obsequiously to the older man, trying to deflect his anger from his own poor efforts with the Napier. 'Having someone like you here to keep an eye on things.'

Winter began to intone gently, jeering at himself as much as at the boy.

> 'Our Father which art in Plummerton
> Offy be Thy name – '

– the words belonged to a blasphemous prayer he had once made up to chide himself. It had had great success at the time among the half-ashamed sycophants of Offy's court.

> ' – Thy kingdom hum,
> Thy will be done,
> In the Sidings as well as in West – '

'Cut that out, Winter,' Kitto said, glaring at him, the stamp of a dogged belief in God on his face, a belief as fierce and unimaginative as his courage and his pride.

'Sorry,' Winter apologised. 'I'm getting a little on edge, that's all. Tired perhaps, sorry even – '

'Sorry? What for?'

'The fox, when the hounds are after him.'

'Dammit, Winter,' Romanis said, swinging round on him and sending the leather coat flirting out, still trying to placate Kitto. 'You're not going to start sticking up for a sickening white-gilled little smous, are you?'

Winter gestured wearily, conscious of a growing difference in the attitude of all of them. 'What is it in your background, Romanis,' he asked, 'that makes a Jew so distasteful to you? How different would it have been if he'd been a Gentile?'

Romanis waved a hand vaguely, still irritated. 'Well, good God – ' he said.

' "*Hath not a Jew eyes?*" ' Winter quoted. ' "*Hath not a Jew hands, organs, dimensions, senses, affections, passions?*" '

Romanis stared at him. 'I don't know what the hell you're talking about,' he growled.

'I don't suppose you do,' Winter said. 'It's *The Merchant of Venice*.'

Romanis turned on him triumphantly. 'Well, wasn't he *another* bloody Jew?' he demanded.

Winter laughed, and Romanis flew into a rage.

'Look here,' he said, 'who're you for?'

'Me,' Winter shrugged, 'I'm for me.'

The words, spoken sarcastically, nudged at him again, reminding him how he had once vowed years before that he would spend only a short time up here in the hinterland, and then return to the Cape. But somehow, Offy had come along then and the newspaper job with the *Examiner* had got lost under all the private work he'd done for Offy's organisation and the return journey had never materialised. He had promised himself on more than one occasion, lying in some dusty hotel room, weary with Offy's work, that he'd do just one more job and then leave, settle down, get away from the crowd. But he never had. He'd gone on doing what he'd been told to do because curiously he liked Offy and pitied him, and he hadn't had the will to make the break; because it had become easier just to go on whenever Offy begged him not to let him down, living in an unholy loneliness in the middle of a life crowded with people.

Kitto had moved away now, to superintend the salvaging of the Napier, driving his men to work harder, then in disgust, he swung into the saddle of the horse again and trotted over to where Winter was sitting.

'I'm going to round that lot up,' he said, indicating the stragglers. 'They look like Sanger's Circus, strewn about like that. I think I can leave this job to that useless clown, Romanis.'

He threw his weight back and loosened the reins and the tired horse broke into a canter, then he whacked it across the rump with his crop and it swung into an unwilling gallop and headed off to the north. Winter could hear him shouting angrily as he reached the isolated groups, and immediately the column began to reform into some semblance of a unified body. The lorry with their supplies drew closer, followed by the few Kaffir guides huddled together in a bunch on their ponies, wretched after the rain.

As Kitto returned, his face was dark and bitter. 'I'm going to scout out on the flanks now,' he said to Romanis. 'I might pick up their tracks again. Le Roux can take the other flank. It's my bet the shrewd little bastard's turned north to throw us off. We've got to get between them and Plummerton again and sweep west. Then they'll *have* to move before us.'

'Right into German South-West,' Winter pointed out sarcastically. 'And if they get that far they'll be interned and our job will be over. Hallelujah!'

Kitto turned bland blank eyes towards him. 'Well, what's wrong with that?' he demanded. 'At least they'll be out of the way. We'd be doing the country a service. It would answer all our problems.'

He swung round and wheeled his horse away. Winter could see the splashes from the puddles on the drying earth as he slammed the animal into a hard gallop. Then the Napier was freed abruptly and as it lurched forward its crew climbed on board and started shouting at him to join them.

twelve

They came up to the river at midday, a deep strip of water beyond a patch of scrub and bastard camel thorn, flooded after the rain and running over rocks as black and shiny as anvils that were set in ripples below steep banks, overhung with red-berried bushes and studded with small flowers like shrunken daffodils.

Polly stood by the cart, holding the reins, watching the blind-eyed police horse picking its way through the broken ground along the bank towards her, through flocks of gay little blue, crimson and emerald birds which kept starting up from the water's edge. Sammy seemed thoughtful as he halted alongside the cart, and for a while he ignored her, staring back the way he had come, then he pushed his hat back and swung round towards her.

'Better cross here,' he suggested. 'It's steep, but it's the best spot. I've scouted a mile each way. We'll have to off-load and work her down gentle.'

He swung from the saddle, and between them, they began to unpack the cart, stacking their belongings among the rocks alongside the river – the bedding and the blankets, then the pots and cooking utensils, and their few hard stores, Polly's trunk and the water barrel. Then Sammy began to lash a rope to the rear axle of the cart and, leading the other end around a thorn tree just above the stream, fastened it to the saddle ring of the Argentino.

'What are you going to do?' Polly asked.

'Use it as a brake,' he explained. 'I can hang on to this. She'll go down easy then. We'll maybe have to haul you up the other side too.'

He put his hands under her arms and lifted her up on to the cart again. For a moment he kept his hands on her waist and she looked down at him and smiled. There was no make-up on her face – and her skin was brown, her hair bleached at the ends by the sun.

'Sammy?'

'Yep?'

'I'm sorry I complained so much when we started. Honest, I am.'

He released her and pushed his hat back on his head, avoiding her eyes. 'That's all right, Poll,' he said. 'I expect you'd got good cause to.'

'No, I hadn't. You've done all the work up to now. I've done nothing much except get in the way. But it's just the change, that's all. Just the change, Sammy. Not knowing what's going on. Not having everything handy – water and that – having to do everything for myself. I'm a bit of a townie, I suppose, especially compared with you, but I'm getting used to it now.'

He nodded and began to turn away.

'Sammy,' she called.

'Yep?'

She paused before she spoke, as though she were faintly embarrassed by what she was going to ask him. 'Sammy,' she said, 'you ever thought you'd like to take me out on one of them shoots of yours some time? I'd drive the cart and cook for you. You could perhaps even teach me how to use the rifle. Maybe I could be a help.'

He smiled. 'Suppose I could,' he said, pleased at her offer. 'It's not hard. Just got to learn how to do it, that's all. There's a different way for everything. Bush, for instance. It telescopes things. Gun barrel looks a mile long. Open flats and across water brings 'em closer. You've got to halve the distance then and aim low.'

He talked slowly, with a soft hunter's sibilance, like the footfall of a stalking animal.

'Messy job for a woman, mind,' he pointed out. 'Ten to twelve wildebeest a day's nothing. Strips of meat drying on trees and the grass covered with blood, and flies everywhere.'

'I'll learn. Will you teach me?'

He grinned. 'You're learning already. At least you don't talk all the time any more. You're doing all right.'

He moved away from the cart and began to examine the rope, while Polly sat above him, pleased at the compliment.

'Hold her back, Poll,' he said at last as he straightened up. 'Shove the brake on hard and sit back on the reins.'

She nodded.

'Right,' he said. 'Let's try it. Giddup, hoss! *Voertsek!*'

The Argentino leaned on the rope and the cart began its slow descent of the donga, creaking slowly forward, the iron frames that carried the canvas rattling in their sockets as the wheels bumped over the rocky ground.

'We're doing fine,' Polly shrieked, dragging at the reins until the leather cut at her fingers. 'We're nearly down.'

Just when they thought they were safe, one of the wheels dropped off a rock and the cart lurched unexpectedly, so that the little grey mare lost her footing immediately and began to slip, her hooves digging at the muddy surface of the bank.

'Look out!' Sammy's voice brought Polly's head round. 'The tree's bustin'!'

The white thorn, its roots in thin rain-softened soil, was beginning to lean towards the river. Polly glanced round, her eyes scared, as she heard the sound of wood cracking; then Sammy kicked his mount forward until its feet scrabbled in the dirt, kicking up great lumps of clayey mud as it leaned on the rope.

'It's going,' Polly shrieked.

She felt the Argentino being dragged backwards, its hind feet fighting to get a grip, then Sammy whipped off his hat and banged it down hard against the horse's flanks, and the Argentino's eye rolled wildly as the flecks of foam from its mouth spattered its chest. As the tree gave way, the cart rolled the last five or six feet with a crash, and the water shot up in a sheet of spray that caught the sunshine in a thousand diamond-points of light. Then the Argentino was slithering backwards, its legs tangled up with the broken thorn tree, and Sammy leapt from the saddle just as it rolled on its side in the water. Immediately, caught by the excitement, the bony mare started to kick in fright, her hooves ringing against the shafts, and Polly jumped down into the water and waded to the animal's head.

For a moment the drift was full of the clattering of wood and iron as the horses struggled, then when the muddy water began to settle into place again, the wagon was standing lopsidedly among the rocks, the Argentino still attached to it, trembling violently with the wreckage of the thorn tree between its legs, its one eye rolling wildly.

'Well, we're down!' Sammy splashed towards Polly through the water, grinning. 'We're down and no bones broken.'

The grey was quiet now, quivering in the shafts, reacting to the soothing noises Polly made.

'All we've got to do now,' Sammy said, 'is get up the other side.'

He led the police horse across the stream and attached it again by the rope to the front of the cart, then Polly called out, pointing to the off rear wheel.

'You aren't going to shift that far,' she said.

The fall into the river had split the ancient axle and the wheel now lay over at a crazy angle, up to the hub in scummy, stirred-up water.

Sammy stared at it, his face unemotional.

92

'Take us a long time to repair that,' he announced, turning to Polly. 'Looks like we got to leave her here.'

He bent and, scooping up a handful of water, threw it over his head and rubbed it in his hair. Then he released the grey mare from the cart and gave both horses water from his hat.

'We've got to leave something behind,' he said, looking apologetically at Polly. 'It's going to be no featherbed ride from now on.'

Polly shrugged, sturdily indifferent. 'I can manage,' she said. 'It wasn't before.'

They began to carry their belongings across the stream, wading knee-deep in the muddy water and dumping them in an untidy pile at the other side, making trip after trip through the muddy water, Polly with her skirt caught up round her waist.

When they had almost finished, Sammy paused and looked at the coffee pot he was holding in his hand. 'Might as well eat,' he said.

He filled the pot from higher up the stream where the water was still clear and kicked the top off a small ant heap. Watched by Polly, he dragged out his knife and started to scoop a hole in the side, uncovering the galleries of teeming ants and their eggs. Stuffing dry grass into the hole, he lit it and the flames swept through the passages, roasting the ants and coming up in solid heat through the hole at the top where the coffee pot rested.

'Might as well start with something inside us,' he said. 'Then I'll take the Argentino and look for a route home.'

An hour and a half later they were ready to move on. The wagon still stood in the stream, lopsided and forlorn-looking, with all around on both banks the belongings they had not been able to load on to the horses.

Waiting alone among the bushes, surrounded by assorted packages, abandoned pots and pans and scattered cardboard cartridge boxes, Polly stared at the open trunk and the few clothes she was leaving behind, regarding them with a lazy good-natured regret. Clothes had always been important to her but she found, to her surprise, that she could face leaving them behind with far more composure than she had thought herself capable of.

She picked up the concertina and stared at it, fingering the notes, trying a few snatches of melody, her face nostalgic as her mind went back to all the things the tunes meant to her. There was nothing of much value in the possessions she was abandoning but for a moment she had a superstitious desire to hang on to the concertina. It was symbolic of her life in Plummerton and, since it was the only life she had ever known, the loss of the instrument gave her an uneasy sense of self-sacrifice.

Then she realised that the unhappiness of the past had always outweighed the fragmentary joy and she found she was suddenly glad to be putting it all behind her. Since she had forsaken it, it had seemed to grow more and more meaningless with every mile she had travelled, and the present had grown more and more real.

In the few days she had spent in the Wilderness, labouring across the saddle-back folds of ground and struggling through the deep dry dongas, she had seen a wider world than she had ever known existed. She had seen pure clear mornings when all the veld was still and the air was cold and stimulating, rinsed with the same heavy dew that soaked their clothes. She had seen vast cloudy herds of game – duiker, steenbok, hartebeeste and springbok, Indian files of wildebeeste and dramatically-striped zebra. She had seen heron, stork and flamingo round the salt marshes, a secretary bird dancing a queer long-legged dance round its victim, strings of guinea fowl like grey drops of quicksilver in the grass, widow birds trailing their long tail-feathers across the dusty earth, and red and gold finches that rose in clouds from the spruits as the pink flush of dawn flooded the tawny grassland with ruthless daylight.

She had felt the immensity of the veld right to her bones, and the clean clear sense of elbow-room that came from the wide expanses of gently rolling land and the sight of the blue and purple hills, the absence of other people, and the wide bowl of the sky above her, cruel in its harsh brightness but surprisingly satisfying once you got used to it.

There were better places in the world than Plummerton West, she decided, and hopefully set her face to the future and the problem of achieving them.

It was without regret that she tossed the concertina into the water, watching the spreading circles of ripples moving swiftly, as though they swept the past away from her into a faded unreality as insubstantial as the dying wavelets.

The bony grey was waiting quietly by the stream, tethered to a thorn tree, wearing a device across its back which Sammy had constructed of rope and pieces of blanket. The parcels with which it was slung seemed to indicate a bleaker life but Polly felt no twinges of regret.

While she stood staring at the old horse, Sammy came scrambling along the river bank on the Argentino. As he reached the cart, he plunged into the stream, sending the water flying, and stopped abruptly beside her.

'Poll,' he panted, 'they've got south and west of us !'

Polly's heart sank, all the warm enthusiasm of her day-dreams lost in a twinge of fear. 'I thought we'd thrown 'em off,' she said heavily.

'So did I. But I rid in a big circle looking for a track, and I saw 'em. The main party's west of us, but there's some horses to the south as well.'

'What the hell are they up to?' Polly snapped, her temper rising.

'I dunno. I think they're trying now to drive us over to German South-West. But we've made 'em think a bit because we've got on the wrong side of 'em.'

'What are we going to do then?' Polly asked. 'I wish we could do something. I'm tired and I'm fed up with hiding.'

There was a sick sensation of disappointment in her heart, a conviction that somehow her newly-discovered ambitions were not to come to fruition.

Sammy was thinking, and when he raised his head, there was something in his eyes that withered the remaining hope in her. His face was calm and expressionless as he spoke, as though he had been thinking hard and had come to a decision that hadn't been easy to make.

'Polly,' he said quietly, 'I'm going to head back to Plummerton Sidings.'

Polly's jaw dropped, and she stared at him for a moment, drained of emotion and emptied of ambition.

She brushed back a lock of hair from her face, her features devoid of enthusiasm, her eyes blank with a look of defeat.

'Back?' she said. 'The way we came? After all we've been through?'

Sammy nodded, his gaze honest with the strength of his conviction. 'We were wrong to come out here in the first place,' he said.

'Have you got the wind up or something?' she demanded suddenly angry.

His eyes rested on hers, begging her to understand. 'You know I haven't,' he said. 'I mean, we should have gone to Plummerton and got it over with in the first place – not tried to dodge it.' He gestured unhappily, as though he felt he was letting her down. 'Maybe if they'd left us alone and let us go quietly to Kimberley,' he went on, 'I might have forgotten all about Willie Plummer. I was going to. God knows, *I'd* no reason to shop him. But this sort of thing kind of makes a man stubborn.' His eyes seemed to grow oddly paler as the determination took hold of him. 'They're getting me mad now,' he said. 'I'm *not going* to be driven to German South-West. I'm not even going to Kimberley now.'

She stood staring at him, twisting a fold of her dress between her fingers, her eyes soft and tragic.

'It's my fault, Sammy,' she said. 'I shouldn't ever have persuaded you.'

'Forget it, Poll,' he said shortly. 'I'd probably have changed me own mind, if you hadn't changed it for me. But that's finished with now. I'm going back.'

'I thought they wanted you out of the way, Sammy.'

'They do. They still do.'

'Suppose they tried to knock you off, Sammy. They might have a go.'

Sammy's face grew hard. 'They wouldn't dare,' he said. 'They'd better not try. Damn 'em, they've tried everything short of pushing us off the edge of the earth. Well, they've brought it on themselves. They should have left us alone. I'm going right back to Plummerton and they can sort it out as it pleases 'em!' He paused. 'I'll see you safely to the Sidings and on your way, Polly,' he ended flatly.

She gazed at him for a while. The exultation she had felt that they had put Plummerton behind them had died, and she could taste the acid sourness of disillusion. But Sammy's face, with its pale ugly eyes determined, made her bite back her protest. She wiped her sweat-damp palms on her skirt.

'That's all right, Sammy,' she said slowly. 'We'll go back to Plummerton.'

She tried to smile but managed only a twisted shadow across her lips. When she didn't stir, he moved restlessly in the saddle.

'We ought to get moving,' he pointed out.

Polly was looking at the concertina in the water and, ignoring him, she waded out to it and picked it up, watching the bright streams fall from it.

'Looks like I'm going to need it after all,' she said heavily.

She laid it across the back of the little mare then, releasing her skirt so that it fell into the water and clung wetly round her ankles, she held the instrument in place with one hand and reached up for the reins with the other.

'I'll pick up a train to Kimberley from the Sidings,' she said, knowing that once she returned, she probably never would.

Sammy was trying to read what was going on behind the fleeting expressions on her face, then he swung down from the saddle and pointed.

'We'll ride north from here,' he said, 'then turn east and see what happens.'

'They'll pick up the tracks, won't they, Sammy? Same as before?'

He shrugged. 'Mebbe,' he said. 'What's the odds though? I'm not bothered much either way any more. I'm going back. I've made up my mind.'

She scooped up her dripping skirt again and waded towards him, leading the grey mare.

Sammy was stuffing the last of the cartridges into his pockets now. He had on the old pepper and salt coat which was too small for him again, and she could see the pockets were stuffed full and heavy, and she guessed it was ammunition.

'I could do with a bunk up,' she suggested, eyeing the assorted packages draped from the mare. 'It's going to be awkward climbing up there with all the hardware in the way.'

As he moved beside her, she turned towards him and unable to stop herself, suddenly began to cry quietly.

'It's all gone wrong, Sammy,' she said. 'It's all gone wrong!'

He put his arms round her, clumsily trying to comfort her, and for a moment she leaned against his chest, feeling sheltered and secure, then she pushed him away resolutely, knocking the tears from her cheeks with a clumsy hand, and put one foot in the stirrup. He helped her up and stood back, slowly rubbing his hands up and down the seat of his trousers.

She gave a ringing sniff. 'Well, come on,' she said loudly. 'What are we waiting for?'

He started out of his trance and came to life. Stooping, he picked up his belongings and swung to the saddle of the Argentino.

'It's going to be faster from here on, Poll,' he said. 'But less comfortable.'

The old grey moved forward as Polly dug in her heels and Sammy nudged the Argentino after it. He glanced upwards at the limpid, diamond-clear sky beyond the stark branches of the white-thorn trees, his eyes squinting at the sun.

'It's going to be hot,' he said.

thirteen

The heat of the afternoon had closed down on them like an oppressive weight, the sky like a brass lid over the earth. They were moving more slowly now, as though even Kitto's driving urgency had slackened under the boiling power of the molten sun, strung out in small bunches of two and three on either side of the cars, scattered by the greyish-black karroo bushes that got between them and broke up their formation.

The wide land was sloping down to where they could see the whitened branches of a belt of thorn trees, stark as bleached bones in the sun, and ahead of them Le Roux was casting long circles in an incredible trot that never seemed to waver, wheeling his horse backwards and forwards, constantly stopping to examine the ground. Here and there over the car bonnets, they could see the flattened strips of dust where the iron rims of cart wheels had pressed and the stirred earth between them where the horses had put their feet.

Winter, jolting around in the back of the Rolls-Royce, was watching the driver hanging on to the steering wheel to keep his seat as the vehicle swung and rolled to skirt the ragged karroo bushes, his teeth clamped, his head jerking as they traversed the rough ground. Behind them the dust plumed out for a mile or more and settled on the thorn trees, turning them to the same yellow-red as the earth. Clinging on with one hand, he wiped the sweat from his face with a soiled and dusty handkerchief, his eyes wearily sweeping the horizon ahead.

He could see Kitto just in front of the vehicle, on a horse again, impatient and eager, as he was every time the cars were slowed by poor ground, trying to wave instructions to Le Roux, who was pointing to the earth in front of him; then his eyes flew to the horizon again beyond the strip of thorn bushes and willows, as though he half-expected to see tiny fleeting figures, the scrap of movement that would tell him they had caught up at last with their quarry.

The horsemen, tired and unshaven after several days' riding, were grumbling at the speed of the chase, complaining loudly about stiffness and soreness, and one of them kept looking anxiously down at his mount which had put its foot in a meerkat hole and was slightly lame. Tempers were growing rapidly shorter with every weary mile. They were all eager now to get it over and done with and return.

The tension had tightened as they had moved on after the storm, picking up the wheel tracks of the cart again with some difficulty, the land empty and silent beyond their own oasis of harsh sound, the thud of hooves and the tacketing roar of the engines as they pulled up the slopes.

With the contrariness of a romantic confronted with a lost cause, Winter found himself half hoping that they'd been given the slip completely, but he could tell from the way Le Roux kept his eyes glued to the ground that the trail had not grown cold.

The scout was riding far ahead now and had neared the thorn trees, ranging well into the distance, and Winter saw him disappear over the saddle of a ridge a mile away. Then he immediately reappeared and Winter saw he was right in among the trees. For a few minutes he was out of sight, then he reappeared, waving frantically and Winter was almost thrown out of the car as the driver turned and increased speed.

Suddenly, they were all of them elated and shouting, and Winter was startled to realise that the faces around him now wore expressions of delight and greed and the violent excitement of a mob. The horsemen, their emotions heightened by the frustration and the killing pace Kitto was setting, had lifted their mounts into a hard flat run, their hooves drubbing the earth, their tails streaming, and they were storming over the saddle of the ridge like a charge of cavalry, bunched together on either side of the cars, standing in their stirrups and even pressing ahead in their eagerness. Some of the men were cheering now and Kitto, in the lead, was lashing his horse with his crop, forcing it into a staggering gallop.

They swung over the last rise, crashing in and out among the thorn trees, then as they reached the top of the drift, Winter saw Le Roux appear in front of them, waving and starting to shout, and he saw the land fall away steeply, abruptly, in front of them, in a horrifying unexpected drop.

Romanis, on the wheel of the Napier which was leading, dragged it to the right and the high vehicle almost flung its crew out as it rolled heavily on its springs.

'It's a donga,' he yelled. 'Nearly didn't see her!'

'Christ, man,' the Army Service Corps mechanic beside him shouted. 'There'd have been hell to pay if we'd lost her!'

The horsemen on their right in a strung-out line, confronted by the swinging motorcar heading across their front, heaved on their reins and crashed together in a bunch, the horses jostling frantically.

'Pas op,' someone yelled. 'Keep going! Keep going!'

A horse went down with a frightened scream, rolling down the bank and landing in a sheet of water, the rider, half-blinded by a branch which had hit him in the face, falling from the saddle with a flat splash.

Winter jumped out of the Rolls as it came to a stop, and ran with knees stiff and trembling with weariness, to where

Romanis and the crew of the Napier were scrambling over the bank. Below in the stream, the horsemen had dismounted and were whooping around the abandoned cart, taking flying kicks at cooking pots and broken boxes. Romanis was laughing at a man standing waist-deep in the water, wearing a woman's hat and a pair of long, cotton, lace-edged drawers, and another man was aiming heavy blows with a rifle butt at a battered trunk. Somehow, suddenly, there was violence in the air.

Then Kitto came scrambling along the bank, and was among them shouting and lashing out with the crop. 'God damn it,' he was yelling. 'Get out of it! Get these men back, Romanis! Give Le Roux a chance, damn you!'

Romanis jumped into the water, yelling orders in his high voice, and the troopers pulled back, splashing downstream and wading heavy-footed through the pools. Kitto stared round at them and at the group who were sitting their horses in a restless half-circle, some on the bank, some standing fetlock-deep in the shallow river.

'This operation's going to be conducted as *I* want it,' he roared. 'By soldiers in a soldierly manner, and not by a bloody mob of hoodlums!'

He turned away abruptly and rode towards Le Roux. 'What have you got, Le Roux? Let's have it.'

Le Roux indicated the cape cart with its broken wheel standing just upstream, its scattered contents, and the few hoof prints in the clay; the abandoned cooking pots and clothes and the cardboard cartridge boxes strewn over rocks and under the thorn bushes. Then he urged his horse forward to the opposite bank, studying the ground carefully.

'They've moved north-east along the stream,' he said. 'They're using the two horses now. They'll move faster.' He grinned suddenly. 'Ag, she'll have a sore backside when she squats down at night. *Magtig,* what a sight!'

103

Kitto glanced at his grinning face, and brushed away the aside in his eagerness to get on.

'How close are we?' he demanded. 'How far behind?'

'Four-five hours, I reckon,' Le Roux said. 'That's all. Looks as though they had their midday meal here.' He indicated the top of the broken ant-heap on the far bank and the flattened, muddy dust where someone had thrown away the dregs of a cup of coffee.

'Right!' Kitto made up his mind quickly. 'We'll stop here for an hour or two to eat and rest the horses. There's water, and we might pick up some fresh meat. There's always game near water. Romanis, send a couple of men upstream to watch the pools. There are always guinea fowl or duiker in the reeds. If they've gone north we'll keep the motors on this side of the river till we find 'em, and let the horses go over the other side. If they've turned west again we'll have to get the cars across somehow. Pick up some rations and get on ahead, Le Roux.'

'I'll take a couple of men to flank me and cut north and get up close to 'em,' Le Roux said. 'They're goin' to be surprised, man, when they see me – especially the woman!'

'Cut that out,' Kitto snapped and Le Roux grinned wolfishly, his expression suggesting all sorts of indecencies.

A man whooped as Le Roux called his name, and Winter shivered a little, his head aching. Le Roux's attitude seemed to go with loot and pillage and all the other horrors of war.

The scout was waving, whirling his horse on its haunches in a showy pirouette.

'Trek ons,' he shouted. 'Tot siens.'

Followed by his companions, he scrambled up the opposite bank of the stream and vanished over the ridge, the hoof beats dying away across the veld.

By this time someone had kicked a heap of dust together and poured petrol on it and a fire was already winking, a thin wisp of blue smoke spiralling upwards in slow curls to the sky. The Kaffirs began to break sticks and unpack the cars, and a few famished men were already squatting in a gulley at the top of the bank, cooking bacon and beans in a mess tin.

The horses, unkempt and exhausted by the chase, were glad of a roll and the chance to get what nourishment they could from the withered grass, and the Army Service Corps mechanics and drivers were humping petrol tins and cans of muddy water from the stream for the radiators. Winter could see one of them with his head in the bonnet of the Napier, cursing with a soft weary persistence.

Kitto and Romanis had a blanket spread on the ground, a map unfolded on it, held down at the corners by binoculars, compass and a couple of stones, and were on their hands and knees staring at it. One of the Kaffirs brought them a meal of potted meat, sardines and biscuits, and they sat back, brushing away the flies, and began to eat.

Winter watched them, eating himself. In his nostrils was the aromatic smell of coffee, mingling in the breathless air with the horse smells of leather and sweat and hot human flesh, laying over the scent of wet soil, the crushed thyme tang of the smashed karroo bushes and the night perfume of flowers along the bank. Beyond the river, the brown kopjes had already melted into violet islands with topaz tops and farther up the stream he heard the hoarse cry of a heron and the sharp whistle of a still-questing kingfisher above the monotonous buzzing of legions of cicadas in the dry grass and scrub. Over his head, the turquoise sky was studded with the first brilliant stars. He looked up to find Kitto and Romanis alongside him.

'What's worrying you?' Romanis asked. 'You look as doleful as a shop with the shutters up.'

'I don't know,' Winter said thoughtfully. 'Nothing, I suppose. Everything. I find I don't like this damned business, Kitto. I was wrong to suggest it.'

Kitto stared at him, puzzled, unable in his forthright directness to understand his fears. 'Is it so wrong to serve your country?' he said. 'That's all we're doing, isn't it?'

Winter shrugged. 'All right, then, we thought right and acted wrong.'

Kitto's face wore the contempt of a man who knows what he wants out of life for one who doesn't, the contempt of a man who had never been actuated by the deviousness of intrigue, and had always seen his objectives clearly before him, unmarred by any doubts.

'If one boy,' he said, 'one Yid whose record shouts out loud that nobody will miss him anyway, if he's unfortunate enough to be in the way, then we have to harden our hearts and get rid of him – for the good of the whole. I'm fighting for unity, one land, not a couple of Crown colonies and a bunch of piddling little republics.'

' "The brittle rights of primitive peoples must shiver to pieces on the rocks of a more advanced society," ' Winter quoted with a smile. 'That's what Offy said when they made him Administrator of Dhanziland. He pinched it, I think. From Rhodes or Shepstone or someone like that. But all it ever meant was that Offy felt he'd a right to spit in the eye of everybody who didn't fit in with his plans. I still think it might have been wiser to recruit the boy, not chase him. He's got courage and it's a rare commodity not to be squandered through mismanagement. I think we set about this affair the wrong way.'

He sat back, chewing at a biscuit, aware of the weakness of his protest compared with the virile hatred that was clearly growing in the minds of the pursuers for someone few of them knew but who had managed by his cunning to bring them all to this far pass of weariness and frustration.

Kitto glanced round him at the men who were unsaddling and rubbing down the horses with handfuls of dry grass.

Someone had started playing a mouth organ and one of the
Boer troopers was singing in a throaty baritone –

> *'Vat jou goed en trek, Ferreira,*
> *Vat jou goed en trek –'*

The song came over the small noises of the camp, the
crunching of heavy boots on the stones, the chink of harness,
the rustle of a thorn bush on the slopes, the splash of a horse
moving through the stream.

'Don't worry,' he said sharply, 'I can handle it all right. I
was with Makepeace in Dhanziland and Jameson's mob
when they rode up to Bulawayo. I've seen more damn'
fighting than most people *dream about,* and I'll handle this
business properly. I've *got* to.'

There was a curious hint of loneliness in his voice behind
the boastfulness, a rare crack in his ferocious military pride
that revealed his sense of failure over the years. 'Time moves
too damn' fast,' he said. 'Before you know where you are,
you're too old. This is my last chance. I shan't be around next
time.'

Somewhere beyond his words, Winter heard a tormenting
certainty that somewhere, somehow, his life and his luck had
slipped through his fingers, ungrasped. And with it, Winter
sensed a frightened awareness that this chance he was
groping for now had turned out to be bigger than *he* was,
something he was going to be rid of only with difficulty.
Behind the bold, resourceful Kitto, Winter knew, there
seemed now to be another man, suddenly puzzled, uncertain
and a little hurt, and Winter tried to take advantage of it.

'This isn't what Offy wanted, Kitto,' he persisted. 'We're
beginning to look like a pack of hounds.'

Kitto turned his handsome, sun-lined countenance
towards him and the other Kitto had vanished again as
quickly as it had come. With the heroic legend of the

youthful Hector Stark Kitto behind him, he was always a little more real than the real thing.

'You're not facing facts, Winter,' he said sternly.

Winter shrugged, realising Kitto was probably right. He *never had* faced facts. For a moment, he sat still, thinking of all the things he had always dreamed of that had never materialised, all the ambitions that had ended like a lot of damp fireworks when he had met Offy Plummer. He fished in his pocket for a cigarette, conscious of having made his protest and failed to convince anyone.

He pushed it out of his mind hurriedly, knowing it would end in emptiness and the incredible fatigue of frustration, and Kitto turned away and stopped, one foot on the bank, looking like Napoleon before Austerlitz.

'There's only one important thing for us now,' he said. 'And that's winning the war. As far as I'm concerned this became an affair for soldiers long ago.'

fourteen

Sammy Schuter had been moving faster for some time now. Trailed by Polly who was trying hard to ride as he did, relaxed and easy, he had long since left the bed of the stream. They had camped the night among the broken country on the way back towards Plummerton Sidings and were now heading through the line of kopjes leading to Sheba.

Polly sat on the bony shaft-horse, drooping with weariness, and stared curiously ahead at Sammy who had dismounted and was standing in the track, coated with red-yellow powder, a dust-caked figure with a stubble of beard on his face. He had set off in front of her, circling a small group of buck he had seen, and as she had followed him she had heard the report of the old Martini-Henry and moved slowly in the direction of the sound.

He was standing now, way up in front of her, the carcass of a buck by his feet, his slender horseman's body somehow incomplete without the Argentino, staring at something in the track. Polly dug her heels into the grey and moved forward, jangling and clattering like a tinker as the cooking pots around her rattled together.

'What is it, Sammy?' she asked.

Sammy looked up, and she saw the pale eyes in the young-old face were hard as ice. He pointed to a pile of horse-droppings at his feet and stirred them with his boot.

'Still warm,' he said. 'Not more than a couple of hours old, I'd say. I found a dead fire out there too.'

He nodded towards the south-west where the veld shimmered in the rays of the sun.

'He's looking for us. He's been ranging backwards and forwards. I found the tracks a mile or two away. He's looking for our spoor. Judging by the way he's heading, he's somewhere behind us now. It'll be Le Roux, I suppose. He'll swing back east, I reckon, and pick up our spoor about where we camped, judging by the way he's workin'.'

'Could be someone shooting for the market,' Polly pointed out without really believing what she said. 'Maybe some prospector. We're near enough to Plummerton now.'

He glanced up at her. 'On his own?' he asked. 'There's no prospecting here, Poll. No water. And he's not shooting for the market. He's got no cart with him. Where'll he put the meat?'

He looked up at Polly and smiled a quick mischievous unexpected grin.

'I'll make him think,' he said. 'Get up ahead there beyond that clump of rocks at the bottom of the kopje.' He indicated the low hillock, broken at its base by the mass of granite rocks like tombstones.

'Keep going,' he said. 'Keep going behind the kopje so he won't be able to see you. I don't want him to swing off west or east. I want him to come straight through here.'

Polly looked down at him. The days in the sun had cut tiny lines at the corner of her eyes and bleached her lashes white, and the print frock already seemed faded.

'What are you going to do, Sammy?' she asked.

He scratched the stubble on his cheeks and fidgeted in his sweaty shirt. 'I'm going to give him a surprise, whoever he is,' he said. 'We could use his hoss, maybe.'

Polly watched him, her face anxious. All the posturings and artificiality had gone from her long since and left her with her emotions undisguised.

'Sammy,' she asked, 'wouldn't it have been best to go where they wanted us to go?'

'What? Into German South-West? *That's* what they're trying on now.'

Polly shrugged, body-weary, her mind stupefied by fatigue so that she couldn't absorb the meaning of their increasing importance to the men just over the horizon behind them, couldn't grasp its significance. 'Perhaps internment wouldn't be all that bad,' she said. 'Maybe they'd treat us all right.'

'And maybe they wouldn't.'

She seemed to droop in the saddle. 'Sammy,' she pleaded. 'I'm getting awful tired. I can't go on much longer.'

His face set. 'Hang on, Poll,' he encouraged her. 'We can't let them get away with this. It's just not right, and we've not so far to go now.'

She tried a new approach. 'Well, then,' she begged, 'can't I stay with you? Don't send me on, Sammy. Let me stay.'

'No.'

'Why not?'

'It's not safe.' His voice was gruff as he answered, and he tried not to look at her.

'I'd like to,' she pointed out.

'It's no job for a woman,' he insisted. 'I'll look after meself all right.'

Her eyes grew soft and appealing. 'I looked after you long enough in the past when Pa first brought you home,' she said. 'I'm older than you, remember.'

'Two years,' he pointed out.

'Three,' she persisted. 'Let me stay, Sammy.'

'No.'

'Sammy –' she paused, staring down at him. 'I wouldn't want anything to happen to you.'

'Why not?' He looked up quickly, irritatingly remote still.

'Oh Lor',' – she groaned at his blindness – 'why do you think I *always* looked after you, fixing your things whenever

111

you appeared? – not seeing you for months and then having all your clothes washed and ready when you came home? I didn't have to – especially the way you kept disappearing. Look what it let me in for.'

Sammy frowned. 'What you getting at, Poll?' he asked.

'Dammit, you great clown, don't you know I love you?'

He looked up at her sharply, then his eyes fell and he began to move his hand up and down the gun.

'You loved lots of blokes,' he said quietly.

'Not like you. God help me, I don't know when it started or why. I only know that you don't worry for friends or your own flesh and blood as I used to worry for you, Sammy. You and me were brought up like brother and sister but no woman ever felt for her brother what I started to feel for you. Why'd you think I made an effort to put up with everything out here? I'm not a backvelder, Sammy, I'm a townie, but I've tried heavens hard to keep up with you so's I could be near you.'

Sammy studied her for a long time, his pale eyes on her face. 'Whyn't you ever say?' he asked.

'It's not my job to say,' she pointed out, her head up, her eyes unashamed.

His hand was still moving slowly over the gun and he looked uncomfortable, shifting awkwardly from one foot to the other. 'I didn't know,' he excused himself. 'I never thought of it like that. I always felt you might laugh at me. You were older than me and knew too much about me. I wouldn't have gone off shooting if I'd known. I might even have took a job in Plummerton.'

'Not you, Sammy,' she said with a smile. 'I can't see you behind a store counter selling sheep-dip and pearl buttons.'

'Well, I *might*. If you'd only said – '

'Same as me, Sammy,' she pointed out. 'There's lots I *might* have done if *you'd* only said.' She stared down at him, the small smile still playing round her mouth. 'Seems we ought to have got together a bit and talked things over, the both of us,' she commented.

He stood alongside the grey mare, then he reached up and took her hand, his face alive with sincerity.

'Let's get this behind us, Polly,' he said. 'Then we might be able to start again.'

Impulsively she leaned over and kissed his hand as it held hers, then she straightened up and kicked the mare into motion.

'How'll I know when to come back?' she asked, turning in the home-made saddle, her face resolute and courageous again.

'Don't,' he said. 'Just keep going. I'll catch you up.'

She was still staring backwards when she passed the rocks, watching Sammy as he hoisted the buck to his shoulders and began to walk slowly towards the clump of stone, leading the Argentino, his thin body moving with the litheness and grace of a wild animal.

He waved once and she waved back, then she was out of sight on the south side of the kopje.

As she vanished, he stopped, staring after her, his face expressionless, then he pushed his hat back and, humping the rifle, began to walk again, the Argentino plodding after him, its footsteps heavy in the dust...

He picked a spot near the outcrop of rocks and tethered the horse behind a pile of boulders that leaned together like some vast cathedral. Then he walked towards the kopje and began to climb, carrying the rifle.

Choosing a spot where the shade fell and glancing round at the sun, he cocked the weapon and pushed his hat forward over his eyes. The bright glints caught his rifle barrel disconcertingly and he stooped and, picking up a handful of dust, rubbed it along the metal to dull the glow, his movements slow and methodical, for he had performed them a hundred times before out on the bare veld.

He laid the weapon carefully in front of him, butt end on the ground, the muzzle resting on a low rock, and finally leaned back against the rock and prepared to wait.

For a long time he didn't move, frozen into easy immobility, then as the sun dropped farther towards the west, he shifted to find a patch of shade, moving quietly, and squatted down again.

An hour later, he saw a feather of dust across the plain.

Le Roux came towards the kopje, riding the chestnut slowly, his eyes on the ground, then he kicked the horse into a canter as his eyes saw the trail stretch between the rocks at the foot of the hill. As he reached the kopje, he slowed down again, staring at the ground, puzzled.

As Sammy cocked the rifle, Le Roux's head came up. His horse's ears pricked, and he gathered the reins in his hand, looking round him suspiciously.

'Mr Le Roux,' Sammy said, 'I got my gun pointing straight at you. Get off that hoss.'

For a second, Le Roux sat motionless and frozen. His head turned slowly, his narrow eyes hard and ugly, trying to pick Sammy out from the tangle of shadows among the rocks. Slowly his hand moved towards the rifle in the saddle bucket.

'I wouldn't if I was you, Mr Le Roux,' the patient voice came again. 'I can drop a running duiker at three hundred yards without damaging the hide. Better get down.'

Le Roux's eyes glittered with fury and he swung slowly from the saddle.

Sammy rose from behind his rock and moved slowly down the side of the hill among the rocks, his feet silent in the veldschoen. Stepping into the dusty track, he grinned at the scout.

'Mornin', Mr Le Roux,' he said. 'Been a nice mornin'. Afraid I'm going to have to take your hoss.'

Le Roux's flat blank face went dark but he said nothing, standing rigidly, his big hands hanging down by his side. Sammy leaned across the chestnut's saddle, the Henry still pointing at Le Roux, and took the rifle from the saddle scabbard.

'Mauser,' he said, glancing at it. 'Nice gun, that.' He glanced in the saddle bag. 'Plenty of ammunition too. That's handy. Better sling your bandoleer across as well.'

Glaring, Le Roux slipped the heavy bandoleer of cartridges off his shoulder and threw it into the dust in front of him. Sammy knelt, one eye all the time on the scout, and carefully picked out the cartridges and slipped them into his pockets.

'You can have what's left,' he said, rising.

He put a foot into the stirrup and swung up into the saddle of the chestnut.

'Nice hoss,' he commented. 'Them army people certainly mount and kit their men nice. Who's in charge? Kitto?'

Le Roux nodded.

'He knows his stuff, that Kitto,' Sammy observed. 'Bit of a fire-eater, but he's all right. I've scouted for him once. Who else's with you? Winter?'

Le Roux's head jerked.

'You're not too talkative this morning, are you?' Sammy said. His voice suddenly went hard and the youthful respect he had shown towards the older man vanished abruptly.

'See here, Mr Le Roux,' he said. 'I've not harmed anybody, ever. You leave me alone. You tell Kitto that.'

He fished in the saddle-bag and withdrew a few sticks of biltong which he tossed across. Then he unwound the strap of a water bottle on the saddle.

'Here,' he said. 'It's more'n I ought to leave you. Your pals'll be up with you before long, I expect. Tell 'em what I told you. Any single one of 'em tries to interfere with me and mine, and I start shooting. That's a fair warning.'

115

He kicked with his heels and the horse moved forward. Le Roux swung round, squinting into the sun as the animal passed him. Sammy trotted between the rocks at the foot of the kopje and vanished from sight, then a moment later he reappeared, pulling the Argentino on a lead rein, and as he turned behind the kopje, Le Roux ran quickly to the gap and stared after him. But Sammy was already a couple of hundred yards away and riding hard.

fifteen

Kitto's column were straggling badly again when they picked up Le Roux. The cars were steaming and hissing and the horsemen were sore and grumbling under their breath, disappointed that they had not caught up with Sammy Schuter as they had confidently expected after finding the abandoned cart. They rode stiff and swaying in the saddles, their teeth clamped against weariness, the horses moving slowly with drooping heads, stumbling under their burdens, more than one of them lame.

Kitto's face was stiff now with anger whenever Winter turned his eyes towards him; gnawed and nagged by the urgency that possessed him.

When the flank riders returned without Le Roux, Kitto called all the horsemen together and, separating them into groups, sent them out fanwise in splinters, looking for the scout's tracks. Within an hour, one of them had returned with Le Roux clinging on behind the saddle.

Kitto's face was thunderous. 'God damn it, Le Roux,' he said. 'What happened?'

Le Roux's sun-blackened features and dark hair gave him a look of evil as he replied.

'*Ach,* he stole my horse, man,' he said. '*Daar agter,* by the kopje.'

'What the hell were you doing to let him?'

Le Roux gestured, his bony red wrists raw-looking below his sleeve. 'I was close behind 'em,' he said. 'They'll only have gained an hour or two even now. That's all. He offered to shoot me.'

'Where is he now?'

'Heading for Plummerton West.'

'Plummerton? He can't go back there!' Kitto seemed suddenly on the point of panic. 'My God, Winter, you were right! Get in the motor, Le Roux. We can move faster here. The ground's good.'

Winter, leaning over the dun-painted side of the car tried to protest again. 'Offy said there was to be no violence,' he pointed out.

Kitto frowned, on his face an expression of angry bewilderment. So long as the fugitives had accepted the chase and fled before it, his task had been straightforward, even if difficult, but now that they had clearly decided to turn round and head back to Plummerton, the whole operation had been carried beyond the bounds of simplicity. In his strict Calvinistic way, he struggled with his conscience, striving to reach a decision that was effective and at the same time honourable. Somewhere, vaguely, he thought he saw a solution, but uneasily he felt it wasn't the right one.

'He's stolen one of His Majesty's troop-horses,' he said, as though he were thinking aloud. 'This was an armed patrol into Dhanziland when it started, in search of rebels who were aiding the King's enemies. Anyone who interferes with it's a damned renegade and has to be dealt with accordingly.'

A look of surprise came on to Romanis' face. 'Good God, man,' he said. 'What are you contemplating?'

Kitto paused and Winter guessed he wasn't certain himself what he should do.

Then he slapped at his boot with his crop and moved to the car. 'I'm contemplating nothing,' he said. 'But let's be realistic. This damned man's a threat to established order here. If he gets back to Plummerton he could be worth two or three thousand men to De Wet. And for every two or three thousand who join 'em there'll be two or three thousand more waiting for the example of others to encourage *them*. It's a vicious circle and, make no mistake about it, if Botha and Smuts fall, there'll be nothing to stop the Germans walking straight through South Africa as they have done through France and Belgium. And that would be a major victory for them. Don't let's blind ourselves with idealism. This boy's become a menace to more than just Offy Plummer. We've got to get a move on.'

He turned away and spoke to Romanis, and the men standing by the horses swung up into the saddles.

Le Roux appeared alongside the Rolls and grinned at Winter.

'Got to reserve my strength, *jong*,' he said as he settled back on the dusty seat. 'We'll be up with the woman soon.'

Kitto had come striding back now and climbed into his seat at the front of the Rolls. The Army Service Corps driver swung on the starting handle and the engine roared.

Quickly he returned to his seat and adjusted the lever on the steering wheel. The engine of the Napier behind started with a howl, dying away to a throbbing popple from the exhaust as Romanis dragged back the throttle. The horsemen were spreading out now on either flank, some of them already moving away.

'Pass down the car please,' the driver of the Rolls called out gaily, releasing the brake. 'Have your fares ready!'

'Cut that damn' nonsense out,' Kitto said, no room in his mind for levity until the job was done. He waved, pointing forward and as the car jerked he fell back into his seat and the little cavalcade moved off, trailing its plume of dust behind it, moving swiftly east again, away from the falling sun.

sixteen

Sunset at Sheba.

Sammy reined in and stared up at the strange mysterious shape, its burden of stone like battered forts and castles, joined by bastions of gritty earth and clumps of aloe and cactus and rough thorn scrub. He turned slowly and glanced behind him at the bare veld, then swung his gaze back to the orgy of rocky sentinels, his eyes narrowed, his face sombre.

'A man could see a long way from up there,' he mused.

He sat still, as though he were loath to pass the great pile of rock, as though it fascinated him, and Polly watched him silently, listening to the soft hiss of the horses' tails as they swept at the flies. The golden veld was ripening now to apricot and in a short time would be blood red as the sun disappeared.

Sammy still sat in silence, staring first at Sheba then back at the veld over which they had just passed.

'Reckon we'll stay here for the night,' he said at last. 'Plenty of shelter here.'

Polly slipped from the grey, her thighs aching from knee to groin, still feeling the horse between her legs.

She knew that shelter was not the reason why he had chosen the spot, for they had camped without worrying at spots out on the bare veld where there were no rocks within miles to set their backs against. But behind that taut bleak look in his face she could see a troubled stubbornness, as though he had selected Sheba to make a stand. From his next words she knew she was right.

'I'm going up,' he said, pointing to the slopes. 'It's my guess they'll try to get between us and the Sidings again. I could maybe see from up there.'

He slipped from the horse and passed her the reins and she watched him scrambling up the shallow south side, avoiding the boulders, slipping between them on the rough stone-covered surface.

After a while, she lost sight of him and waited in silence, awed by the sombre majesty of the kopje, the legends that had grown up around it frightening her with their suggestions of ghosts. Then she heard a stone roll and saw Sammy scrambling down the slope again.

He stopped by the horses, panting a little.

'See 'em?' she asked.

'Not yet. But they won't be far away. They'll be getting scared now – they'll have guessed by now that we've turned back – and when people are scared, Poll, they do funny things.'

Polly began to unfasten the ropes which held their belongings, oppressed in a way she couldn't explain.

'Hold it, Poll!'

She turned, her eyes questioning, and Sammy gestured towards Sheba.

'Not here,' he said. 'Up there!'

Her eyes opened wide.

'Up there?' The words were jerked out of her in startled amazement as she stared at the precipitous sides of the kopje.

Sammy nodded and pushed her up on to the grey's back again. 'I'm sitting the night out up there,' he said. 'They might easy miss us in the dark, then we can cut down again and head for Plummerton.' He jerked a hand at the kopje 'It's shallow enough at first,' he pointed out. 'We can get the horses up among the rocks. Some of 'em are big enough to hide an elephant.'

He nudged Le Roux's tired chestnut into movement and edged into the deep shadow of the hill, setting Le Roux's horse at the first simple slopes and trailing the Argentino behind him. Polly stared after him for a second, her weary brain unable to take in this new demand he was making on her muscles, then she dug her heels into the grey's flank and followed.

After a few minutes of following the narrow path Sammy had picked out, they stopped in a shallow depression, where the rocky outcrop overhung a flat clearing, a small valley in the side of the hill almost like a kraal. There were small caves in the rock, the homes of the dassies, and Sammy stood still, staring round at them, the grey horse nuzzling his hand. 'We can leave the hosses here,' he said. 'We'll knee-halter 'em so they can't get out. They won't be seen from below.'

'Suppose they come up?'

'They won't come up.'

Something in his voice made her swing round, but he had begun to off-load the horses and rub them down with his shirt, his face turned away from her. For a moment she stared at him, then she started to life again and began to untie the ropes that secured their belongings.

Hoisting as much as they could carry on their backs, they began to struggle higher up the slopes, their feet slipping and stumbling over the loose scattered stones, their faded and dust-caked clothes snagging on the thorn bushes that grew through the cracks between the boulders. After ten minutes, Polly halted and pushed the hair from her eyes.

'Sammy, let's stop,' she pleaded, wiping the sweat from her face with the hem of her skirt. 'I've had enough. Honest I have.'

Sammy stopped and turned towards her. 'I'll take the pack,' he said. 'You get on ahead.'

She shook her head. A moment before she had felt she had no more strength left to struggle but now, as he offered to take her burden, she summoned up reserves of courage she didn't know she possessed.

'I'll take it,' she panted. She tried to take the pack back from him again but he pushed her hand away gently.

'I'll take it.' Her voice was pleading and insistent, and she was near to tears with a weary determination that she should do her share, but he took her wrist in his hand and pushed it gently away again.

'*I'll* take it,' he insisted.

She was too tired to argue any more and she faced the slope without it.

'How much farther, Sammy?' she pleaded.

'Up among them rocks,' he said, pointing to a half-circle of granite crags, their bases sunk in a thicket of cactus and thorn. 'They make a sort of cave. I sheltered there once in a hailstorm.'

'Sammy,' she asked, 'why are we going up here? We've never had to climb before. What's wrong with the veld?'

'Just think it's safer,' he said. 'Got a feeling, that's all.'

He pushed past her and pointed higher up the slope to a cluster of grey shapes like broken teeth above them.

'That's where we want to be,' he said.

Polly was watching him with frightened eyes.

'Sammy' – her voice sounded thin and small in the silence of the kopje – 'are you reckoning on staying here for a few days?'

'Might.'

'Sammy, why?'

He had slipped back into the taut taciturn mood of the beginning of the affair and he looked up slowly and flipped a hand towards the veld.

'Polly,' he said; 'I'm not running any more. If they want me, they've got to come and fetch me.'

123

He pointed and, looking back, she could see the clump of mimosas and the winding path of the stream beyond the rocky hump of Babylon where they had camped on their way out. There was water in it now after the rain storm, a shining strip of steel between the high banks as it curved towards them.

'There's height here,' he said. 'There's water. I can fill the canteens and the barrel and if they try to interfere, I'll give 'em something to think about. Maybe then they'll leave us alone. Polly, we're thirty miles from Plummerton and getting on over a hundred from Kimberley. They're right on our tails and baying like a lot of hounds, it seems to me. I'll feel better with something at me back.'

He indicated the slope of Sheba and she was silent for a moment, appalled by what he was suggesting.

'But, Sammy, it's not legal.'

'There's no law when there's no police.'

She grabbed at his arm and swung him round.

'But Sammy, Sammy, why? Why? Why should they do this to us? We've done nothing to them.'

He looked down at her, his face calm and unafraid. 'Polly, we're dangerous,' he said. 'Both of us. Me because I know what Willie Plummer did, and you because I told you. And now that we've turned back, we're more dangerous still, I reckon.'

She said nothing, her eyes frightened, and he nodded at the slope again. 'They might keep us here for a day or two,' he said. 'But they'll never get up that slope, Polly. They'll have to go away in the end. We've got all the view. And with the sun behind us, we can see 'em sharp and clear while we'll be in shadow and in broken ground all day. The slope faces north and the sun'll be in their eyes except at midday.'

Polly had got most of their belongings set out in the cranny of rocks when Sammy returned, struggling with the water.

He nodded approvingly and placed the canteens and the barrel under the overhang that formed a cave.

'We'd better eat now,' he said.

Polly turned quickly, trying to be helpful to hide her fears from him and from herself.

'I'll make a fire,' she said.

Sammy shook his head quickly. 'No fires, Polly. No smoke. Not tonight.'

She stared at him for a second, but she said nothing and reached for the meat they had cooked earlier in the day.

'It's going to be cold up here,' she said.

Sammy grinned, a short brief grin that lit up his thin face. 'Sleep close together, Poll,' he suggested. 'That'll keep us warm.'

He untied the yellow bandanna he had tied round his throat against the dust and tore it into strips.

'I got a little job to do before we settle down,' he said, and Polly watched him move down the hillside again, the strips of yellow hanging from his hand.

Near the bottom, on the east side, he placed one of the strips of cloth on the south side of the rock, so that it was clearly visible from where she stood, and set a small stone on top of it. Then he moved slowly round the hill towards the west, selecting small rocks that were visible from the upper slopes and placing the yellow rags on them, holding them in place with other small rocks. Every now and again he paused, glancing up the slope as though trying to make up his mind about something, before he moved on patiently.

When she looked round again, he was out beyond the bottom of the slope, a long shadow stretching sharply from his feet, placing small, innocuous groups and patterns of stones in the grass, all of them plainly visible from where she stood. Working slowly, watched by the puzzled Polly, he placed a wide ring of the inconspicuous cairns round the foot of the kopje, then he turned and began to climb back towards her.

He jumped into the shallow hollow behind the rocks where she stood and caught the puzzled look in her eyes.

'Makes shooting easier,' he explained, 'when you know the ranges. That's where most people go wrong, but I've just been measuring it out. That's all. First lot are two hundred yards. Second lot are four hundred. The stones are way up beyond that.'

'Sammy, *will* there be any shooting?'

'Not unless *they* start it.'

'How many of 'em are there?'

He grinned suddenly. 'Not enough,' he said. 'You wait and see.'

She was moved to an explosion of anger by a sudden hatred for their pursuers. 'I hope you kill all of 'em,' she said violently. 'I hope you kill every single blasted one – chasing people up and down Africa like this, not giving 'em any peace. I hope there isn't a single *one* left when you've finished, Sammy.'

He grinned and, turning away from her, began to empty the ammunition from his pockets, tossing it in small shining groups among the rocks. He moved quietly and surely, like an animal that knows it has suddenly become involved in a hunt that can end only in death.

After they had gnawed at a piece of biltong and washed out their mouths with water, he sat back and began to clean the rifles, taking out the pull-throughs and working slowly and skilfully with them. Polly sat beside him, watching him, shivering from time to time, partly with excitement and partly with fear, her eyes on the subtle wiry muscles of his hands. He seemed to ignore her and went on working silently, his thin bony fingers moving over the weapons until he was satisfied. Then he replaced the pull-throughs and the oil and wiped the weapons on a piece of rag. The determined sureness of his movements had a frightening significance.

He caught her eyes on him and returned her gaze without blinking. Something inside her responded to his look, some trick of their sexes that had sparked in her from the first day she had seen him so that the very thought of him had always been a stimulant for as long as she could remember.

'Sammy – !'

She stopped dead, unspoken words dying in her throat, and slowly he pushed the weapons aside, and reached out to her...

For some time, she clung to him, a great tenderness and passion flooding over her as she leaned against his shoulder, content to let him touch her, responding impetuously when he kissed her mouth with a raw unexpected violence, his fingers in her tangled hair, both of them drowning in the darkness of the emotion that flooded over them.

Then, after a while, she sat up, shaken and cold, shivering as she held on to him, caressing his thin features, unable to take her eyes off him, and she was crying, softly and secretly, as she hadn't cried for years.

'Sammy, Sammy,' she mourned. 'What's come over me? I've not done this since I was a kid.'

He pulled her closer, stroking her forehead with the back of his hand.

'Wind up, Poll,' he said. 'It'll soon go.'

She stirred in his arms, unhappy and afraid.

'It's you I'm scared for, Sammy,' she said. 'We're up against it now and no error.'

'Nothing to be afraid of,' he said confidently.

'Isn't there? I don't know so much.'

On her face there was the look of woman throughout the whole of history, hating conflict, wanting only warmth and love and roots deep in the earth, a look that was impossible to answer with words.

'We just happened to fall on the wrong side of the fence, Poll, that's all,' he said inadequately.

Her body shook again in a new paroxysm of misery and fear. 'Sammy, why did we waste so many years? Why didn't you ever take me with you before?'

'I will next time, Poll,' he promised. 'Next time I'll take you with me.'

'Or I could maybe run a little bar to keep me while you were away,' she said. 'Somewhere you could come home to, when you were sick of shooting or when you were tired. Then there'd always be somewhere if you decided to leave the veld.'

He laughed. *'Me* leave the veld, Poll? It's in my blood.'

He grinned and she saw that, like all men, he came from a different world from hers, a world that was as remote from her own desire for security as it was from the moon.

'There might be kids,' she pointed out anxiously, trying with all her woman's skill to give him roots, trying to entwine him, however unconsciously, with the vines of domesticity, trying to tie him down to something. 'You might be glad to come home once in a while.'

'I *might,'* he said unconvincingly.

Polly sat back, forgetting her discomfort and the growing chilliness as she busied herself with daydreams she hadn't ever dared to dwell on before, preoccupied with the idea of houses and homes, seeing him as a new tamed Sammy, accepting ties and roots, attentive in a way she could never in her heart of hearts remember him and never honestly expected to; then, looking round for him, reaching out for him, wanting merely to touch him, she realised he had moved quietly away from her.

She sat up abruptly, but he had moved to the edge of the rocky ledge out of reach – restless even now – and was scanning the russet veld below them.

They could see over a dozen miles in most directions, except north. The evening light was extraordinarily clear, better even to see by than the full flare of the afternoon sun which set the plain dancing with heat shimmers and water-patches of mirage and made it hard to spot sudden movement.

But the faint roll of the ground was deceptive nevertheless. A whole column of buck could hide itself at a distance of a few miles in a place that seemed as flat as a plate, and he was looking for small things that indicated men, a layer of floating dust among the scrub and the scattered thorn trees, a running antelope, or a movement of quail.

He glanced back at the place he had selected for them. Above them the kopje rose gaunt and bleak with high krantzes of stone, buttress on buttress of it, with sparse grassy slopes between. There was only one way to the top, he knew, and that was directly past where he was standing.

He saw Polly watching him, her face still flushed, but her eyes frightened. He grinned at her to reassure her, and laid the two rifles out on the rocks in front of them, their muzzles facing towards the north, protruding through the screen of monkey thorn and cactus that filled the gap between the boulders.

The two weapons had a wicked look about them, the old Martini-Henry, a discarded mounted police weapon years old, with its short barrel, well pitted with rust scars, and the shining new Mauser. Alongside each he had laid the ammunition.

He saw Polly still looking at him and he stooped to pick up the Mauser and one of the clips of ammunition. He held the weapon in his left hand and pulled back the bolt. For a second he stood, balancing the rifle, then he pushed in the clips of bullets and drove the bolt home.

'Nice gun,' he commented and Polly shuddered with an unknown fear.

He laid the rifle down again slowly, then he straightened up and stood in front of her. Lifting her to her feet, he placed his hands on her hips.

'No need to be scared, Poll,' he said. 'There's nothing they can do. Not a thing. Only' – he paused – 'maybe a bit of a prayer might help if you're any good at it.'

She forced a twisted smile, then clutched him to her, her arms round his waist, her face against the rough material of the old salt and pepper coat.

'I'll pray, Sammy,' she said. 'I'll pray tonight.' She looked up at him. 'What will they do, Sammy?'

He picked up a stone and tossed it down the slope. It landed in a flat puff of dust that drifted slowly away. 'Wind's coming from the west,' he observed. He looked at her, shifting on his feet. 'I don't know what they'll do, Poll,' he went on. 'I don't know at all. Only thing I know, I don't trust that Kitto. I feel best up here with him around down there. There's nobody better'n me with a rifle. And I know this land like a springbok does. That lot are city dwellers, for all their hosses and their guns, and one Boer was always better than ten Englishmen when it come to this sort of scuffling. And I've been brought up to the veld like any trek-Boer. Just trust me, Poll. Just try to trust me.'

She looked up at him, her eyes shining. 'I trust you, Sammy,' she said. 'Oh, God, I trust you. I always did, I think.'

He smiled at her, then he pushed her gently aside and moved towards the rifles. Picking up the Mauser, he glanced along the sights and felt the weight of the weapon. Then he pointed with it out across the veld.

In the amazing clarity of the evening, she could see a thin layer of dust rising out of a shallow depression and striking sharply off towards the east at a speed that indicated antelope. Then behind, rising out of the same fall of ground but heading straight towards Sheba, another cloud of dust came, slower, heavier in a way that told them it was men and horses and motorcars.

'We've got company, Poll,' he said.

PART TWO

o n e

The scout cars arrived at Sheba just as the light was beginning to give way to the greyness of dusk. They were moving swiftly, the horsemen driving their jaded mounts hard to keep in sight of them.

The Rolls was in the lead, with Kitto in the front seat, fidgety and unable to keep his patience in check. Several times he had changed to horseback, ranging back and forth across the veld as though the straight course of the vehicles wasn't sufficient for his restless energy, dragging a rifle from the saddle scabbard again and again and thumping his mount across the rump to urge it to greater speed. By the time they arrived at Sheba, he was back in the Rolls again, watching Le Roux as he hung over the dun-painted side, studying the hard earth of the veld which seemed to echo the roar of the engines and the clatter of small stones under the mudguards as they approached.

When they were almost past the kopje, Le Roux flung up his arm and shouted.

'*Pas op,*' he said. 'We lost 'em!'

The Rolls slid to a halt, its rear wheels locked, and seemed to shed men in all directions. The Napier, steaming badly, altered course to avoid them, then while they were all standing in a group, still feeling the motion of the cars as a sailor does when he steps ashore, the cavalrymen arrived, breaking into an unbalanced trot as the horses bumped each other. One of the animals swerved violently in the jostling, flinging its tired rider from the saddle. He swore as he hit the ground, then scrambled to his feet again, his face livid, lashing at the frightened animal with his hat in an outburst of the frustrated fury that had set lines of strain across all their features.

They were every one of them exhausted now and it was beginning to show in explosions of unexpected temper. The horses were worn out, their withers prominent after the pounding they had received, their ankles puffed with hard work. More than one of them limped badly and the complaints against Kitto's hard driving were rising in a crescendo.

There had been a considerable amount of jeering from the hard-pressed horsemen as they had had to help construct fascines of brushwood to enable the cars to cross the deep courses of streams, or had had to haul the heavy vehicles up the steeper slopes or out of the soft dust of the hollows where they had sunk hub-deep, screaming in low gear. More than once there had been a short-lived scuffle as one of the Army Service Corps men, driven to an extremity of fury by the sarcasm, had flung himself at his tormentors, for the car crews were as jaded now as the riders, the drivers weary from the jolting that tore the steering wheels from their grip and left them with blistered bleeding hands.

As they spread out, waiting for Le Roux to examine the ground, they worked their stiff limbs and the Army Service Corps men wandered round their vehicles, gazing anxiously at them. Engine trouble and mechanical defects were beginning to develop after the miles of rough ground. They had been obliged to roar over the bad patches to avoid getting stuck, rushing at them at an unsafe speed for fear of having to call on the resentful horsemen, and rocking over the hummocks in a style that seemed fatal to the chassis. On one occasion, the front bracket of one of the Rolls' springs had snapped and they had had to stop to jack it up, wedging it with baulks of timber on the running board and wiring the whole hurried job together; and time and time again the tyres, heated in the grinding low gear stretches, had burst, so that first one car and then the other had had to halt, their crews sweating under the repeated leverings and pumpings.

Now, as cigarettes were reached for and water-bottles were raised, the Napier driver unscrewed the cap of the vehicle's water tank and the concentrated steam roared out.

'Christ,' he said, staring at the rising cloud, 'we only want railway lines. We've got a big enough head of steam on to pull wagons as far as Jo'burg!'

Oblivious to the activity behind him and the angry muttering of men pushed too far by an over-zealous commander, Le Roux was still prowling round the foot of Sheba. Sitting on the running board of the Rolls, smoking a cigarette, Winter could see him studying the ground among the rocky shale.

'They've turned off,' he announced as Kitto approached him. 'The tracks stop here.' He turned and walked slowly back until he came to a saddle of rock which stretched from the foot of the kopje into the veld. Around it was broken stones and thin flat pebbles, and Le Roux knelt and examined the hard surface. Kitto watched him, knocking the dust from his clothes and out of his hair.

'Came as far as here all right,' Le Roux said, looking up.

He straightened and walked a little way to the north-east, staring at the ground.

'That's funny, man,' he said uncertainly.

Winter saw him return to the flat table of rock and begin to walk to the west.

'For God's sake, put a jerk into it,' Kitto said impatiently.

Le Roux had stopped again, ignoring him, then he turned and stared up at Sheba, whose battlemented summit towered above them into the saffron sky, grey-blue in the fading light.

'I think they're up there,' he said. 'The prints just *disappear* here. *Kyk daar!* Look!'

Kitto stared. 'Up there? In the name of the good Lord Harry, man, they wouldn't go up there!'

Le Roux stared round him again at the ground. 'Only place they *could* go,' he said.

'Up there? Horses and all?'

'*And* the woman!' Le Roux chuckled. 'Calling for volunteers to go after 'em?' he asked.

'You sure?' Kitto demanded.

'I'll make sure.'

'Well, look slippy,' Kitto barked. '*Mak gou, ek is haastig.* We can't wait round here like mashers at a stage door. They're a damn' sight too near the Sidings now for my liking and I want it over and done with. So far we've ridden twice as far as he has and all we've done is make a damn' big circle. My God, with two cars capable of doing sixty miles an hour we ought to be able to catch up with a kid on an old shaft horse!'

Le Roux's square face was eager as he moved slowly in a half circle round the foot of the kopje, away from the horsemen, squatting by their blown mounts, glad of the chance of a rest. None of them spoke as they watched him work. One or two washed their dry mouths out with water from their canteens and spat, or wet their bandannas and wiped the dust from their stubbled faces. Several of them had taken their rifles from the saddle scabbards and one man, glancing nervously round and up at Sheba, slipped the safety catch off his weapon.

Winter stared up at the brooding bulk of the kopje in the failing light, like all of them oppressed by the silence, and he found himself wondering what lonely battles had taken place in the past on the silent amber-tinted crags.

Romanis approached him, his leather coat swinging, his goggles on his forehead, the dust on his face like a weird mask. 'Bloody queer place, this,' he observed uneasily.

Le Roux had walked back a little way now in the direction they had come from, then he approached the kopje again in a shambling run, following the tracks until he reached the flat slab of rock again. Once more, he glanced upwards, puzzled, then he stared at the ground and abruptly began to climb.

The report of the rifle came simultaneously with the metallic twang as a bullet struck the rock near his head. Winter saw the chips of stone fly into the air as Le Roux dropped flat on his face in an instinctive dive for safety, and the sharp whine came to his ears as the bullet ricocheted, buzzing angrily as its twisted shape went up in a tight singing lump of metal spinning out over their heads.

Within a second, before the echoes had finished rolling and clattering through the clefts and fissures of Sheba, the mounted men were all off their horses and crouching on the blind side of them, using them as shelter, clinging to the reins with one hand and feeling for the rifles in the scabbards with the other, eyes peering under necks and over saddles, their gaze straining upwards towards the spires of rock.

Winter found himself conspicuously and bewilderingly alone as the crews of the Napier and the Rolls crouched behind their vehicles, gripping their rifles, huddled in little groups behind the wheels.

'Get down, you bloody fool,' Romanis yelled from behind the Napier and Winter came to life at once and ran, doubled up, for the rocks. Diving into the dust behind a patch of scrub grass, he landed spread-eagled, his face close to the earth, breathing the dry hot smell of the soil, aware of the silence again, a deep new tremendous silence broken only by the chink of harness, and the click of metal shoes as the horses tossed their heads and tried to wheel and back, sniffing the excitement.

For a long time nobody spoke or moved, then Winter realised that Kitto was near him, also sprawled behind a rock, staring keenly at Sheba, his eyes suddenly bright. After a while, Romanis joined them, running bent double.

'Hallo, Romanis,' Kitto said and Winter saw he was grinning. 'The fun's begun!'

Romanis laughed. 'Wouldn't miss this for anything,' he said. 'By God, he's a game little bastard, Jew or not! – game as a pebble!'

Kitto lifted his head slightly and shouted to Le Roux just in front of them on the first slopes.

'You were right,' he said. 'Can you see 'em?'

The scout, on his knees now behind his rock, waved his hand in a sign of negation.

'Keep under cover, boys,' Kitto called to the crouching men behind him, 'and keep your eyes open. You should be able to spot him if he fires again.'

He ducked from his rock and ran stooping for the foot of Sheba to join Le Roux. Then he turned and sat with his back to the rocks and shouted his orders. 'Tell off your horse-holders,' he yelled. 'The rest of you take cover!'

Winter scrambled from behind the patch of grass and dived into shelter alongside Kitto.

'Kitto, surely to God you're not going to go up there after him. Offy said no violence.'

Kitto swung sharply round. 'You politicians are always good at thinking up situations for soldiers to deal with,' he said, 'but you always start bleating when things go wrong and we lose our tempers.'

While they were still staring angrily at each other, their faces only a foot apart, a faint voice came down to them from above.

'I wasn't shooting to hurt anybody then,' it said. 'But if any of you tries to interfere with me, I shall.'

Kitto's face darkened as he gazed up the slope.

'Samuel Isaac Schuter,' he shouted, as though making a formal announcement, 'you're a damned renegade! You've fired on His Majesty's troops in time of war. I'm going to fire back.'

'I bet you haven't seen me yet!'

'I've got thirty-odd men here who say I *will*.'

'And I've got the slope in my favour and a good rifle that says you're wrong.'

Winter grabbed at Kitto's arm. 'Kitto, what in the name of God are you up to? Offy didn't say you'd to shoot the boy.'

Kitto pulled his arm away irritably. Suddenly, he could see quite simply where his duty lay. It had crossed his mind several times in the last few difficult days that the death of Sammy Schuter was the only safe solution to the problem Willie Plummer's stupidity had raised but it had always been one which he could never have reconciled to his sense of honesty. Now, however, there was no longer any question of right and wrong. He was on surer ground and could put politics and politicians safely aside.

The minute Sammy Schuter had pulled the trigger up there on the slopes of Sheba, his course had become clear. The situation could now be resolved outside the dubious issues of humanity and without any stain on his honour. He was a soldier and he was at war.

'If Offy hasn't the guts to do what's necessary,' he said sharply, his face still turned towards the summit of Sheba, 'then *I* have.'

'You'll make a martyr of him,' Winter pointed out. 'Let me go up there and talk to him.'

'It's too late for that now.' Kitto was still staring at Sheba, not taking his eyes off the ground in front and above where his enemy lay. 'We're committed. He's perpetrated an act of war.'

'Fabricius will call Offy a murderer if he finds out about this.'

'He'll *never* find out. It'll be finished within an hour.'

'Kitto, for God's sake, there's a woman up there!'

Kitto turned his narrow face towards Winter again. 'Dammit, this is war,' he snapped.

'This is a lynching.'

'Don't be so bloody spineless!' Kitto lost his temper. 'If a German fired at us, we'd be fully entitled to fire back and kill him. Anybody who fires on the King's men in wartime becomes an enemy immediately and we're quite within our rights to finish him off.' He jerked on to his side in the dust to stare at Winter. 'Thirty years ago,' he said, 'I thought I might reach the highest rank in the British Army. Then things went wrong. I got the medals but none of the rank. Maybe I made a few mistakes in the last war. I don't know. But I'm not going to make any mistakes in *this* one. I've got my duty to do and I'm going to do it.'

'My God,' Winter said helplessly, 'the messes that have been made by people who had to do their duty! You're another damn' De Wet. You've got pride and patriotism all confused.'

Kitto was gesturing irritably now, impatient at what to him had become an arid intellectual brawl. 'He fired on us,' he said, as though that ended the argument, 'and we're reacting in the only possible way – by firing back.'

In spite of himself, Winter knew that he was right, and that his own arguments carried no conviction. Kitto's sense of justice was just too much for him. He could feel himself beating his head against a brick wall.

'Dammit, Winter,' Kitto was saying with frosty self-righteousness, 'what right have *you* to elect yourself as the conscience of the mob? It was your suggestion in the first place that we follow him.'

'It was wrong,' Winter said hopelessly. 'You know it was. I know it was now. I never dreamed he could be manoeuvred into this damnable position! My God, Kitto, I think you're going to murder that boy just to satisfy your own ego!'

Kitto turned away. 'I don't know what you're talking about,' he said. 'But I do know that it would probably be best for all concerned.'

Nobody was moving and there was no sign of life on the high sides of Sheba.

Men were crouched behind every rock, staring upwards in the fast-fading light, their rifles in front of them. The Kaffirs had taken the horses round to the shelter of Babylon and the two motorcars had jolted out of sight without any attempt from the boy on Sheba to stop them.

Kitto was crouching behind his rock with Le Roux and Romanis, staring at a watch he had dragged from his pocket.

'Are you going on with this murder?' Winter demanded.

'I'll give him five minutes to come out.'

'You know he'll never come out.'

Kitto nodded. 'Yes,' he said calmly, 'I know.'

'I believe you want it that way.'

Kitto gestured angrily, surprised that Winter didn't see it his way. 'Of course I do, man,' he said. 'How else can it end? I couldn't *ever* have taken the damned boy back to Plummerton.'

He lifted his head and shouted, his words echoing back off the sides of Sheba.

'This is Kitto speaking, Schuter. Hector Stark Kitto. You'd better come out, or we'll come and get you!'

The voice came back to them, thin and disembodied, hidden among the clefts of rock

'I'm waiting.'

141

'I'll give you five minutes. I'm timing from now.'

Again there was silence for a while, then they heard the boy's voice once more, faint but steady.

'I'd stay where you are, if I was you. Next time, I'm shooting to hit somebody.'

'I hope he does,' Kitto murmured. 'We wouldn't miss one or two of that damned rabble down there and it would give me the best excuse I could wish for.'

He crouched below his rock, studying the men waiting behind him. Their faces were keen and fierce, the faces of men with nothing to lose.

'Can you see him, Romanis?' he asked.

Romanis peered upwards through his binoculars, half-covered by a patch of thorn. 'Not a wink of the filthy little bounder,' he said.

'Can't you tell where he is by his voice?'

'Not a chance.'

'Never mind,' Kitto nodded. 'We'll go in anyway.'

He raised his binoculars to his eyes and swept the rocky slopes above him.

'Stand by,' he called out. 'Wait for the signal.'

He raised his eyes to the hill. 'Time's up, Schuter,' he shouted. 'We're coming.'

'I'm waiting.' The reply floated down again, faintly contemptuous and taunting; and Kitto waved and started to scramble from behind his rock.

Someone started to cheer and two dozen men made for the kopje. When the first of them reached the slope, his hat flew off as a shot rang out, and went spinning backwards among the rocks, its owner dropping flat into shelter in alarm. Another man, his rifle across his chest, was spun round as a bullet smacked into the stock, shattering it, sending him sprawling on his back in a puff of dust.

The man immediately behind him, a great ginger-haired giant, leapt over him and went on scrambling up the slope, swearing heavily, his long legs carrying him well ahead of the others, ahead of Kitto even. For a long time, there was no sound from above and Winter began to think that the show of force had frightened the boy, then as the red-haired man reached the top of a boulder and paused to cheer his friends on, another shot rang out.

It was as though Sammy Schuter had needed time to make up his mind to kill.

The red-haired man seemed to be lifted bodily off the rock, bent back like a pulled bow, then he crashed back on to the slope below, his heels drumming, and rolled down into the hollow at their feet, drawing painful rattling breaths in his throat.

Immediately, it seemed as though Sheba was stricken with silence again. With three of their number down, the rest of the men dived for shelter and the shouting died away. For a second, Kitto stood on the slope, seeing his force melt away behind him, then he too dived for safety and scrambled back to where Winter and Romanis lay with a couple of other men.

'Mr Kitto,' Le Roux called, 'Fred's dead!'

'The bastard's using a Martini-Henry!' A shout went up from the huddle of figures round the body, a howl of rage that demanded revenge.

'Soft-nosed bullets !'

'The dirty Jew! By Christ, he'll pay for this!'

There were a few more angry yells, then the men fell silent, even the bunched soldiers round the corpse seeming to have no tongues left. Sheba descended again into the brooding stillness from which their arrival had only just lifted it.

Kitto was the first to recover, undisturbed by the disaster, staring to the crest of Sheba again with his binoculars. 'Romanis,' he said briskly, 'send the sergeant here, and get that man down. We're stuck for the night, it seems. We'll have another try at first light in the morning with every available man. The advantage's with us. It's easier to shoot up than down and we can be halfway up the slope before he spots us. As soon as it's dark enough to move, we'll back off and move a couple of men to the north side to watch, in case they try to escape in the night.'

Romanis nodded and for a long time they continued to stare at Sheba, muttering together.

Around them, the soldiers were huddled in little groups behind the rocks. One of them was dragging the body of the ginger-haired man into shelter by the feet, his jacket rolling up round his arms as it snagged on the small stones.

'I hope you're satisfied, Kitto,' Winter said bitterly and Kitto nodded slowly, still gazing at Sheba, fortified by his certainty of lawfulness and right.

Winter stared at him, then he scrambled to his feet and ducking from the rock, ran towards Babylon and the group of horses.

'What's that damn' fool up to?' Romanis said, staring after him. 'Got the wind up or something?'

Kitto lowered his glasses and turned. His dark eyes glittered as Winter scrambled on to a horse, his shabby figure awkward in the saddle. For a second, he wrestled with the startled animal, wrenching the reins from the fingers of the Kaffir who was holding it, then he swung it round, dragging savagely at its mouth.

'Let him go,' Kitto said. 'We're well rid of him.'

'Suppose he tells somebody?'

Kitto shrugged. 'What's it matter?' he said confidently. 'We're behaving according to the rules.'

t w o

Sammy Schuter's eyes were cold as he lowered the Mauser.

Polly was crouching alongside him, her face pale and shocked. Long after the running figures below had vanished, she caught a glimpse between the rocks of someone dragging away the body of the ginger-haired man and even from that distance she saw the blood that stained his chest. For the first time she realised he was dead.

'Sammy, you killed him!' Momentarily, she had a picture in her mind of the duiker they had shot on their first day out of Plummerton Sidings, one moment full of enormous pulsing life and the next snuffed out of existence. There was a man below like that now, a big, raw-boned man with red hair who had leapt up the slope full of confidence in his own strength, a man who probably had a wife or a girl friend somewhere, and perhaps even children. He was as dead now as the duiker was. She remembered then how the flies had come from nowhere, clustering round the blood, horrible and obscene, and she shuddered as she connected it all with the man below.

She stared at Sammy and drew away from him quickly, horrified, as though the dead man's blood were actually on his hands.

'Sammy, you killed him,' she said again.

Sammy nodded, still gazing below at the empty plain. 'I could have killed any one of 'em, Poll, at this range. Any time I wanted.'

She swung round, staring at his face. It was lean and hard, mercilessness showing in the angular thinly-fleshed features and pale blue eyes, while his mind remained obscure and silent as a wild cat's behind his inscrutable eyes.

'But he's dead,' she said, her voice breaking. 'Sammy, you don't even seem to care!'

He glanced at her briefly, his eyes resting on her for a second before they turned back again to the plain, searching unceasingly for any sign of further movement.

'That's what I came up here for,' he said flatly. 'I gave 'em plenty of warning. You heard me. If they try again – '

'Oh, God,' Polly moaned. 'No more of 'em!'

The words were wrenched out of her in her horror. She had seen him kill a man with the same air of professional detachment he had employed to kill a buck. Those same thin bony hands which only a short time before had held her, now held the Mauser lightly across the rock, and the blue eyes which had been warm when he had looked at her were now glittering with menace. She saw him suddenly as a different individual, as solitary and self-dependent as the beasts he hunted, and it seemed impossible in that instant to imagine him as a domestic animal, moving about a farm or a house, attending to the duties of a home, living with other human beings.

She drew away from him, feeling as distant from him as if he'd been on the moon, cold and hard and ice-brilliant in his skill.

He looked round sharply, sensing the change in her. 'What's the matter?' he asked.

He reached out a hand to touch her but she pulled away from him.

'Leave me alone,' she said, her voice high and shrill.

Sammy stared at her and, as she saw he didn't comprehend, couldn't even hope to understand her horror, it came home to her how different a man's world and a woman's world were, so different as almost to belong to different planets. While her own lay with warmth and love and all the sensualities of life, he was as set apart from that aspect of living as if it never existed. His home had been too often the veld, his companions only his horse and his gun.

The light was fading rapidly now, and the rocks below were merging slowly into the darkness of the veld. As they watched, they heard a rolling of stones and they saw a bunch of men move away and dive in a scuttling run towards Babylon from the lower slopes of the kopje.

Sammy pushed the rifle forward, his eyes cold again, and Polly flung herself across his arms, staring up at him.

'No, Sammy,' she begged. 'For God's sake, no more!'

He tried to pull the rifle away from her but she refused to let go and he slowly relaxed, lowering it. Finally, he put it down and moved into the shelter of the rocks.

'Better eat,' he said heavily.

He fumbled among their belongings and, bringing out the remains of the cold meat from the saddle bags, he pushed it towards her with one of the water bottles.

'Easy on the water,' he said.

She raised her eyes, saying nothing.

'We might be a long time,' he pointed out.

His face was suddenly strained and tired as he knelt beside her and tossed a blanket across her. Her eyes followed him but she made no attempt to speak. For a while, he knelt by her, looking at her, his expression as enigmatic as the distant aloof hills, then he sat down.

'Reckon it's safe to sleep,' he said. 'They won't trouble us till daylight now. And I'll be waiting for them then.'

Her eyes were still on his face and for the first time he saw the horror in them.

'Polly,' he said, desperation in his voice, '*they* started it. *I* didn't.'

three

There was an air of tension about Plummerton West when Winter arrived, clattering on to the newly-made surface of Theophilus Street from the dusty earth that was all that paved the rest of the town.

He was surprised to see police about, uniformed and plain-clothed, waiting in the shadows, and small groups of soldiers sitting on the wooden stoeps, smoking, their horses tethered in bunches to the pepper trees and swishing at the inevitable flies. Saddles lay along the walls with piles of blankets and cooking tins; and a fire was glinting briefly by the brick wall of the livery stable.

As he arrived, hammering at a staggering horse that he knew would never recover, two men ran out from the darkness and grabbed at the bridle of his mount.

'*Wie gaan?*' one of them demanded in guttural backveld accents. 'Where do you think you're going, man?'

'Into town.'

'Oh, no you're not!' the other chimed in, in the chirpy tongue of a Londoner. 'We want no visitors, mister! Not after this afternoon. It was a cross here between the Charge of the Light Brigade and Saturday night at the Palace. Them Boers is out,' he went on. He indicated the street, and then Winter noticed broken windows, an overturned cart and a dead horse lying under the trees. 'There was some talk of treachery, mate. I don't know whose side they were on, but

148

the police couldn't control 'em. You wouldn't be one of 'em, would you?'

Winter shook his head. His horse stood with its feet astride breathing heavily in snoring gasps and Winter heaved up the long head. 'I want Sir Theophilus Plummer,' he said, 'and I want him quickly, so let me go.'

The two men glanced at each other, but Plummer's name carried sufficient weight for them to release the bridle.

'*Goed Genoeg,*' the Boer said. 'Fair enough.' He stared at the horse. 'Hi, you've come a long way, man.'

'Fast too, by the look of your nag,' the other chipped in.

'Look, I'm in a hurry – '

The soldier studied him for a moment, then he hitched at his belt. 'I'll come with you, or you might be stopped again.'

He disappeared into the shadows and, returning with his horse plodding behind him, swung into the saddle and rode alongside Winter into the town, through the scattered groups of soldiers camped under the trees.

The bright cold starlight was glinting on the iron roofs and the flat brick façades of the new buildings, giving the dusty road an icy tint as they pulled up outside the Plummerton Hotel.

The Cockney soldier swung to the ground and reached for Winter's bridle. 'I'll look after your horse,' he said. 'Not that he's going to be worth much now.'

'I'll need another,' Winter said as he dismounted, staggering a little from weariness. 'I'm going back.'

The trooper stared at him. 'Christ, what's the hurry, mate? De Wet come out?'

He stared at Winter's shabby clothes, and at the dust which lay in their folds and in his hair, but he nodded. 'I'll tell 'em to have one ready,' he said.

Winter pushed into the hotel, stumbling with stiffness, and saw at once there were sleeping figures on the floor of the bar, as though they were refugees from the uproar that had clearly been taking place in the streets. The Portuguese clerk rose from behind the reception desk, blinking, his face strained with tiredness.

'Mr Plummer?' Winter said, and the Portuguese cocked a thumb at the billiard room and disappeared out of sight again at once, yawning heavily.

They had brought a cot into the room and Plummer was stretched out on it, fully clothed, and in the shadows Winter could see Hoole lying awkwardly on the horsehair bench, his face covered by an old copy of the *Illustrated London News*, his pince-nez on a chair beside him.

They were both on their feet in an instant as the glass crashed in the door, Hoole reaching for his spectacles, Plummer's heavy face drawn with weariness, his hair on end, as he swung his feet to the floor.

'Frank! What the hell are you doing here? Where's Kitto and the rest of them?'

'They're at Sheba.'

'Sheba?' Plummer ran his hands through his hair. 'Good God in Heaven, haven't they got any farther than that? What are they doing there?'

'They're trying to blast the life out of that boy there! They've got him pinned up on the slope, and they're shooting.'

'Shooting?' Plummer looked shocked. 'I said no violence. For God's sake, what's going on, Frank?'

Winter gestured wearily with a heavy hand, his back against the door. 'Offy, that damned old fool Kitto'll destroy you,' he panted. 'You've got to come and stop him. I can't. They're out to kill the boy.'

'Kill him?' Plummer looked ill, his plump face veined and sagging. He began to button up his waistcoat quickly, and reached for his collar. 'Good God,' he said, 'that's murder!'

'Not quite. They've got their excuse all right. It's all nice and legal. The boy fired on them first. There's one dead already. One of the troopers. Offy, we took the wrong path in the beginning. We've got to get back on the right one.'

Plummer gestured helplessly. 'What the devil was the boy doing firing on them?' he asked. 'He must have been mad.'

As he turned from the heavy gilt mirror, his face red with the struggle to fasten his collar over the stud, Winter swayed, dizzy with fatigue, and Plummer dragged up a chair quickly.

'Here, sit down, man,' he said, concern in his face. 'You look all in. Hoole, damn you, get him a drink! If they're asleep, knock 'em up!'

As Hoole disappeared through the clashing glass door, Plummer pushed the chair forward and Winter dropped into it, trying to explain what had happened.

'Offy, I told you,' he said. 'He's death with a rifle.'

Plummer sat down and grunted as he reached for his bootlaces.

'But why did he do it, Frank? Why? It don't make sense.'

'I think he just grew tired of being told where he'd got to go. He just grew tired of us, Offy – me, and Kitto, and you. We made a mistake, not leaving him alone. He'd probably have kept his mouth shut anyway, if we had.'

Plummer tugged at his moustache, his pale eyes popping. 'Good God, what have I done?' he said.

Winter knocked the dust from his face with a clumsy hand. 'It's my responsibility,' he pointed out. 'It was my suggestion that we encourage him to get out of the town. It's my responsibility that he's turned round and bitten us.'

'Couldn't you have called 'em off, man?' Plummer looked agitatedly at his watch with the instinctive movement of a busy man, and shoved it back in his pocket again, his thick fingers trembling.

Winter had loosened his tie now and was wiping the dust from his eyes.

'Kitto's in charge,' he said, 'not me. I was only there to watch but it's got beyond watching now. It wants some strong action from someone with enough authority to override Kitto.'

'Who?'

'You, Offy. You. And even then I'm doubtful.'

Plummer gestured. 'Good God, man, what can *I* do? If Kitto considers it's in the best interests of the country –' He stopped uncertainly as the door rattled and Hoole returned with a bottle of gin and a couple of bottles of soda.

'Hoole' – Plummer looked around – 'go and arrange for a meal to be brought in.'

Hoole nodded, and putting the bottles down on the edge of the billiard table, turned back to the door again. Plummer rose and poured a drink.

'By Snuff, Frank,' he said, 'this is the worst thing that could happen to us. There's been hell to play here today. I didn't let Hoole leave for the Cape in the end. I thought it best to hang on to him. Willie'll have to sink or swim on his own. A runner came in to say that Ackermann from Brits' Commando had run into De Wet's rearguard and was on his way back here for supplies. He'd had casualties.' He clashed the bottle back to the metal tray and turned round, holding out a glass to Winter.

'Hertzog's been at it again in the House,' he went on, recovering his confidence as he found himself dealing with something he understood. 'It was in the *Cape Times* that came up yesterday. Said the rebels were being murdered. Murdered, by Ginger! After what they've been doing in the Free State! Fabricius organised a meeting here last night as a follow-up. He knew about Ackermann and he soon picked up Hertzog's phrase. He even hinted pretty strongly that De Wet had got support from the British element here – meaning me, of course! He was damned careful to say nothing seditious but what he was suggesting was plain enough for his followers to smash the town up. He's heard about Willie all right. They tell me he's been turning the place upside down, looking for that boy.'

'He'll find him quickly enough if he goes to Sheba. He might even meet him coming back.'

Plummer gestured angrily. 'He *can't* come back,' he said.

'Kitto hasn't been able to stop him yet!'

Plummer banged his fist down on the table. 'Fabricius is going to love this,' he said. 'And so are a lot of other people! We're going to be busy, Frank, you and me, shoving up the barricades. We've got to be ready for 'em.'

As he moved back to the mirror, smoothing his hair into place, prepared to give battle, Winter looked round the billiard room, remembering other meetings he'd seen in there, meetings like this and the one of several days ago, with Offy and his minions standing around, a different man for every facet of his business, sometimes Hoole, sometimes others; politicians and businessmen all mixed up together, each trying to see to Offy's tangled affairs at the same time, all of them demanding Offy's attention. Inevitably there was always some frightened offender too, some businessman who'd opposed them, some politician who'd been threatening; and Winter, always Winter, in the background, complete with the dirty work in a notebook in his pocket, the evidence, the goods; half-ashamed of himself and trying to pretend that it didn't matter what a man did with his life, that pride was unimportant.

Somehow now, though, it all seemed different.

'Offy,' he said slowly, 'not me. Not this time. You're on your own now.'

Plummer turned, his expression incredulous. 'On my own?'

Winter nodded. 'There've been many things I've done for you, Offy,' he went on. 'There was Abbey and Mrs Williamson's husband, and van der Stel, and a few others. I've fixed 'em all for you, Offy, fixed 'em so their

153

grandchildren will burst into tears every year on the anniversaries. I dug out the dead dogs on their consciences, or buried yours according to the circumstances. But it's over now. I've finished.'

Plummer was standing over him, his thick neck bulging over his collar, angry and disappointed. 'You could manage it just this *once* more,' he said, pleading as he always did when Winter rebelled.

But this time Winter shook his head. 'No, Offy,' he said. 'I've knocked too many nails in the coffin of my conscience, and for once I'm crying enough.'

'Frank – '

Winter shook his head. 'There hasn't been much you've asked me to do that I let you down with,' he said, 'but I'm backing out of this one now. Offy. When we can condone murder by calling it duty, I've finished.'

Plummer's eyes were hurt and he looked old and lonely and deserted. 'Don't leave me now, Frank,' he begged. 'Don't back out at this stage. I'm going to need you. I've always relied on you because you've always told me what I ought to know, not what I wanted to know. I've trusted you even though we haven't always agreed, and my God, I need someone now – not some smooth legal josser like Hoole but somebody who knows what makes me tick. I want you around because there's trouble and there's going to be *more* trouble.'

He poured himself a drink and swallowed it quickly. 'They've been selling shares on the Stock Exchange in Jo'burg,' he said. 'I'm losing money. They've heard of the riots already and they know the signs. The market's gone down with a bang. There's talk of an inquiry here.'

Winter didn't reply and Plummer grabbed his arm.

'If there *is* an inquiry – and the boy comes into it – whose side are you on, Frank?'

'Not yours, Offy,' Winter said soberly. 'Perhaps mine, perhaps that boy's, but not yours and not Kitto's.'

'You were in it from the start, Frank.'

'I'll take that risk. I'll be prepared to tell the truth, Offy. But it won't be *your* truth or *my* truth. It'll be God's blessed and unflyblown truth for once. Somewhere inside I find I'm human after all.'

Plummer sighed and poured himself another drink.

'I've told you many times before, Frank,' he said slowly, suddenly calm, 'and you know it, that we who were here in the early days were guilty of more than one sin before we got into the saddle. We had to be. There were too many others like us. Those who weren't went under or ended up in a coffin made of gin cases. Reputations as well as manners decayed quickly in those days. You washed in soda water because there wasn't anything else and a punch on the nose came to be regarded in the light of a receipt stamp. And we who survived rose from the ruck and the muck with a load of the dirtiest money on earth and the memory of as many sins as are chronicled in the Newgate Calendar.' He paused and drew a deep breath, the agitation gone at last from his face, his manner calm again. 'But I like to think that even if my money wasn't clean when I got it, I've tried to cleanse it a little by putting it to the best use I could – for the country, for my fellow men who weren't so lucky. Not since those early days have I tried to bully anyone who wasn't trying to bully *me*, and I don't want to bully anyone now. I said no violence and there'll be no violence. I'll go, Frank. I'll go at once.'

Winter's expression softened. 'Thanks, Offy,' he said quietly.

Plummer began to collect his belongings, then he turned, and stared ahead of him, talking to himself.

'God, this couldn't have come at a worse time,' he said. 'Ackermann'll be nearing Plummerton any time now and De Wet's still free.' His shoulders sagged. 'Just another worry, Frank, on top of all the others.'

As he struggled to smile, Winter realised that sometimes he felt that his complex empire of politics and finance had grown too big even for him.

Plummer smiled wryly and, patting Winter's shoulder, turned for the door.

'I'll be going now,' he said. 'Hoole can drive. Never managed to find time to learn meself. Get some sleep.'

Winter shook his head stubbornly and forced himself out of the chair.

'I'm coming with you,' he said. 'If we hurry, we should just make it back by daylight.'

Plummer pushed him back. 'You're all in,' he said. 'I know Sheba all right. We can find it on our own.'

'I'm still coming. As soon as I can find another horse. I've killed the one I had.'

Plummer looked at the grey pallor of fatigue on Winter's face, then he shrugged. 'Have it your own way,' he said. 'But get a couple of hours' sleep first. I'll leave a message for them to wake you. And don't worry about horses. Take the Vauxhall. It'll be gentler than a saddle and a lot quicker.'

He paused, his face full of compassion as his mind flew to Sheba and the drama that was being enacted there. 'Poor old Kitto,' he said, as he stood with the door open. 'I always guessed he was a fool. He never did know how to do anything any other way than getting his head down and rushing at it like a bull at a gate. That's why he collected all the medals and all the casualties in the last war. That's why I never did anything when he complained he was being neglected. I could have helped him a lot but I always did feel he had more guts than brains. He wouldn't even have become the legend he did if Chief Jeremiah hadn't guessed wrong that day thirty years ago. He'd have been just a heap of powdering bones on a hill in Dhanziland. This'll finish him. He'll be right back to what he always should have been – the everlasting subaltern.'

four

The sky was already saffron yellow in the east when Polly woke up, drenched with dew. To her surprise, she found she had both blankets over her, and she felt round in sudden terror for Sammy. Then she saw him sitting behind one of the rocky krantzes, holding the Mauser, his eyes calm with the bland blankness of a dog in the sun, the same controlled fatalistic expression on his face that she'd seen often on the faces of the backveld Kaffirs, unmoved and faintly touched with boredom.

She sat up, turning eagerly towards him, then she remembered with horror the events of the previous evening, the picture of the big raw-boned ginger man spread-eagled against the plain, teetering backwards, and finally crashing to the rocks, the red stain spreading across his smashed chest, and she drew her feet up under her and pulled the blankets tighter round her, staring at Sammy, sick and confused.

Sammy had opened the Mauser now and was cleaning it. As she watched, still in the blankets, she saw him pick up the bullets, wipe them on his shirt and reinsert them. Then he laid the weapon down, wiping the barrel carefully.

As he picked up the Henry, he saw her staring at him. 'Dirty rifle's dangerous,' he commented. 'Kicks like a mule. Might even burst.'

He made no attempt to move towards her, to touch her, or even to explain himself, as though he understood that nothing he said would ever make any difference. His eyes had returned to the floor of the veld as he worked and he was picking up the cartridges by the feel of them, his fingers moving over the breech mechanism and sighting arrangements with a deft certainty. He cleaned each bullet carefully, as he had done with the Mauser, then he laid the weapon on a rock in front of him.

Below him, a scant half-mile away, he could see the shadows beginning as the sun appeared over the horizon, long dark shadows on a red-gold veld. As the light improved, he caught a movement beyond the rocks of Babylon, and saw a man stand up, smoking a short clay pipe, then another and another. Imagining Sammy to be farther to the west than he was, they thought themselves unseen.

He lifted the Mauser, fingering it, sighting on each of them in turn to get the feel of the gun. Then he noticed Polly watching him and he glanced briefly at her again.

'Should be starting again soon,' he said unemotionally. 'Reckon we'd better eat something.'

Still keeping one eye on the veld below, he rummaged in the saddle bags for the biltong, and passed her a twisted piece of dried meat that looked like an old root. He threw the water bottle after it.

'Chicken and champagne,' he said.

As she took it from him, he lay down flat on his face again among the rocks, watching the shadows shortening on the veld below. Then a man ran from behind the pile of rocks that formed the end of Babylon and dived headlong into shelter at the bottom of Sheba, and Polly saw Sammy lift the Mauser and push it forward. Another man ran from shelter and took up his position behind a rock, and Sammy again lifted the Mauser and laid it down again, waiting. In the quiet patience of his silent stare there was something of a cat waiting for a bird to move within killing distance. From being a civilised human being he had become just as much a part of the veld as the animals he had hunted, as cautious and as cruel, knowing only the law of survival and the power of the strong.

Another and yet another man had found a place among the rocks at the foot of Sheba but he continued to hold his fire. He had set out a row of bullets alongside him and she knew well from what she had seen of him that he could use them all and not miss with any of them.

Then a rifle popped somewhere below them, strangely small in the vastness of the plain, and she ducked as the echoes went rolling round the krantzes. The bullet struck a boulder away to their left and went whining up into the air, and she lay with her face among the dusty grass, sick and petrified with fear.

'Nothing to worry about,' Sammy said, unmoved, his position unchanged, his eyes unwinking. 'They don't even know where we are.'

He didn't move a muscle as the firing increased and even Polly eventually lifted her head as she realised it was all directed well to their left.

'They'll be coming any minute,' Sammy said flatly. 'This is just to make us keep our heads down.'

She saw his face had suddenly tightened as he stared down and as she scrambled to her knees and peered between a crack in the rocks, a car appeared over the fold of ground, trailing its long plume of red-yellow dust. It was a bright yellow vehicle, square and heavy, its paint and brasswork dulled with dirt. The men at the foot of Sheba, preoccupied with their shooting, clearly didn't notice it as it pulled to a stop in full view of Sammy, and she saw the door flung open in a flash of yellow as the rising sun caught it, then there were two men running towards the base of Sheba where the soldiers were concealed.

They made no effort to hide themselves, the biggest of them, a broadly-built man with a moustache, lumbering heavily as though he were unused to exercise.

Polly watched him start to scramble among the rocks, waving his arms and shouting. For a moment, he disappeared, then he reappeared again, higher up, still scrambling ahead, turning round and waving to the others, shouting all the time.

Her throat constricted as Sammy leaned forward and adjusted the sights of the Mauser and she put her hands over her eyes, unable to watch.

Sammy pushed the rifle forward and slowly the sights came into line. Through the V of the backsight he could see a small triangle of grey which was the big man's jacket. The foresight moved up slowly, then it paused for a tiny instant of time as Sammy steadied his breathing, and took the first pull of the trigger. The soldiers had risen from behind their rocks now and appeared to be cheering and waving too and Sammy's finger began to tighten on the trigger.

Then Polly screamed. Drawn by a horrified fascination that wouldn't let her shut her eyes, she had been staring through her fingers at the men below again, and it struck her suddenly that the heavily-built man wasn't cheering the others on, as she had thought, but was trying to reach a position in front of them where he could be seen, and that his gestures were not of encouragement but of discouragement. He was waving to the men around him to stay where they were and then she realised that his shouts were orders to withdraw.

Then it dawned on her who he was, and as he paused by a rock where she saw the bright gleam of a strip of yellow bandanna, she shrieked out.

'Sammy, no – it's Mr Plummer!'

five

They had risen to their knees, crouching, as Kitto waved; tensed, waiting for his signal to move forward, all of them feeling glad to get on with it, willing to take a chance to get the job done; and none of them saw Plummer come up behind them.

They had been so engrossed with what they were doing, with shooting and keeping their heads out of sight, with shouting instructions and advice to each other, they had never noticed the Daimler arrive, the shots and the clatter of stones rolling down the first slopes of Sheba drowning the sound of the engine.

The first they saw of Plummer was as he passed them, running, half-turned towards them, ungainly, scrambling awkwardly up the slope, his big body clumsy on the difficult surface.

'Get back,' he was shouting. 'Get back, you lot of madmen!'

He was waving frantically, his face purple with exertion.

'Kitto,' he was shouting, 'call them off! I'll have no more killing!'

Romanis was standing up now, waving his arms. 'Get down,' he shrieked. 'Get down, man!'

As Plummer turned, they rose to their feet in surprise, as though to follow him, and at once they heard the thump of a bullet striking home and immediately afterwards the report of a rifle, which ran menacingly round the half-circle of Sheba's rocks.

Plummer had stopped dead, his arms still wide in protest, balanced on top of a rock he had mounted so he could be seen. They saw the stain start immediately in the centre of his chest, and for a second he drew a few painful breaths that made the blood throb out of his lungs and ooze through the linen of his shirt. The anger in his face had changed to surprise, as though he couldn't believe what had happened.

They were all standing up now, heedless of the rifle above them, all of them staring at Plummer. His hat fell off and he took a staggering step backwards, his eyes directing a worn reproachful gaze towards them; then with his arms still open wide as though he were diving, he plunged backwards over the edge of the rock and dropped almost flat.

He landed directly in front of Kitto and Romanis and slid sideways down the slope, his arms and legs spread-eagled, until his body was stopped by a small boulder. Still indifferent to the rifle above, they left their cover and crouched over him.

He was still conscious, his blue eyes open and gazing upwards, though there was dust now on the staring pupils. His restless fingers were picking aimlessly at the pebbles, and a strange whispering rose in his throat.

Whether or not he recognised them, it was hard to say, but after a while he opened his mouth and spoke slowly and firmly to them.

'Don't use me to start a vendetta,' he said. 'There must be no spirit of revenge.'

Then his head rolled back, and Romanis began to feel under the blood-soaked jacket. Kitto shook his head.

'That's no good, Romanis,' he said sharply. 'He's dead.'

He looked up, his face at first shocked, then slowly becoming suffused with anger. As he looked round, it

dawned on him they were all out from behind cover and that
the deadly rifle up there on the slopes was still unsubdued.

'Get down, damn you,' he roared, coming to life at once.
'Get down!'

The heads bobbed out of sight quickly, and Kitto and
Romanis pulled Plummer's body into the shade alongside
them, the blood blackening the dust as it moved. Slowly
Romanis stripped off his jacket and laid it over the dead face.

The sour sickly smell of blood was still in their nostrils
when they heard a scrambling of feet on the stones behind
them, and they looked round just as Hoole dropped alongside them, his pince-nez lopsided, his face white with shock.

'Offy? Is he – ?'

'Offy's dead,' Kitto said in a harsh flat voice.

'By God,' Hoole said. 'The swine shot him. Just as he was
trying to save him too.'

'Save him?'

'He'd come to call it all off. Winter came in last night and
Offy came at once. He was hoping to stop the whole
business. He talked of it all the way.'

He moved the jacket gingerly and stared with horror at the
grey shrunken face, then up at the rocky slopes of Sheba. 'I
don't know now – ' he ended uncertainly.

Kitto's mouth closed tight. 'There'll be no calling it off
now,' he snapped. 'Offy's not going to go unavenged.'

Romanis broke in. 'Offy said no vengeance,' he pointed
out.

'Offy was always too soft-hearted.' Kitto's eyes were sharp
and glittering. 'By God, man, you don't think we're going to
let him get away with this, do you? Offy was a KBE. He was
Administrator of Dhanziland. He brought *all* this area under
the Crown. We annexed it together. He raised a regiment of
horse for the Government in 1899 and paid for it out of his
own pocket. He was raising another one now. He made
Plummerton West and Plummerton Sidings, and many other

places besides. There'll be a lot of weeping when they hear about this.'

He stopped, as though he'd run out of elaborate praises. 'It might have been called off yesterday,' he said. 'It might have been called off this morning. But not now. No damn' Sheeny renegade's going to get away with this. It's become our duty now to hang that bloody murderer as high as we can get him.'

Hoole looked at him, and then at the body and the spatters of blood seeping into the greedy earth. He took off his spectacles and began to polish them nervously.

'Vengeance won't do him much good,' he said uneasily. 'It won't even save his companies. This time tomorrow, they'll be manoeuvring for control of his shares.' He looked up nervously. 'I never did like this affair,' he said. 'I was against it from the start. I said so.'

Kitto was tapping his boot with his riding crop, his dark angry eyes flickering about him.

'We've got to get him down from here,' he said. 'We've got to give him a decent burial.'

'Here?' Hoole looked up. 'Won't they want him back in Plummerton?'

'How do you propose to take him back?' Kitto demanded hotly. 'Slung across a saddle like a common thief? We'll get him below. Anybody got a white handkerchief? I wonder if that bastard up there will accept a flag of truce.'

Hoole shook out a neatly-ironed square and Romanis tied it to the barrel of his rifle. For a while he waved it to and fro over the rock, but there was no indication of whether it had been seen or not from above. Kitto stood up abruptly, impatiently, waiting for the shot.

'Get up, Romanis,' he snapped. 'Stop cowering down there like a savage! You've been a soldier, haven't you? Stand up!'

Romanis stood up uncertainly and Kitto nodded towards the body.

'Take his legs, man. We've got to get him down. Hoole, stay here. It's safer. Keep an eye on things for me. I'll be back in a moment then we'll try to carry the place.'

Ignoring the possibility of further shooting, they started down the slope, stumbling under the weight of the body, the slow-dripping blood making poppy splashes in the dust as they walked. Though Romanis kept flinging glances over his shoulder towards Sheba, Kitto's back was straight. On any other battlefield, he would have won them both a medal.

They laid Plummer down alongside the wagons, watched by the goggle-eyed Kaffirs whose chatter had been completely silenced. They all of them knew him. They knew him as the man who had subdued the tribes of Dhanziland, and had destroyed the power of Madewayo in the last century; of M'buladhanzi to the East, and his son Jeremiah. They knew him as the man who had brought them prosperity, giving them work where before they had quietly starved with their thin cattle on the veld round the original Madurodorp. They knew him as the Great Father, who had played fairer, after he had conquered them, than anyone else they knew, they knew him as Bright Hair and Red Neck and by half a dozen other names they had given him. But above all, they knew him as the man who had gathered all the strings of power in Plummerton and all the wide country around into his thick fingers and held them firmly and fairly and without corruption.

Helped by a couple of troopers, Kitto and Romanis laid Plummer in the shade of the Daimler and placed a blanket over him, then Kitto straightened up and stared at the slope.

The troopers nearby watched him, their faces hard and unemotional. They could all of them feel the atmosphere changing. The thing had grown, the excitement of it feeding on itself until it was suddenly completely out of hand.

Originally, it had been merely a chase, but anger and frustration and finally murder had swollen it like the ugly body of a leech, until the desire to capture had become a desire for retaliation, and Kitto's wish to achieve success had become in all of them a lust to kill.

Kitto's thin face was hard as he glanced round at the group of men. Then he slapped his boot with the riding crop. 'We'll attend to the murderer first,' he announced. 'There'll be no stopping now until he lies here with Offy Plummer.'

s i x

Polly had watched Plummer stand spread-eagled, his arms outstretched as though in an appeal against fate. She had watched with horror each of the stiff-legged steps backwards until he had disappeared, crucified against the sky, over the edge of the rock and crashed to the earth below.

Sammy had made no attempt to fire again but his face had grown tight and thin and there was a muscle twitching at the edge of his jaw.

'You've shot Mr Plummer,' Polly breathed.

For a while, neither of them spoke again as they watched the movement below, then Polly put into words a last faint hope she still harboured in her mind.

'You didn't kill him, did you?'

Sammy nodded without speaking, and she knew then there could be no doubt. He had waited until Plummer had stepped within range. There on the rock, near where Plummer's white hat had fallen she could see the spot of yellow rag, standing out glaringly against the dun-grey of the rock.

'Sammy,' she breathed, 'why did you do it?'

He shook his head. 'You shouted too late,' he said flatly.

'You murderer, Sammy,' she breathed. 'You murderer!'

He turned to her, startled, making a forlorn movement with the gun, pain in his eyes, bewilderment, and a lack of understanding.

'You're worse than a wild animal,' she went on, her voice rising. 'You're worse than all them jackals, all them vultures. All them lions and tigers. Killing and killing. All the time. You've hunted so much, you're just another of 'em.'

'Poll –'

He reached out a hand but she cowered away.

'Don't touch me,' she said sharply. 'You're not fit to touch a decent girl! Not with blood on your hands, like you've got!'

He dropped the rifle and seized her quickly by the arms.

'Polly, have you gone mad? They started it. Not me. Didn't they? Didn't they?'

'You shot first,' she screamed, wrenching herself free. 'I saw it plain as you please! You were the one that fired the first shot! Last night, you did! *You* started it!'

In the shocked horror of the killing, she had forgotten the wretchedness of the last few days when they had crossed and recrossed the veld like hunted animals.

He was staring at her, hurt and angry. 'Polly, you don't know what you're saying.'

'I know all right. I know. I know you killed Mr Plummer. He was a good man, Mr Plummer was.'

'Poll, I *didn't know* it was Plummer.'

'I told you. They'll never stop now. They'll never stop till they get you.'

Her words seemed to remind Sammy of his relaxed vigilance and he turned quickly away from her, scrambling for his little parapet and grabbing the Mauser, his eyes glued to the cleft in the rocks.

'They'll never get me, Polly,' he said over his shoulder. 'They'll never get me in a million years. I can hold out here for ever.'

'You've not got that many bullets,' she said. 'You couldn't hold out against that lot down there. You haven't a chance. They'll bring up more of 'em. And more – and more and more till there's an army down there with flags and cannons and horses and everything. They'll stay there now till they starve you out.'

Sammy was calm once more now, not heeding her. 'Well, I'll take some of 'em with me,' he said quietly.

His calmness seemed to drive her nearer to the edge of hysteria. 'They'll never stop,' she shouted. 'Not now! Not till they've hanged you as high as the highest tree they can find! They'll never stop till they kill you!'

She rose to her feet and before he could reach her, she was scrambling out of the rocky little valley.

'Polly!'

'I wouldn't stay here for anything now,' she shouted. 'Not after what you've done!'

As she began to run down the slope in and out of the rocks, wrenching her dress free with a despairing movement every time it snagged on thorns, a shot rang out and a bullet whined away above them. Polly fell on her face in terror, sliding in the dust, sobbing and shrieking at the same time, then someone below shouted and the shooting stopped at once and she was on her feet again, her dress torn, her hair loose and falling round her neck.

Sammy stood up. 'Polly,' he shouted. 'Polly!'

As someone took a pot shot at him, he ducked quickly behind his pile of rocks and lay staring between the chinks, sick with misery and a sudden new loneliness, watching Polly stumbling and running and falling down the slope.

'Don't shoot,' she was shrieking. 'I'm on your side! I'm on your side!'

Sammy lay motionless, the truth of what she had told him suddenly coming home to him. There was no going back now. He couldn't expect mercy and they could keep coming at him again and again and again, and for every bullet he fired they'd be less likely to let him go in peace. His eyes narrowed as he realised he was face to face with inevitable, remorseless and unswerving fate.

As Polly reached the bottom, a man who looked like Le Roux, rose up from behind a rock and, grabbing her round the waist, fell with her out of sight again, and immediately the shooting started once more.

At once the desperate need to survive was borne in on Sammy. His eyes were bright and sharp again, suddenly clean and competent, the hunter turned the hunted.

'I'll give 'em something to think about,' he said aloud.

He scooped up the Henry and a handful of cartridges and rising to his feet, ran stooping behind the rocks out of sight. By this time, more men had emerged from shelter, growing more confident as he didn't fire on them, and when he flung himself down again it was well to the right of his original position. Rolling on his stomach, he pushed the weapon forward and pulled the trigger quickly, without aiming. The Henry barked, and he pumped the weapon. The men below began to run immediately, weaving and dodging and diving for shelter once more.

The Henry roared once, twice, three times, again and again, as fast as he could eject the cartridges, then he scrambled to his feet again and hurried, bent low, back to his original hide-out.

He could hear shouts from below now and saw men pointing to the spot where he had fired the Henry.

'He's up there!' He heard the words come clearly in the crystal air. 'I saw the smoke!'

A veritable fusillade of fire was directed to the spot he had just left and he saw the bullets chipping the rocks and sending the dust spurting. A red-hot ricochet singed his hat and went on to strip the bark off a thorn bush behind him.

Several of the men below were firing steadily now at the point where he had made his brief stand, then, while they kept up their fusillade, half a dozen more of them rose to their feet and began to climb rapidly up the slope. As they approached, Sammy raised the Mauser and carefully pushed it through a cleft in the rock. He was quite calm and in complete control of himself.

The man in the lead, a grey-shirted man smoking a pipe, was climbing quickly, pushing his rifle ahead of him. Sammy raised the Mauser and the sights came into line, fixed on the centre of the climber's shirt where his cartridge belt crossed his breast bone. There it stayed, for a second, unwavering, then Sammy remembered Polly alongside him, staring down with a fascinated disgust and her outburst of shocked loathing, and abruptly he moved the sight a fraction of an inch and squeezed the trigger.

The man in the grey shirt stopped dead, flung back a step or two as the bullet hit him high on the right shoulder. He dropped the rifle and clutched at the wound with his left hand, then he sat down abruptly, an expression of acute bewilderment on his face.

The scrambling men had stopped, staring round at him, then they started immediately for the bottom of the kopje again, out of sight behind the rocks. The firing continued desultorily for a few seconds, then that died away too as the marksmen realised there was nothing for them to fire at.

Kitto was crouching behind a rock, watching his attack peter out, his face livid as he realised it was not going to be as simple as he had hoped and expected. A man so accurate with a rifle as Sammy Schuter was, could take severe toll of a small group of men climbing awkwardly towards him.

The battle had suddenly reached a ridiculous stalemate which neither side was able to break off. The boy couldn't move and they, unable to dislodge him, were held there by their pride and their humiliation.

'Get 'em spread out, Romanis,' he called. 'We're all going up this time. The lot of us.'

'What, *again?*' Romanis stared.

'Yes, and I don't want any hanging back. But we've got to be well deployed.'

'I'll stay back and guard the girl,' Le Roux grinned, one big hand on Polly's shoulder.

She sat with her back to a rock, staring at his flat ugly face, hypnotised with fear, the print frock stained with dust from her descent and torn away at the shoulder where he had grabbed her and flung her to the ground beneath him.

'Shut up, Le Roux,' Kitto snapped. 'Less of that talk!'

'Wouldn't do any harm to throw her to the boys, man,' Le Roux growled. He reached out for Polly and received a stinging clout on the ear as she came to life.

He grinned and shoved her down with his hand on her chest, holding her there easily. 'It isn't as though she wouldn't know what it was all about,' he said.

'Hold your damned tongue,' Kitto snapped. 'You're not a bloody savage!'

Le Roux subsided, growling, his eyes still on Polly, and under shelter of the rocks, Kitto spread the troopers over a distance of fifty yards in a big half-circle round the bottom of the kopje and gave the word to advance.

Once again, however, he over-estimated the agility of his men. With those sheer-faced rocks at the base of Sheba, it was impossible to move forward quickly, except through the spaces of open ground between them. And where these spots occurred Sammy had thoughtfully placed the fragments of his bandanna.

He had selected a hollow beneath two great rocks that leaned together like spires, leaving a narrow fissure between them, which was screened from below by cactus and low mimosa thorn. Cautiously he moved the rifle, watching carefully, the scattered shade of the low tree acting as a camouflage for him, spotting him with its indeterminate shadow like the rocks about him.

As the line of heads below him started moving forward again, he knocked the hat off the nearest with his first shot, then the other heads grew into shoulders and bodies and legs which moved upwards towards him, rising upright as they tried to scramble across the granite boulders, making short rushes through the clear patches of ground but still moving forward at a painfully slow pace. He worked the bolt and fired slowly and deliberately, waiting until a man heaved himself up from behind a sheltering rock before he pulled the trigger. After two more shots the attack died away, none of them wishing to expose himself deliberately, and two more men were moaning and holding wounded limbs.

He had deliberately avoided killing. The memory of Polly alongside him, her fists jammed against her teeth to stop herself screaming, had restrained him. But he had done enough. The survivors below were back behind cover now and lay without attempting to move forward again, firing wildly so that the clatter and rattle of musketry began to echo in every cranny and hollow of Sheba.

The firing was aimless, however, for no one had any idea even now of his hiding place. At a distance of two hundred yards, it required a keen eye to see a dust-smeared rifle muzzle firing modern smokeless ammunition in a thicket of cactus and thorn, and an inch or two of eye behind it.

Bullets began to whine overhead in the hot morning air, scarring the dust, sending chips of rock flying as they struck the granite boulders and stripping fragments off the cactus. None of them came anywhere near Sammy. They were still firing in the general direction of the hollow along the slope where he had used the Henry.

Coolly, dispassionately, he waited until he could see an exposed leg or a shoulder, then took careful aim and fired, moving cautiously to avoid being seen, and as the shots echoed wildly round the slopes, there was nothing in the sound to indicate his position to the men below who could peer over their shelters only with the greatest haste.

Gradually the firing died down again, and silence descended once more on Sheba. The sun clawed its way higher and the rocks began to take on a sharp unreality as they began to shimmer in the heat haze of the sun.

Winter heard the crackle of musketry die away while he was still eight or nine miles from Sheba. He could see the ragged edge of its slopes in the distance, blue against the sky, its base concealed by a shallow fold in the ground.

He had been driving at a breakneck speed over the rolling ground ever since he had heard the firing start twenty minutes before, and the Vauxhall was rattling over the stony surface as though it would fall apart. He was sick with fear at what he might find, for the firing had already told him he might be too late, and he clung desperately to the wheel, half-choked and blinded with dust, his brain numbed by the noise of the engine, his nerves on edge with the jolting.

As he breasted the first of the rises that brought him to the plain before Sheba, he became aware of another cloud of dust over on his right, rising out of the valley and moving up to the fold of ground he was crossing himself. He slowed down and swung the Vauxhall in a wide circle and turned in the seat to peer into the sun.

There was a car there and at first Winter thought he had caught up with Plummer and Hoole. Then for a brief instant of hope, he thought it might even be the boy and Polly managing to make their escape, but he realised the dust cloud was far too big for one car or two horses to make, and he forced himself to be calm. After a while, he saw that in addition to the motorcar there was also a squad of horsemen and for a second he wondered if it were De Wet, smashing through Botha's flying columns and advancing on Plummerton.

Finally, as the dust grew nearer, he decided it must be part of Botha's column itself, for there were about twenty men, three or four of them in the car, the rest riding in two short files with, in between them, the shape of a Vickers-Maxim pom-pom, a relic of the two wars against the Boers.

Somehow, with the sound of firing still in his ears, the little column represented law and order, and he started up the Vauxhall again. As they saw him approaching, the officer in the car threw up his arm and the whole column came to a halt at once, breaking formation as the horsemen crowded round the vehicle and the gun with its spidery wheels. They made no attempt to advance towards him but sat in silence waiting for him.

As he drew nearer, he could see the thick red dust of travel caked on their clothes. Their horses were staring-coated and shaggy with neglect, as though they had been hurrying and had been a long time on the way, while the riders had the hard-bitten wary look of men who had lived too long on the plain and had lost the finesse of civilisation. They were clearly from one of the commandos led by men like Koen Brits and van Deventer whom Botha was using instead of Imperial troops.

As Winter circled the Vauxhall to a halt by the side of the other car, he could see there were sheets of armour plate screwed roughly to its sides in the shape of an ugly iron box, and that a light Lewis gun was balanced on a Scarfe mounting on the stern, like an elongated frying pan with its flat container of ammunition clamped above the breech.

The officer stood up and saluted him briefly, a mere boy, descendant of some Irish adventurer and one of the hundreds who had volunteered for service as soon as war had been declared.

'O'Hare's the name,' he said and Winter saw his face was drawn with weariness. 'Second-Lieutenant O'Hare. We're from Ackermann's Column working with Brits and Botha. We had trouble with the gun carriage and lost touch. The rest of 'em'll be in Plummerton Sidings now, where we were hoping to be shortly. Only we heard firing and thought we'd investigate.' He grinned, young and enthusiastic despite his weariness. 'Ride to the sound of the guns, man! Napoleon's maxim.'

Winter nodded. 'Glad to see you,' he said, thankful for the boy's obvious commonsense. 'My name's Francis Winter.'

'Plummer's man? I've heard of you.' O'Hare grinned. 'Well, when you see him, you can tell him we managed to give De Wet's rearguard a rare mauling at Kadhanzi before he got away again. They won't come out this way again in a hurry.' He nodded towards the distant firing. 'It's from Sheba, isn't it? What is it? Stragglers from De Wet's commandos?'

Winter shook his head. 'I don't know,' he said. 'There shouldn't be firing from there.' He turned and stared at the distant blue crags. 'Plummer's there himself,' he added. 'Or he should be.'

The boy grinned again. 'Well, we'll come along with you,' he said, 'and give him the news about De Wet personally. He might reward me with a medal. Let's go and investigate, shall we?'

He turned and shouted his orders, then raising his arm, swung it over his head and forward, pointing to Sheba, and the little column began to move ahead again, the two cars jolting along side by side.

They came up to Sheba at a tremendous pace, the ground rocking under the pounding hooves, the shaggy beaten horses dragging the light weapon at a remarkable speed after the cars, bouncing it over the stones with such élan that at times every wheel of both gun and gun-carriage seemed to be off the ground.

As the two cars swung into a wide circle before Sheba, the gun crew swerved their horses to a stop just beyond them, the dust rolling away in oily folds as they dismounted. While they were still reaching for cigarettes and water bottles, Kitto came running towards them, his face red and angry, and it was then that Winter noticed the bandaged men crouching behind Babylon.

'My God, man,' O'Hare said, his young face startled. 'What's going on here? Looks as though you've been having a regular battle. O'Hare's the name.'

'Mine's Kitto – Hector Stark Kitto.'

He brought out the name as though it were a flag he was waving and young O'Hare grinned.

'I've heard of you,' he said enthusiastically. 'I used to play at Hector Stark Kitto defying the Dhanzis when I was a kid. I'm pleased to meet you.'

Kitto waved away the outstretched hand, though Winter could see he was pleased at the recognition and the adulation. 'Time for that later,' he said. His narrow dark face turned to Sheba. 'I want you to get your gun into action as quickly as you can.'

Infected by Kitto's energy, O'Hare swung round. 'What against?' he demanded. 'Who is it?'

'There's a damn' young thug up there with a rifle.'

O'Hare's sergeant, a grizzled veteran with an American accent, one of the wandering fortune-hunters who had probably found his way to the district from the goldfields of the Klondike twenty years before, one of those curious accidents of nationality like O'Hare that were found in South Africa, leaned over the gun, smoothed his gravy-dipper moustache and spat.

'Guess there ain't anything effective against good rifle fire,' he said. 'Less it's well outside the range.'

Kitto gave him an angry look. 'He's killed one of my men,' he snapped, 'and wounded six others, two of them badly. We can't get near him. A few bursts from that gadget of yours should shift him though. At least it'll give us covering fire till we can get up there.'

Winter had jumped down from the Vauxhall. 'Good God, Kitto,' he said. 'You're not going to bring artillery against him now, are you?'

Kitto glared at him, his eyes hot and fierce, exuding righteous resentment from every pore. 'He's got to be flushed out,' he said, 'and if we can't do it with small arms, we'll use artillery.'

'But the woman – ?'

Kitto's mouth twisted in a crooked smile. 'She had enough,' he said. 'She came down.' He jerked an arm. 'She's over there somewhere. Drinking tea. For God's sake, get her away from Le Roux. He can't do anything for staring at her.'

He turned to O'Hare. 'We know now what equipment her boy friend's got and how much ammunition. She told us. He's got food and water and a couple of rifles, one of 'em an old Henry. But he's not short of cartridges. Dammit, he marked the range out before we got here,' he went on as though the hidden marksman had cheated, 'and we can't close him. She won't tell us exactly where he is. She says she doesn't know but I think she's keeping it back. I've a good mind to threaten to throw her to Le Roux. That should loosen her tongue.'

'Who is he?' O'Hare asked, glancing up at Sheba. 'One of De Wet's crowd?'

'No. He's English, they tell me. Or a damned smous. Name of Schuter. Get your people moving before he changes his mind and starts shooting again.'

O'Hare's sergeant glanced over his shoulder. 'Bit close here, sir,' he reminded O'Hare.

'You'll be quite safe at that range,' Kitto insisted. 'Dammit, there's only one of him.'

'It's against all instructions, sir,' the sergeant persisted.

'God damn it,' Kitto snapped. 'Are we to argue all day about the niceties of artillery firing? Let's get on with it.'

O'Hare's sergeant shrugged, pulled his hat down over his eyes and hitched up his trousers, but O'Hare made no move, staring at Kitto with a sudden doubt in his eyes.

'Hold it, Hadman,' he said.

'What's the matter now?' Kitto demanded. 'Are *you* worried about the range too?'

'No.' O'Hare shook his head. 'I'd fight at that range if you advised it. You're in command here. But it's not that.' He looked at Kitto apologetically. 'I'm sorry, Major Kitto,' he pointed out, 'but *we're* here to find De Wet. We're recruited to fight against the rebels, not against loyalists – even if they *are* criminals. Much as I'd like to help – '

'Oh, for God's sake,' Kitto interrupted irritably. 'Don't split hairs.'

O'Hare looked uncomfortable. 'We only came along because we heard the firing,' he said. 'We thought it might be a splinter from De Wet's commando setting about someone.'

'I'll take full responsibility.'

Winter pushed between them. 'You've no right to take responsibility for murder, Kitto! Offy's on his way. He left Plummerton last night to put a stop to it.'

Kitto gave a queer warped smile of triumph, and then Winter noticed the plump figure of Hoole in the background with Romanis, and he had a swift sensation of tragedy.

'Come with me,' Kitto said.

He led them in silence to the cars behind Babylon and drew back the stained blanket from the bulky shape which lay there.

'There's Offy,' he said.

Young O'Hare stared at the body. 'Is that Plummer?' he asked. 'The Plummer of Plummerton?'

Kitto nodded and let the blanket fall back into place.

'What happened?' Winter asked quietly.

Kitto jerked a hand at Sheba. '*He* murdered him. Shot him deliberately, while he was standing unarmed in front of us on the kopje, appealing to him to come out.' He swung round on O'Hare. '*Now* will you use your damned fowling piece?'

O'Hare still looked unhappy, an expression of disappointment on his face, as though Kitto wasn't behaving according to the heroic pattern he'd expected. 'It's against my orders,' he said uncertainly.

'Great God, man!' Kitto exploded. 'You can see Plummer there in front of you, murdered by one of his own countrymen, the one man who brought law and order to this district, the very man who was responsible to the Government for raising your damned troop of horse-thieves. Have you no pride? Have you no honour, no patriotism? You're not going to let that damned Sheeny renegade get away with this, are you? If any man in the whole of this God-forsaken country *ought* to be avenged, it's Plummer. This murder's as much a part of the insurrection as De Wet is and I'm going to stay here till I've done my duty.'

He brushed them aside and strode back towards the rocks. Then he turned and stared at O'Hare. 'I expect you to bring your gun into action forthwith, Lieutenant,' he snapped.

For a moment O'Hare hesitated, then he shrugged. 'I suppose under the circumstances – ' he began. He stopped and called out to Kitto.

'You'd better tell me where he is,' he said.

eight

In his eyrie on the face of Sheba, Sammy had watched the little gun swing into position below and stop.

The air up there, with the sun rebounding off the rocks, was stifling. Nothing moved and even the myriad flying insects seemed to be silent. In front of him, down the slope he could see a thin column of ants trudging between the stones, and a lizard motionless on a rock, its throat fluttering with a pulse that seemed too powerful for its fragile body.

As he watched the new arrivals ease their limbs, he reached out for the water bottle and allowed himself a quick swallow. Then he cut off a piece of biltong and gnawed at it for a while, allowing the salty flavour to lay on his tongue before he took another swallow of water to wash it away. He knew now that only a miracle could save him.

He shifted his position and wiped the sweat from his face, smearing the dust that had grimed it across his cheeks. Then he thought of the rifles and took advantage of the lull to clean them with the pull throughs, wiping the breech mechanism carefully free from dust. Finally he laid his cartridges on the wiry grass where he could reach them quickly.

He was hungry now, but not so hungry that he couldn't manage without food, and he decided to conserve his rations for as long as he could. In his days as a hunter there had been many times when he had gone without eating for long periods, through the urgency of a chase or through accident.

Once he had been thrown from his horse and had had to walk back to camp, throughout the whole of a day of scorching sunshine, until his tongue was dry and swollen and his legs were buckling under him with fatigue and hunger, and it was no severe hardship to him to lie motionless in the speckled shade of the thorn bush.

A sudden flurry of movement below him caught his attention, and he saw the gun was being unlimbered. The drivers had trotted the gun team away now and there were four men busy round the little weapon. It startled him a little to realise they were intending to use the gun against him, and for the first time it occurred to him that alone he had held up an assault from thirty-odd men. Now they had brought up a pom-pom and twenty or so more men to deal with him, and if he were to survive long, he had to act now. Once that fussy little weapon with the crackling shells started probing the hillside, there would be little chance to fire back and not much left in the way of shelter.

The increased range didn't worry him. Shooting was something he had been doing all his life and the extra distance meant simply more care and greater concentration. He could see the cairns of stone quite clearly out on the veld near the gun, marking exactly how far away it was.

He pushed the Mauser forward and raised the sights. The tip of the fore-blade seemed to dance in the heat and he quickly withdrew the weapon and, reaching for the water bottle, poured water sparsely along the barrel to cool it. Then methodically, he laid aside the water bottle and pushed the rifle forward again, remembering instinctively all the things about shooting downwards he had learned during his days as a hunter.

The pom-pom crew, their khaki clothes yellowish against the red-brown of the dusty veld, were moving casually, with the hardened indifference of battle-tried men. At that range, they seemed to feel there was little to be feared from a single rifle. So far, they still didn't know where they were going to fire for the very simple reason that neither O'Hare nor Kitto knew either. There were plenty willing to offer advice, however, for several of the troopers had seen what they thought was the glint of the rifle barrel or a wisp of smoke, but none of them was really certain.

The driver of the armoured car watched the operations from his seat with absorbed attention, then, obviously thinking it might be more interesting to take part himself, he climbed into the box-like body and reached for the frying-pan shape of the Lewis.

Sammy saw the lieutenant in charge walk slowly towards the pom-pom, watched by the horsemen he had brought with him and the few figures still crouching at the bottom of Sheba. He waited until he stopped and began to point to the face of the kopje, then he raised the Mauser slowly. For a while, he stared along the barrel, then he blinked quickly against the strong glare and, remembering to aim short because of the telescopic effect of firing over rocks, squeezed the trigger. He saw the bullet kick up the dust just in front of the officer and, finding his exact range, he raised the rifle a fraction, and fired again.

As O'Hare heeled over, his knee smashed by the bullet, there was a sudden flurry of movement among the horsemen. The few who had dismounted leapt to the saddle hurriedly, and the whole bunch of them moved away in a cloud of dust, and all the standing men dived for shelter.

O'Hare, who had fallen on his side, had dragged out a revolver from a holster on his belt and fired a couple of useless, hopeless shots towards Sheba, then one of the gun crew ran towards him and, hoisting him over his shoulder, stumbled with him towards Babylon and out of sight. Immediately the man in the rear of the armoured car, which stood beyond the gun, the sun painting wavering lines of heat over its metal sides, swung the Lewis gun round, his hand flashing over the cocking handle. Then, as Sammy fired again, he toppled backwards out of sight, reaching for a broken shoulder, the gun slowly tilting until it came to a stop, cocked ridiculously upwards. As he fell, another Army Service Corps man appeared from behind Babylon, sprinting for the vehicle in an attempt to rescue his charge.

Sammy's foresight followed him, moving slowly. He knew he could kill the man as easily as pulling the trigger and as simply, but he was suddenly sickened with killing. As the man swung open the door to the driver's seat, Sammy hit him in the hip so that he fell out again at once on his back in the dust, staring at the sky, and beating the ground with his fist in his pain. Sammy could still see the three men who had remained with the pom-pom, trying now to crouch down behind the inadequate shield, twisting brass wheels in an effort to raise the barrel. One of them had a grip of the spade tail and was trying to swing the gun round.

They seemed to have some idea where he was now and, as one of them pointed, Sammy calmly smashed his arm with a bullet and, pumping the bolt of the rifle, followed it up with another which plucked at the clothing of the man at the tail of the gun and sent him diving for cover. As he lay behind the gun, his foot was still protruding, and Sammy put a bullet through his ankle which sent him rolling out into the open, moaning with pain. The gun remained silent, its barrel half-slewed round towards him, the one unwounded member of its crew crouching out of sight behind the shield.

nine

Winter knelt behind the rocks at the foot of Babylon, among the groups of swearing men, staring with haunted eyes across the dazzling strip of red earth towards the little pom-pom and the improvised armoured car, obsessed with the unholy loneliness of guilt that all the shooting and the maiming he was witnessing had sprung from a suggestion of his own.

What exactly he had been expecting he didn't know – perhaps to hear the crack of the gun and the chatter of the Lewis echoing round the crags of Sheba, perhaps to see stones and little landslides come rolling down the slopes as the bullets and the shells hit, perhaps to see a slim figure stepping out from behind its sheltering boulders, its hands empty, a rifle on the ground beside its feet in surrender, perhaps even a body sprawled among the rocks while the blood blackened in the sun and the flies came from nowhere and clustered, ugly and obscene, on smashed limbs and torn flesh.

But there was none of this. In two or three minutes of fantastic shooting, both the car and the gun had been silenced as effectively as if they had been hit by a shell from some heavier armament.

Perhaps the knowledge that there was only one man up there on Sheba had blinded O'Hare in his youth and inexperienced enthusiasm to the accuracy of a Boer-trained plainsman who could hit a field rat in the eye or a duiker at five hundred yards without ruining the good eating flesh of the body, but certainly the hidden boy had shrewdly assessed the value of the car and the gun and with a few sparing shots had levelled off the discrepancy between their fire-power by his pure skill. Like all the rest of them, from O'Hare moaning with the pain of his shattered knee, to Kitto biting his lip in fury, Winter knew that until darkness fell again there would be no chance of changing anything. The deadly accuracy of the boy above them, who could see every movement in the open from his eyrie among the rocks, had reduced them all to impotency.

Behind him, Winter could hear the horses moving restlessly on their pickets, as though the excitement and the mounting fury of their riders had got into them too. The conversation among the crouching soldiers was desultory and fierce at the same time, with the warped indignation of thwarted men.

'The bastard, not giving us a chance at him!'

'He's using soft-nosed bullets, did you hear?'

'Need a linseed poultice to draw that guy outa there,' Sergeant Hadman commented severely, standing by O'Hare, his feet apart and squinting critically at Sheba.

'Knew we shouldn't have tried it,' O'Hare was muttering between his gritted teeth. 'Knew we ought never to have joined in.'

Kitto stormed across to him. 'Can't you get that damned gun firing?' he snapped.

O'Hare pushed himself upright with his hands, brushing aside the trooper who was trying to bandage the shattered knee. The hero-worship was gone from his face now, leaving only a disillusioned bitterness with Kitto. 'If you want the bloody gun to fire, man,' he snapped back, 'go and fire it yourself!'

He called Hadman across to him. 'For God's sake, get those men over there out of the sun, sergeant,' he said. 'Use a white flag if necessary. Get 'em under cover.'

Hadman gave him a salute like the kick of a horse and Winter watched the extraordinary spectacle of a small army of almost fifty men, several cars, an armoured vehicle and a gun appealing for mercy from a single boy with a rifle.

There was no shooting after Hadman shoved up a white tablecloth he had obtained from among O'Hare's belongings, no sign of hostility while he superintended the removal of the injured from the shelter of the gun and the armoured car. But as they turned away, Hadman reached down a great brown fist without thinking for the starting handle of the armoured car and immediately a bullet struck the steel plate guarding the bonnet, and whirled away across the veld, buzzing on a high-pitched uneven note. The sergeant dropped the handle as though it were red-hot and ran after the wounded for the shelter of the rocks.

'By Christ,' he said as he ducked into shelter. 'He's well named. He's sure enough a sweet shooter.'

Kitto was standing over the grimacing O'Hare now, frustrated and furious, a bitter sourness of disappointment in his throat.

'I'd like to call for volunteers to work that gun,' he was demanding.

'Not damn' likely,' O'Hare said through his gritted teeth. 'I've had enough of my men injured for you and your mad-headed schemes, Major. Leave the gun where it is for a moment, man. We should never have tried to fight it from there. We'll try to bring it in with horses soon. It might be done. Then you can pin him down with a few shells over the top of Babylon if you like.'

As he watched Kitto gesturing angrily, Winter became aware of Polly alongside him, crouching close to him as though she drew comfort from his presence as her only apparent ally. Her face was pale and strained, and he was startled at the change in her. The old, painted raucous Polly he had known in Plummerton had disappeared, and in her place was a taut strained girl with an unmade-up face, a suddenly rather plain girl, clutching a torn frock across her breast, her native resourcefulness broken down by the extraordinary circumstances in which she had become involved. More than once he'd seen her rid herself of some persistent drunk with complete confidence but here, caught up in murder and battle and the smell of cordite, she was suddenly younger and frightened, a girl with a heart, and with emotions unexperienced by the ribald woman from the bawdy house behind the Theophilus Street bars.

'Mr Winter,' she said tremulously, 'can't you stop 'em?'

Winter shook his head, feeling inadequate and out of his depth in the battle-line.

'Polly, this is war now,' he said hopelessly. 'It became war the minute the first shot was fired. The politicians have retired to the sideline here just as much as they have in Europe.'

She seemed to crouch nearer to him, seeking comfort and reassurance. 'What'll happen then, Mr Winter?' she asked.

'God knows, Poll,' he said. 'I don't. This thing's growing bigger with every hour. The longer it goes on, the less chance we have of stopping it.'

'Do you think I did wrong coming down, Mr Winter? Should I have stayed up there with him?' She was clearly uncertain now, troubled within herself at her treachery.

'I don't think it would have made much difference either way, Polly.'

'I called him a murderer, Mr Winter,' she went on, her eyes on the slopes of Sheba as though she were watching for Sammy. 'I told him they'd hang him. And I enjoyed telling him. It all seemed so dreadful then. Especially when I saw Mr Plummer drop dead. But now, from down here it looks so different.'

She clutched at his hand. 'It's their faces, Mr Winter,' she said. 'It's their faces. That Kitto' – she shut her eyes – 'and that Le Roux – '

She shuddered as she remembered how Le Roux had caught her in his strong arms as she had collapsed in the dust behind the shelter of his rock, and dumped her unceremoniously flat on her back, his hands roughly grasping at her clothes. She had been immediately surrounded by hard men with bitter faces full of lust, and a hatred that had frightened the facts out of her, so that she had told without intending to how much ammunition Sammy had, how much food and water, how he had used the scraps of yellow bandanna to give him the ranges.

Then Le Roux had twisted her arm and to stop him wrenching at the stuff of her dress, she had told them where the horses were, realising as she did so that with nightfall, they'd take them away and remove the only chance of escape that Sammy still had. It was only the heartlessness in their faces, the thirst for revenge, that had prevented the ultimate betrayal of telling them exactly where Sammy was hiding. Caught by a sudden fear for him, which was as unexpected as her earlier loathing had been, she had pretended she wasn't certain, that everything looked different from below, that she was too shocked to be sure of anything.

'It's their faces,' she said again, repeating it with a kind of wonder, as though she had never believed, even in her own hard life, how incredibly pitiless man could be when corroded by war.

'All this talk of him being a Jew,' she murmured. 'As if it were a crime. He never seemed no different to me, Mr Winter. They look so wild. Like a pack of hounds after their prey.'

Winter glanced round him. What she said was right. There was vengeance now even in the features of O'Hare's newcomers, and the cruelty that lay just below the civilised façade of every man. When it had all started at Plummerton Sidings, he remembered, there had been in the expressions of the troops around him only boredom and the indifferent unconcern of the private soldier doing a duty which only his superiors could explain.

'Polly,' Winter asked, turning to face her, 'are you in love with young Schuter?'

She looked up at him quickly, her eyes big, just a plain pale-faced girl frightened by the terrifying things she had brought on them all.

'I don't know, Mr Winter,' she said. 'Honest, I don't. There *was* a time when I thought I did. Only he vanished and ended up shooting for the market. That was when I changed my mind. Then when we came out here into the Wilderness, and I saw him looking after me, taking care of me, trying to help me, doing things I wanted to do, even though he didn't want to do 'em himself, I felt I'd been wrong. But this morning, when I saw Mr Plummer drop dead, I thought I hated his guts. I thought I could never look at him again without wanting to spit at him.' She paused unhappily. 'Now I've seen it from the other end,' she went on quietly, 'and I can see what he's been up against, and what they're wanting to do to him, now I can see their faces – like ravening wolves, Mr Winter – now I'm not so sure of myself again. All I want to see now is for it all to finish and for him to get away free where he deserves to be. He's only behaving as he's been brought up to behave. If they left him alone, he wouldn't go back to Plummerton, he'd just go. I'd *make* him go.'

'Where would he go, Poll?'

Polly shrugged. 'He talked of going over towards the South-West,' she said. 'He thought he'd be safe there.'

'He'd be safer still if he headed north into Bechuanaland. But it's a long way.'

She managed a faint smile in which there was a trace of pride. 'Not to *him*, Mr Winter,' she said. 'Not to Sammy.

Nowhere's too far for Sammy. He knows the country like the back of his hand. He's shot in the Salt Pans dozens of times. I know he has.' Somehow she seemed to see a gleam of hope in his words and was snatching at it with both hands. 'He knows it all – from the Orange River to Khama's country. He's crossed it all. He told me so. Only the other day. He's carted his kills into Windhoek and those places dozens of times. He's driven horses across the Kalahari for the German Army and up to Bulawayo. He knows it all right. If he could get out of here, he'd make it. I know he would. He knows all the water holes and where to find the game.'

Winter nodded. 'I think you know a great deal more about that young man than you realise, Poll. I think you've been watching him and listening to him more than you knew.'

She looked puzzled and stopped, sitting quietly alongside him, holding the torn dress across her breast, indifferent to the angry arguments going on round the prostrate O'Hare. 'Perhaps you're right, Mr Winter,' she said wonderingly. 'It takes something like this to bring it home to you, I suppose. Not that it's going to do either of us much good now, though, is it?'

For a moment, Winter didn't know what to say, then while he was thinking about it, he became aware of a movement among the horse lines and saw Hadman and three of O'Hare's troopers swing to the saddle.

'It's a gun team,' he said to Polly. 'They're going to try to fetch the gun in.'

'What'll happen then?'

Winter's throat was dry as he replied. 'They'll fire from behind Babylon,' he said, 'where he can't reach them.'

'Will they kill him, Mr Winter?'

'I don't know, Poll.'

'It can't go on much longer, can it, Mr Winter?'

191

She seemed to be appealing to him to contradict her, but he shook his head. 'No, Poll,' he said heavily. 'It can't go on much longer.'

As he finished speaking, he saw Sergeant Hadman raise his hand and sweep it down. There was a sharp clatter of hooves on the stones then the four horses burst out from the shelter of the rocks towards the gun, sending the stones flying as their riders whipped them into an immediate gallop.

Nothing happened for a while, and they found themselves watching, fascinated as the horsemen drew nearer the gun. Then, as they swung round in a half circle to bring themselves up to the tail of the weapon, the rifle on Sheba cracked twice quickly and two of the horses dropped in their traces, going down on their knees without a sound and sending their riders flying over their heads.

'Corked, by Jesus!' Sergeant Hadman's disgusted voice came across to them quite clearly, and Polly screamed with a sudden excited enthusiasm and grabbed Winter by the arm.

Hadman leaned from the saddle and tried to cut the dead horses free, but the rifle cracked again and the fourth rider swayed in his seat and only managed to keep himself upright by clinging to the mane of his mount. As Hadman turned, baffled, and reached across to help the injured man, the rifle roared once more and the sergeant's horse sat back on its haunches, as though it were resting, and slowly rolled over on to its side, its head stretched out, blowing bloody froth from its muzzle. The sergeant stepped from the saddle, an expression of puzzled anger on his face, and signalled with his arm to the two dazed dismounted gunners. The sole remaining horse had been cut from the traces now and three unmounted men were running again for the shelter of the rocks, keeping on the blind side of the animal.

'By the Sweet Jesus,' Hadman panted as he came into the shelter of the rocks again. 'Let me like a soldier fall, by Christ! If it's medals you want, this is the goddamn place to win 'em, sure enough! That son-of-a-bitch up there sure can use a rifle.'

All talk had stopped again as their voices were stilled in surprise at the unreal situation.

Hadman was standing in front of O'Hare now, offering his report, sturdy and efficient. 'Christ, sir,' he said, 'it'll take a bloody army to shift that guy. I dunno how much ammunition he's got, but while he's still got it, there ain't going to be no volunteers. I wouldn't even ask for 'em. He killed them hosses neat as you please. Every bullet in the same place, and if he can kill cattle like that, he can kill men. Mr O'Hare, apart from that sighting shot he took at you, he ain't once failed to put a bullet where he wanted it.'

He pushed his broad-brimmed hat back and stared up at the slopes of the kopje. 'Jesus,' he went on, 'an armoured car and a field gun sitting there, dominated by one guy with a rifle. It just ain't possible.'

O'Hare was growing pale and weak now with pain and loss of blood and when Kitto came up to speak to him, followed by Romanis and Hoole, he raised himself irritably.

'I hope you're satisfied, Major,' he said.

'It's a disgrace to British arms!' Kitto postured, honour and courage rampant on his face, Winter was reminded of Offy Plummer's scathing summing-up of him back in Plummerton West. The everlasting subaltern, he had called him, and he was reacting now as he might be expected to react, baffled, angry, able to think only in terms of forlorn hopes and headlong charges. As he found himself wondering how much Kitto's defiance of Chief Jeremiah thirty years before had been sheer stupid do-or-die bravado instead of the colossal nerveless bluff he'd always thought it to be and how much of the legend had been of Kitto's own making, Winter realised how much shrewder Offy Plummer had always been than the rest of them. He had always known Kitto right to the core.

Kitto was almost stamping with rage now as he walked up and down, talking, his still-slim youthful figure stiff with pride.

'We ought to be ashamed of ourselves,' he was saying. 'Each and every one of us.'

O'Hare raised his head, wincing. 'The British Army spent fifty years in South Africa underestimating people like that boy up there,' he said. 'My men are going to do nothing till after dark.'

Kitto seemed shocked by the turn of events, his bright dark eyes glittering ferociously in his thin face.

'Since I arrived only an hour or two ago,' O'Hare went on remorselessly through his pain, 'I've had six men wounded, two of them fairly seriously, and I've lost three of my horses. You've got one or two wounded yourself, and one dead, to say nothing of Plummer himself.'

'All the more reason why we should press home,' Kitto snapped. 'I for one shan't be satisfied till I see his body lying in Plummerton like a condemned murderer's.'

'I wish to God I'd never seen your damned little war,' O'Hare snapped. 'I'd like you to supply me with a car to remove my wounded to Plummerton.'

Kitto nodded unwillingly. 'I'll provide you with a car,' he said. 'But I'd like a reassurance first that you'll see this thing through. If we let this boy go free now, our prestige won't stand for anything out here. De Wet's followers'll trot out all that old talk of the fumbling British Army, and start quoting lost guns at Colenso, and all the nonsense of Majuba and Spion Kop at us again. And once that starts, De Wet won't ever be short of recruits.'

Sergeant Hadman snapped him a salute. 'Permission to make a suggestion, sir. Mr O'Hare ain't going to be much good around here any more now and, with your permission, he oughta go in one of them cars himself to the Sidings to get hisself soled and heeled. I'll see it through here for him.' He paused. 'If you ask me, sir, though,' he ended, 'it ain't going to help our prestige much now, whichever way it finishes.'

Kitto stared up at Sheba. 'Whichever way it finishes,' he said slowly, 'it'll *be* finished.'

As he moved away, the sergeant saw Winter staring at them. His eyebrows rose and he shrugged, speaking in his deep nasal American voice.

'You Limeys certainly know how to make your lynchings legal,' he said.

The flat-topped hills were folded in the pearly haze of distance beneath a sky of perfect turquoise, and the jagged top of Sheba shone like a diamond as the narrow wheels of the Napier pushed steadily through the yellow grass and dry bushes, crushing the stones and sending the lizards scuttling before it.

Riding one of Kitto's cavalry horses alongside, Polly stared back to the little group of figures clustered round the base of Babylon, and the silent abandoned gun a little way out from where they were standing. The aasvogels had arrived now and had started their work on the carcasses of the dead horses, which sprawled bloodstained and feather-strewn in the sunshine, twenty or more rusty dusty naked-headed birds tearing at them with a strength that set the dead legs kicking.

Once, before she had left, she had seen one of the revolted troopers fire into the mass, miss, and turn his back on the sight. Within a few hours there would be little but bones and bloated tawny-eyed vultures, too heavy to rise, beating at the ground with creaking, tattered wings.

Up in the sky above her other ragged shapes were circling, still gathering, then one of them came swooping over the tender in a long slanting dive that carried it beyond them to the raucous crowd of ugly bodies she could see near Babylon.

They had buried Plummer alongside the big ginger-haired trooper from Kitto's column who had been the first to fall, hacking with difficulty at the thin rock-hard soil with shovels from Kitto's car.

'This is *his* country,' Romanis had said, sycophantic to the end. 'Let him rest here.'

Kitto had recited the burial service, standing at the head of the grave, small, leathery and sombre, playing the part of the commander to the last gesture.

'*Man that is born of woman hath but a short time to live and is full of misery*' – the slow sombre words still hung on Polly's ears – '*He cometh up, and is cut down, like a flower –*'

He had done the thing properly, with a volley of rifle fire and a flag unearthed from his kit making it into a barrack-square ceremony as though they were in the middle of that willow-shaded burial ground near Plummerton instead of out in the veld, tired, dusty and unshaven and beginning to grow frustrated and a little sick of it all.

As they had filed away from the grave, Polly had seen a squad of O'Hare's men under Sergeant Hadman give the wooden cross a smart eyes-left as they passed. Nearby, the Napier with the injured men in it, their wounds crudely cauterised where possible with a heated pistol barrel, was waiting to leave; and beyond it the men who were to remain behind had stood in a group, their faces hard and masked with the dust that was beginning to blow from the Kalahari, Le Roux's snake eyes ignoring the existence of the grave and remaining constantly on Polly.

Now, as she moved away, she could see them all taking up their places again behind the rocks, and even as she watched she heard a short spattering of rifle fire and, sickened, she kicked the gaunt horse she was riding after the slowly moving tender.

As she caught up, one of the wounded men, sitting by the tail board, whistled at her, then another head appeared, grinning broadly. They all knew her and where she came from and as she rode up alongside they began to catcall.

The tender seemed crowded with men, the boots of the injured sticking stiffly over the stern board. O'Hare, who was supposed to be in command was in the front seat, feverish and exhausted with pain, his knee wrapped in first-aid bandages and splinted with sticks broken from ammunition boxes. In front of the car there was a man with an arm wound, riding a dusty neglected horse, and behind a corporal, his right thigh strapped with bandages, all of them victims of the fantastic one-sided battle at Sheba.

O'Hare raised his head wearily at the jeers. 'Cut it out,' he ordered. He turned to Polly with difficulty. 'I'd be obliged,' he said in a cold voice as she came alongside, 'if you wouldn't dawdle, Miss – er – '

'You know me name,' Polly said sharply. 'Parasol Poll, they call me!'

She stared at him aloofly and he blushed before her gaze.

'Whatever it might be,' he said uncomfortably. 'I'll thank you to keep close.'

'Frightened I'll nip off back?'

O'Hare shook his head with the exhausted petulance of a man in pain. 'Personally I don't give a damn if you *do* nip off,' he said. 'But I've been told to get you back into Plummerton and that's what I intend to do.'

Sheba receded slowly into the distance and the men in the tender, stupefied by the heat of the sun and uncomfortable with their wounds, stopped their catcalling. They sat now, smoking, their heads rolling to the shaking of the wheels over the rough ground, cursing at every small boulder that jolted their injuries.

Soon after midday they stopped for a meal of coffee and tinned meat and biscuits, those who could climb down from the tender helping those who couldn't, and afterwards they stretched out in what little shade the tender gave and dragged out their pipes.

'Going back into business in Plummerton, Poll?' one of them asked her as she scoured out the cooking pot with sand.

'None of your affair,' she snapped back, thinking with a touch of misery that what he had suggested was probably what *would* happen to her. There had been a chance once – not so long ago – that Sammy might at last settle down after his fashion, for there was much they could have done together. There was money in Kimberley for a man who could shoot like Sammy could, and plenty of work for a woman without her having to degrade herself. Fifty years old now, its raucous past long forgotten, Kimberley was a growing city with all its wood and iron buildings gone, and the gum trees tall and straight in its streets. There might have been so much hope in Kimberley.

Polly sighed and climbed to her feet as they began to strike camp.

They had loaded their belongings into the Napier again and got everyone aboard when she heard one of the men shout, and looked up to see the occupants of the tender staring across the veld towards a group of horsemen who were riding towards them.

It was obvious immediately that they were Boers. Even at a distance, Boers looked different with their slouching seat. One or two of the men scrambled awkwardly out of the tender again and stood waiting, their pipes in their mouths, their eyes squinting against the sun.

'De Wet,' someone said, putting into words the fear that was at the back of all their minds.

'God help us, if it is,' O'Hare commented. 'He hasn't been showing much mercy round here.'

The Boers approached with dash and pulled up thirty yards away, a group of drab-looking men in broad-brimmed hats, store suits and cord trousers. There was nothing military about their looks, but in the way they handled their horses and guns there was an air of supreme confidence.

'Finest light cavalry in the world,' O'Hare said with a pride in his race he obviously found hard to hold back. 'Every damned man of them springs from the Voortrekkers who fought against the Kaffirs. Weaklings didn't survive that sort of work. Wonder what they're up to.'

He called out to them in English as they approached, asking them what their errand was, and one of the horsemen drew out from the jostling group and cantered towards him. As he took off his broad-brimmed hat and wiped the sweat from the leather lining, Polly saw it was Fabricius. She knew him well by sight, had seen him addressing outdoor meetings in Plummerton and involved in more than one disturbance, calm among the rowdies who were causing the trouble. He had left the smart suit he usually wore behind him now and was dressed in a thick flannel shirt and cord breeches. A rifle lay crosswise on the saddle, and in his belt there was a heavy hunting knife. With that incredibly swift transformation of the Boer commandos, he had left behind the smooth lawyer and become a hard-hitting fighting man.

He stopped his horse before O'Hare sitting in the tender, in his blue eyes the fixed gaze of the political zealot.

'I've got to ask you where you're going,' O'Hare said. 'This is an area of military operations.'

Fabricius wiped the brim of his hat again with his handkerchief and replaced it on his head.

'De Wet's come out of the Salt Pans,' he said bluntly. 'He surprised and destroyed a patrol that Ackermann left behind him at Kadhanzi.'

'How do you know?'

'A runner arrived in Plummerton Sidings last night.'

'Does Ackermann know?'

Fabricius' face altered subtly. 'It isn't my duty to act as informer to the British,' he said.

O'Hare gestured wearily, as though waving aside the hatred in Fabricius' face. 'Where are you going now?' he demanded.

Fabricius' expression changed secretively again. 'With the grace of God,' he said, 'I'm proposing to protect a few relatives in the area of operations – as are also the rest of us – from the depredations of *both* sides.'

'You wouldn't be thinking of joining De Wet, would you?' O'Hare asked shrewdly.

Fabricius paused, then nodded towards the wounded, watching from behind O'Hare in the tender. 'By the look of your party, Lieutenant, you're in no state to stop us if we were.'

'O'Hare flushed. 'Where's De Wet now?' he asked.

'I don't know. But it'll be a couple of days before Ackermann can be up on him again.'

O'Hare frowned. 'We can handle De Wet,' he said with a boldness that even Polly could see he didn't feel just then.

'From what Ackermann said, you had already,' Fabricius commented. 'But he's on the move again, in spite of it.'

He glanced at the wounded men in the tender and at O'Hare's bandaged knee.

'One would almost have thought you'd bumped into one of his outposts yourself, Lieutenant,' he commented.

'Another affair,' O'Hare muttered. 'Nothing to do with De Wet.'

'Schuter?'

As Fabricius spoke Sammy's name, Polly's eyes gleamed. Ever since Kitto had first told her she would have to go back to Plummerton Sidings, her mind had been full of half-formed plans for recruiting help. Almost the first thing that had occurred to her in her misery was that Fabricius might be called upon to assist. Knowing his interest in Sammy, he seemed the obvious man to help, and finding him here now lifted her heart with new hope. Whatever else he might choose to do in the face of Kitto's formidable force, she knew that at least he was in a position to rouse sufficient public opinion to make the activity at Sheba politically dangerous.

O'Hare was looking up at Fabricius now, his hand moving slowly up and down across the bandages on his knee. 'That sounds like his name,' he was saying. 'How do you know about him?'

'People talk. You look as though you've been roughly handled.'

'He's up on Sheba,' O'Hare said sullenly.

' "*Whoever commands the heights commands the plains*," ' Fabricius said. 'An old maxim the Boer nation used to advantage in two wars with the British.'

O'Hare flushed. 'Sheba's a damned awkward place to get at,' he said with a youthful indignation. 'It's only got one slope. The rest's sheer.'

He stared aggressively at Fabricius for a moment then, wearying of the argument, he raised his hand in a brief gesture of salute.

The Boer nodded, accepting his dismissal, and turned away.

'Bastard,' Polly heard O'Hare mutter. 'I'll bet he's going to join De Wet.' His face wore the baffled expression of a man finding himself involved in civil war and not completely understanding the problem of identifying friend from enemy in a land where all men carried guns.

As Fabricius replaced his hat and loosened his reins, Polly pushed past the men grouped round the tender and ran towards the horsemen. One of them grabbed at her but she brushed his hand aside and stopped in the dry grass before Fabricius, who was swinging his horse in a slow contemptuous circle.

'Mr Fabricius,' she called, her eyes bright, her face full of eager hope. 'Mr Fabricius!'

The Boer jerked his horse's head up and waited for her.

'Mr Fabricius,' she said, reaching for his stirrup. 'I'll show you where Sammy Schuter is. They've got him trapped up there on Sheba.'

Fabricius' face hardened. 'I can do nothing for Sammy Schuter,' he said coldly, and Polly's face fell.

'But I thought you wanted him! They're trying to kill him!'

'My authority doesn't cover the military, *mejuffrouw*,' Fabricius pointed out.

'But if you want him –'

Fabricius' face had lost its smooth legal expression and had become icy with the hatred of generations.

'If there's anything that I – or any other true Transvaaler for that matter – enjoys seeing,' he said, 'it's the English quarrelling among themselves and trying to kill each other. "*God hath prepared for the wicked the instruments of death.*" '

'If you don't come soon it'll be too late!'

Fabricius gestured with the rifle, almost as though he were brushing her aside.

'I needed Schuter,' he said, 'for the evidence he could give which might have become a rallying cry for my people. But with the military between us, he's beyond my reach now.'

'You're a lawyer! You know what to do! Isn't there somebody you can tell?'

'It's best that it's left as it is. It was the English who decided it should be resolved in this way.' Fabricius shrugged. ' "*Who so diggeth a pit shall fall therein!*" '

Polly's hands had fallen to her side and she stood before the lawyer, her eyes big and appealing, begging him mutely to help her.

He paused before he went on, one hand stroking his horse's neck. 'With the name he's got and the life he's led, we could easily make him one of us, *mejuffrouw*.'

Polly's face was blank and bewildered. 'I don't understand,' she said.

Fabricius lifted the hand holding the reins and his horse began to move forward slowly.

'Patriotism makes use of the strangest weapons,' he said. 'He'll make a most satisfactory martyr.'

Polly ran after him. 'But he's not Dutch!'

'He will be. *After he's dead.*'

Fabricius put his hat on, his face stony, and kicked his horse into a gallop. As he rejoined his followers, they all turned in silence, swinging inwards into a bunch, and cantered quickly away behind him.

Polly halted, the dry grass brushing her skirt, and stared after them, shocked into muteness by the cold-bloodedness of their politics.

O'Hare watched her come to a stop, then he nodded to the driver of the Napier and the vehicle moved up towards her.

She was still staring after Fabricius, her eyes bright and unhappy, anger and misery flushing her cheeks.

'Damn your bloody patriotism,' she was saying bitterly. She turned away, blinded with tears, to find the tender alongside her.

'What's the trouble?' O'Hare asked gently.

'Nothing! Nothing, damn you! Nothing that would interest anybody who's not human. Only a matter of life and death, that's all.'

O'Hare stared after her as she moved away, his face pale and strained. Then he shifted uncomfortably in his seat, his teeth clamped on his lower lip in pain as his fingers plucked restlessly at his bandages.

'I suppose we'd better push on,' he said uncertainly, half to himself, embarrassed by Polly's remark.

'What about the pom-pom, sir?' The corporal had ridden slowly up alongside. 'Won't Colonel Ackermann want it?'

O'Hare's pain-dimmed eyes clouded, and he paused, unsure of himself, his wound making him unable to make up his mind with any conviction.

'We've got to get this lot to hospital,' he said. 'There's a couple of 'em pretty bad. We'd probably do well to warn Ackermann too.' He stared after Fabricius. 'That damn' lot are obviously going to tell De Wet where he is,' he added shrewdly. 'Their saddlebags were full, I noticed. A sack of meal, biltong and a box of cartridges, I'll bet.'

He stared after the retreating horsemen then back in the direction they had come, uneasy, limited in his knowledge of the wider complications of military strategy and uncertain what to do for the best.

'I reckon we'd better carry on,' he decided finally. 'Ackermann will want to know.'

The Napier's engine roared as the driver moved the throttle and it rolled across the uneven ground to where Polly was standing.

The corporal moved up, leading her horse, and passed her the reins.

'I'll be obliged if you'll get aboard, Miss Bolt,' O'Hare said with a stiff boyish dignity. 'We'd like to get along now.'

She pulled herself slowly into the saddle, and settled herself, not looking at him, her eyes still on the dwindling cloud of dust thrown up by Fabricius and his little commando.

Her mind was stiff with the knowledge that there was nothing she could do now – nothing. Fabricius' refusal had made it perfectly clear that whatever she might attempt when she reached Plummerton there was no one there who could save Sammy Schuter. She stared at O'Hare and the corporal with a bitter dislike then, making up her mind quickly, she swung the horse round, sawing savagely at the reins as she spun it on its heels.

'Here' – the corporal saw the move too late and tried to head her off – 'where do you think you're going?'

She had clapped her heels into the horse's flanks now and was clattering down the rise in a flat gallop the corporal couldn't hope to match with his injured leg, heading away from the cloud of dust Fabricius had left.

'Come back here!'

The Army Service Corps driver circled the Napier up alongside the corporal.

'Let her go, Corporal,' O'Hare said wearily. He indicated the stripes on the corporal's arm. 'You won't lose your skaters for her. She can do no harm and she's not our concern. We've got a job to do that's more important than a little tart who got herself mixed up with a murderer.'

eleven

When Polly hauled in the gasping horse alongside the small Egyptian cotton tent they had pitched for a headquarters, the top of Sheba was already apricot-tinted with the lowering sun.

Soldiers ran up to meet her as she reined in, and one of the troopers grabbed at her bridle as she came to a stop.

The big figure of Le Roux appeared beside her, his pale eyes glittering in a grinning face.

'So you couldn't do without us,' he said, reaching up. 'Let Fricki Le Roux lift you down.'

'I'll get down myself, thank you,' she snapped, lashing at him with the slack of the reins. 'You keep your dirty hands to yourself!'

His face went dark but as he grabbed her and dragged her struggling from the horse, Winter came up behind him immediately and grabbed the collar of his shirt.

Le Roux's grip relaxed at once and Polly stumbled free. As Winter released him, Le Roux rubbed his throat.

'*Ach,* throw her to the boys, *jong,*' he snarled, his sullen face red. 'A woman like her don't deserve mercy.'

He turned to Polly, his pale eyes cold. 'It's a good job for you,' he went on slowly, 'that we've got an audience. I'll see you tonight after I come off duty on the horse lines.'

Polly stared after him as he turned away. 'Thanks, Mr Winter,' she said shakily. 'I suppose he reckons I'm fair game, and maybe I am. All the same, if I'd been properly dressed then he'd 'a' got a hatpin in his eye for his trouble.'

His lean face set, Kitto pushed angrily through the group of men round Winter, and stopped in front of Polly. 'What the devil are you doing back here?' he demanded.

'I came back because you're trying to kill him,' Polly said fiercely. For the life of her, now that she was in the camp again she couldn't think of any other sensible reason for her impulsive valueless gesture, nothing beyond a vague hope that by her presence she might prevent murder. She had an uneasy sense still of having betrayed Sammy and felt the need to make amends by suffering with him.

'We can do without women around at a time like this,' Kitto was saying waspishly. 'I've a damned good mind – ' he stopped, at a loss to know what to do, aware that he couldn't put her under arrest or confine her physically.

'Keep her out of my way, Winter,' he said finally in a harsh voice. 'We'll take her back with us tomorrow. It'll be all over then. The men have got their tails up now.'

Polly choked with anger. 'My God,' she said, 'you've even got a timetable for it!'

The wind was rising a little now, blowing the dust in swirls through the camp, and ruffling the bloody pinions of the few vultures still crouching among the remains of the dead horses, too gorged to move.

The troopers sat in the fading light, huddled in blankets more to keep out the flying particles of sand than for warmth, wiping the dirt from their weapons and drinking strong coffee full of grounds and yellow with tinned milk. The Kaffirs were preparing a meal at a string of smoking fires and the Army Service Corps mechanics probed gingerly at the engine of Kitto's Rolls-Royce alongside which Plummer's two vehicles, as though recruited into the army, had been parked with geometrical precision, canvas covers stretched over the open tonneaus to keep out the dirt.

In the horse lines, the animals had humbly turned their rumps to the weather and bowed their heads, their tails whipped along their bodies by the wind. Kitto was standing alone in the tent, his eyes on the angular shadow of the pom-pom beyond the abandoned armoured car. His head was bent to avoid the flypaper one of the Kaffir servants had hung from the apex of the canvas, and his hand rested on an oil-cloth-covered table spread with maps and scattered with binoculars, compasses and weapons. For the last hour he had been studying his watch, his thin, too-handsome figure fidgeting to finish off the affair before it got out of hand.

There had been no attempt all day from either side to move into the open, and the gun had stood in the sunshine, the heat haze over the metal almost fluidly solid in the glare. Then towards the end of the afternoon the wind had crept round to the north-west, bringing the dust down from the Kalahari, and the sand had begun to pile up against its wheels and find its way into every cranny and corner and sift in little dunes on the mudguards of the armoured car.

There had been very little shooting from the men sprawled among the rocks, just an occasional pot-shot when somebody had thought he had seen a movement on Sheba, and the rare twang of a bullet striking stone as the marksman in the shadows above them had been tempted to fire at a hat raised on a stick. After a while, they had begun to count the shots, Kitto even posting a corporal with a piece of paper and a pencil to tick off the bullets that went singing across the veld.

Polly sat wrapped in a blanket Winter had found for her, watching the moving shapes of the men and catching the acrid smell of coffee that came with the woodsmoke from the fires.

Winter, who was huddled beside her on an ammunition box, looked up and offered her a cigarette. For a moment she hesitated, then she accepted.

'Nice girls don't smoke,' she said, trying to make a joke as she took the light he offered.

Winter said nothing, his face drawn in the fading light, and as a Kaffir brought him a mug of coffee he passed it silently to Polly.

'Wouldn't mind a drink of something stronger just now,' she said.

For a long time she studied his tired unshaven face and the lean body in the shabby clothes, a look of gentleness on her features as she sensed that they were both outcasts now, the only difference between them the levels of society that they came from.

'Why didn't you ever marry, Mr Winter?' she asked unexpectedly, looking at him with soft compassionate eyes.

Winter raised his face to hers with a faint smile. 'Nobody would have me,' he said.

'Why not?'

' "*Villainous company hath been the spoil of me.*" '

'What's that?'

'Quotation. Shakespeare. Ever read Shakespeare?'

'I always had too much to do.'

'Maybe I'd have done better if I'd had *more* to do,' he said with a wry smile. 'I'm a thinker, Poll, without being a doer, and that's worse than being like Kitto, a doer who's not a thinker.'

Polly touched his hand shyly. 'You're all right, Mr Winter. You're a toff. You're labelled a gent like an eighteen-carat gold ring.'

He shook his head and smiled. 'No, Poll,' he said. 'Toffs have clean hands and pure hearts. *I* haven't even got much pride left.'

Polly stared at him and curiously in her tired face Winter saw hope for himself. He'd been with her often in Plummerton, seen her with the cheap peek-a-boo embroidery of her blouses on her breast, and never thought much on her. But now he seemed to see the real Polly underneath the mask of hardness, the other Polly, the one with the heart, humble and trusting, pleading with all men to peer beyond the façade as he was doing now, and see her as she really was. And in her down-to-earth humility he saw commonsense that made his own troubles trivial, all the suffering of centuries bound up in one tired dusty girl.

The rock formations were fusing together in the dusk with the stunted karroo bushes, the square shapes of the motorcars and the few sentries watching Sheba. There wasn't much talk from the troopers near the fire, or from the men moving the picket stakes of the horses to let them get fresh feed, nothing beyond the shrill cursing of the Kaffir cooks who found their tins continually full of dust or the struggling big black ants which had trudged after the sugar. To one side a few soldiers, their eyes and throats sore from flying grit, had stretched out under their blankets, and another sat by the fire indomitably trying to darn a hole in the toe of his sock by the light of the flames. A couple more had crept inside one of the cars and huddled down under the canvas cover out of the knife-edge gusts of wind that shuddered the tonneau and whipped the hissing sand against the windscreen.

There was very little sound beyond the clink of hooves against stone and, once in the gathering dusk, the clicking complaints of the Zulu servants.

Someone started singing –

> *'Who were you with last night,*
> *Out in the pale moonlight   ?'*

The whole camp had fallen into a somnolence that came with waiting.

Then, as the night song of crickets and the hoarse croaking of frogs from the stream beyond the mimosa thorns grew to a mad night-time chorus, they heard a sharp clattering of stones, and in a second they were all on their feet, squinting into the dust, peering towards the shadowy loom of Sheba. A shot rang out and whined off into the darkness and several of them reached for their rifles. There was a wild drumming of hooves, and a couple of troopers galloped past, riding a pair of unsaddled horses, and leading a third.

'Look!' Polly clutched at Winter's arm. 'Those are our horses. That's the grey mare and the police horse Sammy bought in the Sidings. The other's the one he pinched from Le Roux. Now he can't *ever* get away.'

There was a burst of cheering and men came out of the shadows, forgetting about sleep, running towards the two laughing men who were sliding to the ground now, doing a crazy triumphant dance in the firelight at their first tangible success against the hidden boy on Sheba.

'We've got his 'osses,' one of them shouted. 'We've got him trapped now. We've only got to get that old pom-pom in then we can walk right over him in the morning.'

As darkness came with African suddenness, Winter saw a team of horses move up from the horse lines, wearing fresh harness made from ropes, and as soon as it was completely dark, Hadman, O'Hare's sergeant, and two other men moved out silently and hitching up the little pom-pom, brought it safely back to the shelter of Babylon. Then they all heard the sudden cough of an engine rise to a howl and die away again to the dull metallic popple of an exhaust as the armoured car jerked into shelter also, lumbering towards them like some great beetle. In the movement of the machinery of war there was a deadly efficiency, as though the forces of death were ranging themselves against the hidden sharp-eyed boy on Sheba at last.

'Well, thank gawd for that,' Hadman said as he dismounted by the gun. 'I thought we were never going to see old Flossie again. I guess it'd have been hard lines on her, after surviving two wars without capture, to be nobbled by a kid with a rifle.'

He turned and saluted as Kitto approached him and stared up at the shadowy mass of Sheba. 'Never thought I'd live to see a field piece mastered by a single rifle,' he observed. 'The drill book says not to go within seventeen hundred yards of massed fire, but I never seen no mention of a single Mauser. I wish that kid was on our side, sir. We're going to need a few like him if we catch up with De Wet.'

A little later, the clang of spades and the ringing profanity of tired men from the darkness indicated the gunners had begun to dig a gun pit...

It was after midnight when a shaggy berry-brown man wearing the patched khaki jacket and pink puggaree of Ackermann's Irregulars arrived in the camp, spurring and jagging furiously at the mouth of a jaded horse. He was met by Romanis and taken to Kitto in the acetylene-lit tent.

'Corporal Snell, sir,' he panted. 'From Colonel Ackermann. Stumbled on you by a bit of luck. Saw the fire from about eight miles away.'

'What do you want, man?' Kitto snapped.

'Message for Lieutenant O'Hare's detachment, sir, from Colonel Ackermann through Lieutenant O'Hare. It's addressed to Mr O'Hare but I bumped across him at Plummerton Sidings on the way. He readdressed it to his sergeant. He was bad hit.'

'I'll take it,' Kitto said, reaching across the table. Romanis raised an eyebrow but he said nothing.

'It's for the sergeant, sir,' the messenger pointed out respectfully. 'This 'ere other's for you.'

'I'll pass it on to him, man,' Kitto snapped. 'The sergeant's operating under my command at the moment. I'm Major Kitto. Hector Stark Kitto. You can rely on me.'

The rider thankfully took the glass of brandy and water Hoole pushed across to him, and handed over the slip of paper. Kitto pushed an empty ammunition box forward with his foot and Snell sat down gratefully while Kitto glanced at the messages.

For a while there was silence, then Kitto raised his eyes.

'Very well,' he said. 'I'll see to it. What about you?'

'I'm to report back at once, sir.'

Kitto nodded. 'Romanis, see this man gets some food. He can eat it in here out of the wind.'

'That's kind of you, sir.'

Kitto waved a hand, and spoke to Romanis again. 'See that his saddle's put on a fresh horse,' he said. 'Have it brought round here in a quarter of an hour.'

There was some speculation in the camp about what message the rider had brought, for he had obviously ridden hard, but Kitto kept him well inside the tent where all they could see of him was a hand holding the glass of brandy and water that Hoole had passed to him. Then one of the Kaffirs pushed through the flap with food, and half an hour later the messenger was mounted on a fresh horse and swinging away towards the darkness of the veld.

Winter stepped out of the shadows as he reached the edge of the encampment and Snell swerved his horse violently to avoid knocking him down.

'Steady on there, man!' he shouted, struggling with the lean unkempt horse they'd given him. 'You near as hell got knocked over.'

'Never mind that,' Winter said. 'What's your message?'

Snell quietened his startled horse. 'For Sergeant Hadman, sir,' he said shortly. 'I handed it over to Major Kitto.'

'What was in it?'

'Messages is for the eyes of officers and NCO's only, sir.'

'I'm here as a newspaper correspondent,' Winter pointed out. 'It'll reach me eventually.'

Snell stared at him for a moment. 'I didn't realise that,' he said. 'Well, you oughta get moving, sir, if you want to be in on the fight. It's up Waterbury way. General Botha's cornered De Wet. He moved east again, sir. He's in the Salt Pan area. He wiped out one of Ackermann's patrols near Kadhanzi, and the Colonel's mustered his column again and he's on his way back. He wants the armoured car and the old pom-pom. Major Kitto's to leave at once with everything he's got and pick up the column on the way out of the Sidings. De Wet looks as though he's going to make a fight of it and Ackermann's going to cut him off to the west.'

Winter's heart was leaping as Snell gabbled on.

'Botha wants every available man-jack, vehicle and gun, sir, at once,' he said. 'There's to be no fight till we're all there. I think the Colonel's after keeping his forces close so they can support each other. De Wet bites like a snake, sir, and just as fast.'

As he saluted and swung his horse away into the darkness, Winter crossed to Polly and told her joyously of what he had discovered.

'I didn't ever think much of it before, Mr Winter,' she said quietly, 'but there must be a God somewhere up there. I've been praying awful hard ever since I got back that something would happen to save him.' Impulsively, she flung her arms round Winter and hugged him, the tears on her face smudging against his cheek.

'It's only a matter of minutes, Poll, before the gun goes,' he said, 'and Kitto won't dare stay here now. Sammy'll be free then to come down off Sheba.'

Polly's arms slowly loosened round his neck and she glanced round at the darkness. Immediately he sensed her disquiet.

'Mr Winter,' she said, her voice puzzled, 'if the gun's going, why are they still diggin' that pit?'

Winter looked round, suddenly alarmed by her words. 'By God, Polly,' he said, pushing her aside. 'Surely Kitto's not going to risk hanging on to it!'

He found Kitto in the tent by the oil-cloth-covered table, poring over a map with Romanis and Hoole.

' – Ackermann'll take this route here,' he was saying. 'We can join up with him between Plummerton Sidings and Kadhanzi – '

He looked up and nodded as Winter appeared, then turned again to the map, ignoring him.

'There's only a matter of four hours in it,' he went on, 'and Snell could easily have wasted that much looking for us.'

He pushed a bottle of Rhynbende across to Winter.

'Sit down, man,' he said. 'You might be interested. There's a fight coming up. We're to meet Ackermann and we're just working out how long it'll take us.' He turned again to Romanis. 'We can go directly north. Ackermann's bound to head that way and we can cross his path.' He looked up at Winter. 'Afraid you'll have to go back to Plummerton, Winter, with the odds and ends. You might have come with us if that damned woman hadn't come back, but someone's got to see her safe and you're the only one available.'

'Why hasn't the gun left?' Winter demanded.

Kitto looked up, his handsome face hard. 'Are you trying to teach me my job, Winter?' he asked slowly.

'The message was that it was to leave at once.'

'How do you know what was in the message?'

'I asked the runner.'

'You'd no damn' right to go poking your nose in. Messages are secret. You're a civilian.'

'Thank God for that. Why hasn't the gun left?'

Kitto's face darkened and Winter saw that he was completely and dangerously obsessed now with the desire to succeed here at Sheba. There had been a blind red rage in the energy he had shown in the last two days, as though he sensed that if he failed in this trivial operation he could never hope to succeed anywhere. Sammy Schuter had become a symbol of his luck – almost as though he regarded his end as the point at which it could change for the better. Beyond the fierce dark eyes, there was the blank stupid anger of a goaded bull.

'In this day and age,' Kitto was saying, 'a soldier's expected to use his commonsense and interpret his orders as they fit the situation. I know what I'm doing. I don't have to answer to any lily-livered civilian who confuses the issues of war with what he calls justice for a murderer.'

His anger drove Winter back a step, but he persisted.

'Have you given the message to the sergeant?' he said.

Kitto began to shout. 'Your job's to report on what you see, Winter, not to question my orders! I have to remind you again that this is a military operation! Leave the army to soldiers, and stick to your blasted pen pushing...'

Polly was waiting outside when Winter left the tent. He shook his head at the question in her eyes, unable to meet her stare.

He heard the gasp as she caught her breath, and he threw away his cigarette. 'There's only one thing now, Polly,' he said. 'I've been thinking about it all day. We've got to cut a horse out from the horse lines – two for safety – and place 'em where he can find them easily. Then I've got to get up there to warn him.'

'He'll shoot, Mr Winter.'

'That's a risk I've got to take. I wish I could be certain the Kaffirs would leave the horses exactly where I want them.'

Polly's head came up. 'Let me do it, Mr Winter,' she said at once. 'I can do it better than any Kaffir.'

He smiled in the darkness. 'Bless you, Polly, I thought you might. You've only to get them to the mimosa thorn near the stream and stay with them until he comes. Then get back here as quickly as you can.'

'I can do that, Mr Winter.'

'Won't you be frightened? You'll be out there on your own.'

She shook her head. 'I'm not frightened, Mr Winter. Only about what'll happen to me if they find out. I'm not a man and I can't fight against people like you can. They've chased me out of Plummerton once already.'

'Polly' – Winter spoke impulsively – 'don't let that worry you. Stay with me. We'll get away from here. We'll go to the Cape. We'll go together – we'll get a train as soon as we've got Sammy away from here.'

She looked at him strangely, her eyes soft, her lips trembling, her expression a mixture of gratitude and joy. 'You mean that, Mr Winter?'

Winter nodded. 'Yes, Poll, I do,' he said.

Her eyes had a distant look in them. 'I always wanted to go to the Cape, Mr Winter,' she said.

twelve

They waited until the camp was quiet, holding on to their patience until they could move into the naked veld that lay cold and eerie under the empty stars. Polly was tremulous in her excitement, her face lit with bright new hope. All the time, as they crouched together just beyond the firelight, she talked of Sammy and what he could do when he reached Bechuanaland, and how she would find a job in the Cape until the war was over and he could come back to her.

She even established herself in Winter's house, as some sort of housekeeper, prepared out of sheer gratitude to work for him without pay and for as long as he wished her to stay.

'There's lots of things I can do, Mr Winter,' she said eagerly. 'I'm not as stupid as I look and I can clean up and do anything you ask.'

He could feel her trembling with pleasure alongside him, at the thought that she might save Sammy yet, unable to halt her whispered chattering or the dizzy plans she was making, staggered by the prospect of security and some sort of rooted existence at last.

She required no encouragement when the time came to move, and was on her feet before he was, the blanket over her shoulders against the flying dust.

Digging a couple of saddles from the pile of equipment among the rocks, they carried them with a sack of oats and biltong and flour, and containers of coffee and salt they had bribed from the Kaffir cooks and hid them carefully away from the light.

'We'll have to be careful,' Winter said. 'I don't know quite how we're going to do this but we can only try.'

Polly was straining her eyes in the darkness. 'There won't be lions out there, will there, Mr Winter?'

'There aren't any lions round here, Polly,' he reassured her. 'Nothing that'll worry you.'

'How'll he know which way to go?'

'Sammy'll know. He'll know the stars.'

She became curiously quiet.

'It'll be lonely,' she commented in a whisper.

'Sammy's used to being alone,' Winter said.

'I didn't mean it that way. It's just that the veld's such a big place and there'll be no one he can turn to. Not one single solitary person on his side.'

'*You'll* be on his side, Polly. I know you will.'

'I wouldn't be much help in Cape Town. What if something happens to him?'

'Sammy's too smart for that.'

'I dunno. There were times when even Sammy was glad of a helping hand. On the way here, for instance.'

'Polly' – Winter touched her hand – 'it'll be different this time. There'll be no one on his heels.'

She didn't reply and he was aware of a sudden difference in her demeanour, as though the excitement had gone from her and left her doubtful and uneasy about what they were doing.

As they drew nearer the horse lines, Winter stopped and emptied his pockets of all the money he had on him.

'Here, Polly,' he said. 'Take this. Give it to Sammy. He'll need it.'

She looked startled as he pressed it into her hand.

'Mr Winter, Sammy's not short of cash. He's got all you gave him before we left Plummerton.'

'For all we know, Polly, that might not be enough. He may need all he can get. Give him that and tell him he's welcome to it.'

'But Mr Winter – '

Winter closed her hand over the money, feeling that it helped in some small measure to soothe his sense of guilt that the disastrous affair at Sheba had all sprung originally from his own half-sarcastic suggestion to Plummer.

'Don't ask questions, Polly. I'd rather he had it.'

'I don't like taking money – '

He smiled. 'All right, Polly,' he said, humouring her. 'You can pay me back then, if you like. You've been working it out all evening.'

She paused, still oddly subdued. Then she pushed the money back at him quickly. 'You'd better keep it, Mr Winter,' she said abruptly in a firm voice. 'I shan't be coming back. I'd like to go with you to the Cape – you know that. It's what I've always wanted and it was nice of you to ask me. But it's no good, I've *got* to go with Sammy.' Her eyes were steady, begging him not to be angry. 'It's better that way, Mr Winter,' she ended. 'It's the only way really.'

He said nothing for a second, feeling disappointed and grieved. He had begun to feel he had something to look forward to at last. There were oaks and magnolias and hydrangeas at the Cape, and rich flowering proteas, away from this bleak land of tumbledown houses and bleached dorps where the ground was sour with sunshine. Down at the Cape, away from the fierce pride that ran like summer lightning among the empty plains and flat-topped hills of the Orange River, life had more dignity, and with Polly's rich character nearby to give it purpose, there had seemed some point at last in getting away and starting all over again. All his ties with Offy Plummer had fallen away from him and left him in a void of indecision from which Polly's sturdy mind offered a strange spiritual security missing from a life too cynical to be quite real.

Instinctively he attempted to dissuade her, not wishing to be alone again. 'It'll be hard going, Poll,' he said.

'No harder than it was before we came to Sheba,' she said laconically.

Winter paused, faint stirrings of jealousy in him, wondering what it was in a man that could produce such loyalty in a woman, then he nodded, accepting the situation.

'It'll be better for us all, Mr Winter,' she explained quietly. 'Him and me's the same sort. We're common folk. We understand each other. I love him whatever he is and whatever he does and I've got to be with him. I know that now. I belong to him, see, and he belongs to me and no other. Till death do us part, everlasting, amen. Dead or livin', that's the way it is. I ought to have known it all along, but I didn't. When he comes, I'll stand and look at him and the tears'll run down my face, never stopping, and no word'll be said. But *he*'ll understand. He'll know all right. It's always been this way, Mr Winter, but I've been too soppy to realise.'

He nodded again, and patted her hand. 'I understand, Polly,' he said awkwardly. 'Don't worry.'

As they drew near the horse lines, Polly became silent and he put it down at first to a sense of guilt at letting him down, but as they crept closer she grew even more withdrawn and remote, as though she weren't even aware of his presence.

When they could catch the acrid stable scent of the horses and hear the soft footfall of the man on duty, Winter put a hand on her arm, doubtful of his strength and full of indecision.

'The sentry's awake,' he said, and Polly stopped dead in her tracks.

'Mr Winter,' she whispered.

'What is it, Polly?'

'Can I kiss you good-bye?'

'What, now, Polly?'

'If you will. There might not be time later.' Her voice seemed to be trembling. 'I might never see you again and you've been real good to me and Sammy. Better than you realise.'

He felt touched.

'I know you and me's kissed more'n once,' she went on, 'but not that way. I'd like to kiss you proper. You're a toff, Mr Winter. A real sport.'

Her lips were cold on his and somehow, behind the feeling of loneliness the gesture brought to him, he had the sensation of some vast emotional disturbance inside her, something that made sense of the incredible tranquillity that had suddenly come over her, smothering her excitement.

As he released her, she turned away and he saw her face was strained and pale in the dim light of the stars, and she was standing very erect.

'God knows how we're going to go about this,' he said, glancing towards the spot in the darkness where he could hear the soft snorting of horses and the chink of iron on stones.

She was standing a little in front of him and as he moved forward again, she turned round to face him, her eyes hard and calm.

'You stay here,' she said quietly. 'I've thought of that, Mr Winter. It shouldn't present no difficulty.'

'What do you mean?'

She was picking nervously at the rough stitching with which she had repaired the torn neck of her dress and he saw the whiteness of her skin in the starlight and the shadowed hollow between her breasts.

'Polly, what are you up to?'

'It's that Le Roux what's on sentry go at the horse lines, Mr Winter.' She spoke in a flat numb voice. 'The one who's been doing all the shouting. It shouldn't take long for me to shift him.'

223

'Polly, what are you contemplating?' Winter felt shamed by the calm dignity on her face.

'It's no hardship, Mr Winter,' she said quietly. 'It's no sacrifice to me. I'm giving away nothing that I haven't given away already. There've been plenty of times when I'd rather spit in their eye, so I can do it for Sammy now. I'll meet you here.'

Winter was at a loss for something to say. For a moment, he tried to speak, but the words stuck in his throat. Dumbly he laid his hand on her arm and nodded, and turned away quickly.

Polly remained where she was, straight and slim, her figure casting the slightest of shadows under the stars. She was still fiddling with her dress as she called out.

'Le Roux! Fricki Le Roux!'

A burly shape appeared from the direction of the horse lines.

'*Wie da?* What do you want?'

'You been shouting the odds all day,' Polly said. 'You're good at that, when a girl's alone in front of everybody. You ask me, though, I don't think you're man enough when it comes to the pitch. I reckon it was all wind.'

Le Roux was staring at her, his arms slack by his side, his rifle hanging from one big bony hand, then he grinned and, whipping his hat from his head, he sent it skimming away and swept her to him in the darkness.

It was only a few minutes' job to cut out a couple of horses from the horse lines and lead them off silently, the soft flapping sound of their feet in the dust hidden by the stamp of iron-shod hooves and the whinnies of half-fed animals. From the fire by the rocks of Babylon, there was laughter and some singing and no one took any notice as Winter saddled the animals.

After a while Polly appeared. Her face was expressionless and there was something in her eyes that made Winter hate himself. She said nothing as she emerged from the shadows beside him, pushing a strand of hair into place.

'I'm ready, Mr Winter,' she said quietly.

'Polly – '

'Better not say anything, Mr Winter. It's done and there's nothing we can do to undo it.'

'Polly – '

'Damn it,' she said, her voice suddenly harsh and irritated. 'I don't want any mealy-mouthed apologies. What do you think I am? It's nothing new to me. I'm no bloomin' angel. Give me a leg up.'

His mouth dry with salty distaste, Winter bit back the vague apologies he felt were demanded of him, humiliated by the frigid impassivity of her features. Pushing her on to one of the horses, he attached the other by its reins to the iron ring behind her saddle.

'You know the spot, Polly?' he asked, speaking briskly, trying hard to forget what she had just put behind her. 'See that star up there? – the bright one – keep it right in front of you. Don't lose sight of it and you'll run straight to the stream. Turn to your right along the bank and you'll reach the mimosas. It should take you about ten minutes or a quarter of an hour. No more. Wait there for Sammy coming.' He looked up at her calm stony face. 'You aren't afraid, are you, Polly?'

She shook her head, still staring in front of her. 'There isn't anything in the world left to be afraid of now,' she said slowly. 'Nothing. Not ever.'

She paused, gazing down at him, then without looking back, kicked the horse into movement and moved away from him into the darkness.

For a long time he stared after her, his mind confused and reeling, then he managed to get control of himself and, turning away, still trembling, walked rapidly to the base of Sheba.

The rocks where the troopers had hidden all day were empty now, faintly outlined by the starlight. Winter stopped and stared upwards towards the black loom of the kopje, ragged and ugly against the indigo night sky, wondering what other ancient forlorn rearguards had fought there. Somewhere up among the rocks in the stark silence was young Schuter, sharp-eyed, clear-headed, that deadly rifle of his close by.

He crouched for a while behind the rocks, conscious of his heart beating furiously in the terrifying absence of sound. His pockets were stuffed with as much food as he had been able to cram into them, jammed hard on to the top of what Mauser cartridges he had been able to find. Soldiers were notoriously slovenly about their bullets and never troubled to pick up what they dropped, feeling there were always plenty more, and it had not been difficult to find a couple of pocketfuls.

For a moment, he waited in the darkness, trying to make up his mind to move. He had no idea whether Sammy was alert or not. He could only hope he was sleeping. He had already fixed in his mind's eye just where he was hiding and he only needed to get within calling distance. At least, Sammy had known him in the past and had trusted him. He could only hope he would continue to trust him.

He tried to convince himself again he was right in what he was doing. All his life he had suffered from an amiable inability to move forward with certainty in himself, lacking always the sort of blind confidence that had made Offy's fortune and enabled Kitto to feel that what he was doing was honourable without any qualms of conscience, the same certainty of right that had held Sammy Schuter up on Sheba for two nights and a day now, holding at bay almost half a company of infantry, an armoured car and a field gun.

In a confusion of emotion, he thought of Polly and what she had done, not considering it a sacrifice, and he felt his own share was small.

Certainty swept over him. There was to be no Polly after all, none of the things he had been vaguely forming as hopes in his mind, mere reflections of warmth without the reality of fire, but he knew he was now as sure of what he was proposing to do as he would ever be. Sammy Schuter must have *something* in him to produce such faith as Polly had, whatever he was or had become through the militaristic single-mindedness of Kitto.

Winter thought briefly of the hot-eyed little soldier behind him awaiting the morning with eagerness, certain that he was doing his duty, convinced that all he had done was right. Poor Kitto – the everlasting subaltern! Winter found he could be sorry for him. It was the Kittos of the world who always carried the blame, honest, humourless, rigid in their ideal of duty to the point of being a nuisance. They were the sacrificial goats of the world, who saved their fellow men in times of emergency, the sort of professional soldiers who willingly accepted death or disgrace until the amateurs were ready and the first complicated choreography of opposing armies was over and the battle lines were set up.

Winter stared up the slopes again. From behind him he could hear the sounds of the camp and see the glow of the fires over the rocks of Babylon. Somebody laughed back there, and a horse whinnied, and suddenly, from that bare bleak side of Sheba, it looked incredibly warm and welcoming, with the red glow coming over the top of the stones and the sound of laughter. There, beyond Babylon, were company and shelter. Here was only bareness and emptiness and a big question mark.

Winter buttoned his jacket tightly around him and stood up, a stone chinking softly by his feet. He listened for a second, but there was no movement from Babylon. As he moved again, the pebble rolled down the slope, then he turned his face firmly towards the summit and began to climb.

227

thirteen

Sammy Schuter woke abruptly. He was cold and tired and thirsty. Above his head, softening the blackness to a watery mistiness, the distant stars were vivid against the silent sky that backgrounded the summit of Sheba, rising like some fantastic castle behind him.

He turned slowly on his side, the blanket sliding from his shoulders, and listened. Something had disturbed him and with the hunter's instinct which let him sleep while all his senses were not switched off, he was awake immediately.

For a moment, he lay silently, still listening, catching the thin cheeps of the bats that darkness had brought out of the caves of Sheba into their twisting complex flight, and the breeze moaning shrilly through the clefts and stones lower down. A prickly pear just in front of where he lay clapped its flat leaves together and his nerves tensed as he strained his ears. Then he heard the thin rattle of a pebble rolling, and he sat up abruptly, letting the blanket fall to the ground. Turning over on to his stomach, he peered between the two rocks that had sheltered him from sight all day.

He could see the glow over the rocks of Babylon quite clearly and could hear the faint bark of laughter from the men camping there. He pulled the Mauser forward and worked the breech silently, catching the acridity of cordite that came with the movement. He was not afraid. He was well aware of what the following day would bring for he knew they had captured his horses, and there was no hope of stealing another. He had thrown a shot in the direction of the galloping hooves, but he had realised immediately that he couldn't see well enough to shoot effectively and he had hung on to the rest of his cartridges, certain he was going to need them the following day. He knew the gun had been recovered now, *and* the armoured car. He had heard the engine start and the dull popple of the exhaust fading as it vanished behind the rocks of Babylon. The engines of war were ranged against him now, inexorable and deadly.

Indeed, he had spent the day exploring with his eyes the surface of Sheba for another position, where he might be safe, but he had not found a better one where he could command the whole of the plain below, and in the end he had grown tired of looking. It would only serve to stretch out the misery of waiting and, suddenly, he couldn't be bothered any more. He had now only seven cartridges left for the Mauser and three for the Henry. That wouldn't stand off a determined assault for long.

For a while, he had hoped they might have been dissuaded by his tenacity and go away, and once when he had heard a horseman ride in and, shortly afterwards, ride away again, he had thought it might be a reprieve of some sort, but nothing had happened and he had settled down again to wait.

All day he had waited in silence, motionless in the broiling heat, listening to the shrill bird-like cries of the dassies. Once a puff adder had passed in front of him, undisturbed by his stillness, golden and shining in the sun, its body flowing in a cold boneless advance. Above him he had seen the kite-hawks and the vultures attracted by the horses he had killed, black and ragged against the sky, floating as though on strings.

He was certain within himself now that the cord of his life was drawing taut, that he had only a few more hours to live, and he was facing calmly the certainty of a lonely trapped death. He had never faced up to artillery fire before but he knew something of its effect on human beings.

He might have made an effort to build up some entrenchment for the morning, but his movements had become lethargic now with hunger and thirst and his mind was numb with too much thinking. He wasn't afraid. He wasn't even bitter. He had absorbed in his years of living on the veld too much of the philosophy of the survival of the fittest, and had spent too much of his life as a hunter to be afraid of being the hunted.

He thought bitterly for a moment of Polly, wondering where she was. He would have liked to have seen her again, if only to make her see that what he had done was the only thing he *could* do, but he knew that his sole hope of a few more hours of life was to stay where he was. Even if he reached the bottom alive – and he felt certain he could if he wished – there could be no hope for him without a horse on the empty plain which could give him no more shelter than a billiard table.

Sammy shifted uneasily, conscious of a sense of loss that he was not to enjoy any more the sunny windless evenings and the silent stars of Africa, the soft crackle of frosty grass as he turned out of his blankets in the morning, the high skies, the light dawns and the golden landscapes of dry grass and low distant hills; the titanic laughter of the Kaffir bearers and the sound of a guitar or a concertina dwarfed by the immensity of the veld.

A stone chinking below him jerked his head up, interrupting his musings, and his light eyes narrowed as he stared through the cranny between the stones. Briefly, for an instant, he had seen a shadowy figure move in the darkness. Slowly, he reached out for the water bottle alongside him and, moving slowly, took a sip. Holding it to his ear he shook it and realised it was almost empty.

He stiffened as he saw the figure move in the shadows again, difficult to make out in the uncertain light. At first he thought the men below were trying a night move against him, then he realised there was only one man there, whom he must have seen twice. The figure was moving with the utmost caution, but clumsily nevertheless, with the awkwardness of a city dweller. It was closer now, moving steadily upwards, keeping always to the shadows so that it was difficult at times to see him. It was an easy shot. Too easy for the Mauser.

Sammy watched for a few moments longer, his eyes glittering, a muscle working at the side of his lean unshaven jaw, then he reached backwards and drew the old big-bored Martini-Henry up to his chin, pushing it forward inch by inch through the cranny in the rocks...

fourteen

The crash of the shot brought them all to their feet. As they leapt for cover, the sock-darner was jostled into the embers of the fire and he scrambled out again, yelling and swearing and kicking sparks of burning wood flying in his haste and anguish.

Sergeant Hadman was out of his blanket in a bound and behind a rock on his hands and knees.

'Christians, awake,' he called. 'We're off again!'

The sound of the shot had gone rolling round the jagged slopes of Sheba, echoing and clattering among the spires of rock in the silence, so that for a moment it seemed as though there were several guns up there. The horses threw up their heads, their ears pricked, listening, and the dozing Le Roux at the end of the horse lines came to life at once and ran to see what was happening.

Kitto appeared at the entrance of the tent with Romanis and Hoole, and stopped there, staring up at Sheba. Around them were men in various stages of undress, some without boots, others without jackets, holding blankets, all staring with them up at the spires of rock that stood out against the sky.

'Wind up,' someone commented in a hoarse voice.

O'Hare's sergeant shook his head. 'That's something *he* ain't got, brother,' he said dryly. 'Something moved. Mebbe a rock rabbit. Thank your lucky stars it was that what he was shooting at and not you. There'll be one rock rabbit less'n there was. That's for sure.'

'It was like this in the last war,' somebody muttered. 'Stuck out on the veld, listening, hearing rifles. You remember Ladysmith, Sarge?'

'Sure.' The sergeant nodded, staring upwards. 'It was me what took her dancing...'

Waiting out among the group of mimosa trees, Polly jumped to her feet as she heard the rifle bark. The horses which she had tethered nearby edged away, their ears back, settling down again as the silence flooded round them once more. She could hear frogs not far away in the low-lying ground near the stream, croaking hoarsely, and the high thin irritating cheep of crickets.

For a while, she stared nervously around her, wondering what to do. Judging by the time that had elapsed, she guessed that Winter must have reached the little krantz where Sammy was hiding out beyond that she knew nothing, and she was desperately tempted to leave the mimosa thorn and head back to camp.

The thought of the crowded circles of men round the fires and the big knotty body of Le Roux held her as she moved towards the horses, then the need to be with Sammy again and some loyalty to Winter drew her down again to the rock where she had been sitting.

With her nerves prickling, she heard someone in the camp call out, then a rifle fired, and there was silence again...

Kitto was still standing by the tent door, staring up at Sheba, his eyes narrowed.

'Tell that damn' fool over there to put up his rifle,' he snapped.

'Accident, sir!' Sergeant Hadman appeared alongside him, the sharp planes of his features glowing in the light of the fire. 'It won't happen again. It nearly took his 'ead off and he'll be more careful in future, I think.'

'See anything, Sergeant?'

'No, sir. Nothing. I been forward a bit but there's nothing moving. I think he musta seen a rock rabbit or a snake or something and mistook it for one of us.'

'Perhaps you're right.' Kitto glanced again up at Sheba, then turned into the tent, followed by Romanis and Hoole. 'Whatever it was,' he said, 'it's one bullet less to face tomorrow.'

Winter lay back in a crevasse between two rocks where he had been flung by the shock of the heavy, soft-nosed bullet which had hit him high up on the right side of the chest and smashed his shoulder blade on its way out.

He put his left hand to his shoulder and was surprised to find that the blood on his fingers was black in the light of the stars. Then the pain began to come to the torn hole in his back where the flattened bullet had made its exit, growing steadily stronger as the numbness of the initial shock wore away. He struggled to sit up and was startled to discover he couldn't do so, and it dawned on him quite clearly and without fear that he was probably going to die.

He struggled back through the mists to complete consciousness and called out softly.

'Sammy! Sammy! Can you hear me?'

He moved his left hand about, trying to push himself upright, and found that his fingers only weakly scrabbled over the uneven stony surface. Feebly he began to pat his pockets and realised they were still jammed with food and Mauser cartridges, then as a wave of pain swept over him he tried to hold his shattered shoulder together again, clutching at the splintered bone as though with his own desperate anguished strength he might stop the bleeding and take the pain away.

He remembered the look of amazement he had seen on the face of the dead Offy Plummer, and he wondered if the same look of shock had been on his own face as the bullet had flung him back among the rocks.

Once again, he struggled to rise, but his fall had jammed him somehow in the crevasse with his useless arm beneath him, and he was unable to shove himself upright.

'Sammy!' he called again. 'This is Winter! Come here, quickly!'

Again he struggled to sit up, wishing he had something at his back against which he could use his legs as a lever to force himself upright. Then, his mind swinging dangerously, erratically, he found himself wishing he had a drink and tried to remember if he'd brought a brandy flask with him. After a struggle to find it, he realised he couldn't get at it even if he had, and he began to wonder instead if Sammy Schuter had saved a few drops of water up there in his rocky eyrie.

'Sammy! This is Winter!' He was horrified to hear his voice come out only in a croaking whisper. 'Come down here, for God's sake!'

He was lying on a sharp-edged stone which dug into his back, but the effort of thinking about it seemed too exhausting and he let it slip from his mind with relief...

With a start and a groan he came back to consciousness from a dark world of peace, back to torment where spinning things of flame-coloured red whirled before his eyes, where a growing thirst and a dreadful agony wrapped him about with iron pinions.

Dimly, he realised he had failed. He had failed Offy and killed him. He had failed Sammy, and now he had failed Polly, to whom he had wanted to give so much. Like so many others, he had the gift of thinking correctly and acting hopelessly wrongly. In fact, he thought in a haze of pain, they had *all* thought correctly and acted wrongly. Offy had been right in principle but wrong in his methods, as indeed so was

Kitto, with his stern belief that Sammy's survival was more dangerous to the country than his death. They had all planned correctly but they were all losers in the end, every one of them, because of a simple inexorable fact that behind every action, every event, there had been an unseen, unmentioned and unconsidered being called God.

If only Willie Plummer hadn't acted so stupidly, if only it hadn't been Sammy Schuter with his skill and courage and cunning who'd been involved, if only he hadn't broken his word and turned south instead of heading west, if only they hadn't all distrusted him and followed, if only they hadn't chivvied him until he had turned round on them like an angry dog, if only the politicians and the would-be savers of humanity hadn't failed to take into account the individuals in their plans. There were so many ifs which had become facts, building up one upon another until the outcome had become as inevitable as the next morning's daylight.

Through his numbed meanderings, Winter heard a faint murmur of disturbed earth, and a pebble rolled down near his ear and finished with a click as it bounced against the rock by which his head rested.

He forced his eyes open and in the faint light that came from the stars, he saw a figure standing above him. As tall as a steeple it seemed, and beyond it towering away to the heavens themselves was the ragged summit of Sheba.

'Sammy, old boy,' he said weakly, 'I brought the rescue party.'

Sammy knelt beside him, laying the rifle down.

'You asked for it, Mr Winter,' he said fiercely, and the voice came booming out at Winter from what seemed a hollow tunnel full of echoes, rising and falling as it came in uneven woolly tones. 'They *all* asked for it. I never wanted to shoot nobody, but they made me. It was them or me.'

'That's all right, that's all right!' Winter gasped the words and struggled to sit up, clarity returning to his mind. 'Pull me out of this bloody rabbit hole, for God's sake!'

Sammy knelt by his feet and Winter felt his strong fingers round his ankles.

'If they hadn't forced me, Mr Winter, I wouldn't have shot.'

'Yes, I know. But never mind that now. For God's sake, get me out! Your bloody bullet tossed me in here. Where'd you learn to shoot like that?'

Sammy's face came nearer, blurred and indistinct, and Winter struggled to focus his eyes on it.

'I didn't know it was you, Mr Winter. Honest I didn't.'

'Oh, for Christ's sake, shut up, and get on with it!'

Sammy's fingers tightened on his ankles and Winter felt himself being dragged out of the humiliating situation in the crevasse. As his shattered shoulder bumped over the sharp-edged stone in the middle of his back, he choked dryly on a scream, but bit it off short as he remembered the waiting men below, already alerted by the shot.

Sammy came nearer, kneeling by Winter's side, uneasy, sensing that things were not as they should be.

'Mr Winter,' he said, 'what were you doin' crawling about on Sheba like that? You ought to have known I'd shoot.'

'I did, you bloody fool! Now shut up and listen to me.'

'I didn't ask to kill anybody – not even Mr Plummer.'

Winter wrenched his eyes round. 'For the love of God, stop indulging in self-sympathy,' he snapped. 'I don't want pity, man. I knew what I was doing and so, I suppose, did Offy Plummer.' He gasped as the pain tore at him with iron-clawed fingers, then he patted his pocket with his left hand. It was a clumsy, awkward movement, for he found his arm wouldn't do quite what he intended it to do, and he was fighting all the time to get his breath against the tearing pain

237

that seemed to stop everything inside him as it dragged at him.

'Listen, Sammy, you know that clump of mimosa out there by the stream. You must have noticed it. You've been staring at it for two days now – '

'Look, Mr Winter, there's no need to talk – '

'In the name of Christ,' Winter said weakly, 'shut up and listen if you want to get off Sheba alive. I'm trying to help you. Be quiet and listen.'

Although the boy knelt beside him, Winter could see him only faintly, but he was silent at last and not full of stumbling excuses and apologies.

'Listen, Polly's there among those mimosas waiting for you – '

'Polly – !' There was anger and contempt in the boy's voice, and Winter stirred weakly.

'Yes, Polly,' he said. 'By God, that's a good woman – you don't know how good! And she's waiting for you. Don't start blaming her for running away. Women do funny things, boy, as you'll learn when you're a bit older. She was probably scared. She'd never seen killing before. She's there among the mimosas – '

'What's she – ?'

'Don't interrupt, for God's sake! I can't go over it all again. It's too damn' painful! Listen, she's got two horses. One each for you. She's got food and forage. Go to her as fast as you can. You can get out that far in the dark without being seen. Nobody'll follow you. They'll be too busy. De Wet's out again and they'll never waste two or three days chasing you now. Go south-west, as hard as you can. Get out towards the Flats. You'll be all right. But, for God's sake, keep to the south! I should hate you to run into De Wet after all the blasted trouble I've taken on your behalf. Now, get going. Take your gun, but for God's sake, only use it from now on to get meat. And don't stop till you reach safety.'

'What about Polly?'

'She's going with you.'

'Why?'

'Oh, for God's sake, why do you think? Why do you think she's willing to wait all night in those damn' mimosas in case you come? Now that you've blown a hole in me, she'll probably think I've failed, and go back. But I don't think so. She's not the type. You're luckier than I've ever been. She's tough and good and honest in spite of everything, and she deserves something better than you.'

'How do I know you're telling the truth?'

'Feel in my pockets, man. Empty 'em. There's as much food in 'em as I could get in. There are cartridges for the Mauser. It *is* a Mauser, isn't it? Take your water bottles and fill 'em at the stream as you go. Don't take anything else, though, nothing that'll hold you up. Polly's got all you're likely to want. She's got money, blankets, everything I could find. You'll be all right if you go now.'

Sammy leaned over him, dimmer somehow now. Winter could feel the blood running through his fingers as they clutched his broken shoulder and he winced once or twice as the boy emptied his pockets quickly, jerking at his body in his nervous hurry.

When he had finished, Sammy paused, staring at Winter. 'I ought to get you down there,' he said. 'Or somewhere where you can call for help.'

Winter turned his head away. 'Don't talk damn' silly. It'd give the game away at once.'

'Well, let me make you comfortable.'

'You'll be better advised to cut and run for it while you can, and stop wasting your time with me.'

'But that's an awful bad wound –'

' " 'Tis not so deep as a well, nor so wide as a church door".' Winter paused before he finished. ' "But 'tis enough",' he concluded quietly.

'Mr Winter, let me just – '

'In the name of God, man,' Winter croaked, 'go!'

The boy straightened up and Winter saw him slip away up into the heavens again, up among the battlemented crags of Sheba.

'As a matter of fact, Mr Winter,' he said slowly, 'I'm afraid it wouldn't be much good whatever I did.'

'I know that, you fool!'

'I'm – I'm sorry, Mr Winter.'

'Oh, keep your bloody condolences!'

'I'll go then now.'

Winter nodded, his face towards the rocks. He knew the boy was still standing alongside him, still watching him with those curious glittering eyes of his which were so deadly sharp behind a rifle.

'Are you still there?' he asked.

'Yes, Mr Winter. But I'm going now.'

'Give Poll my love.'

'You're a toff, Mr Winter.'

'That's what Poll said. I think there must be something in it, after all.'

He sensed the boy move away then, and heard the stones disturbed faintly by those soft veldschoen-clad feet of his, and he felt hysterically like laughing as he remembered his own clumsy efforts to move quietly.

As the little sounds died away, the pain came again, worse than ever now that his job was done and he had nothing to take his mind off it. He wanted to cry out with the agony of it, but he bit his lips feverishly, to hold back the cries.

He awakened after what seemed like a long sleep, feeling nothing and hearing nothing, silent, sunk in the deep sad loneliness of approaching death. At first he thought the day had come, for it seemed much lighter suddenly, then he realised it was only his imagination and that in actual fact he couldn't see much at all, that he was already standing with one foot on the other side of death.

He seemed to be looking down now from far up above, seeing the jagged slopes of Sheba in a brilliance of light, the veined granite rocks and the little valleys, and the scatter of equipment where Sammy had fought them all off so courageously. Beyond, there was the patch of mimosa and the thread of the stream, dark amber where it was stained by its iron-stone bed, and black where the rocks shone under the stars. In his imagination, he could see two small shapes heading out over the veld, two horses, two lonely people, heading westwards and never stopping...

He was in darkness again now, a rising darkness, opaque and unpierceable like floodwater rising in a cellar. For a while he stared, unmoving, absorbed. There seemed to be no sensation anywhere except for that fierce burning that extended down the whole of his right side, but even that was growing insubstantial now, and there was little else left except the mist...

fifteen

Sunrise at Sheba. It came in a faint creeping violet tinge of light in the east across the pure clear morning, throwing a purple haze over the land, touching hollows of the veld where the night mists still hung about. Then the purple turned to grey, a deep lavender grey that began to paint their faces with glowing light, and finally, the first hint of day reached the topmost spires of Sheba.

They had all been up and about some time now and Kitto, irritable and nervous, had had Sergeant Hadman and his gun crew standing by the little pom-pom long before it was light. The armoured car stood on its own in the shelter of the rocks, its gunner gripping the spade handle of the Lewis gun, his jaw clamped tight, his eyes moving backwards and forwards from the slopes of Sheba to where Kitto stood.

The fires had burned to flat beds of grey ashes now, touched in the centre with crimson, and the tent was down and packed. Nobody had known just why Kitto had insisted on striking camp with the first light, before the job was done, but it didn't exist any more now and the horses were saddled up and waiting. The Kaffir cooks were packing the lorry after their before-daylight breakfast, and the motorcars were standing in a row facing to the north, their engines warmed, and ready to go.

The wind had dropped and the last curls of smoke from the fires drifted to the east as the greyness touched the horses and men and machines with weary light.

The troopers were sprawled among the rocks at the foot of Sheba, their rifles in front of them, their eyes exploring the folds and crags of the slope in front, searching for the one from which the bullet might come which would stop them in their tracks. But they were all eager now. After the waiting of the previous day, they were all anxious to get it over and done with, and though most of them were decent men there was vengeance in the souls of all of them. Somehow, this ridiculous one-sided skirmish had lost the cold impersonality of a bigger battle. Here, they were all involved – each and every one of them – in the humiliation they had suffered in their defeat, and there was none of them who felt much mercy.

'Watch us put the kibosh on him this morning,' they were saying to each other.

The niceties of right and wrong and blame didn't dwell in their minds much. They had been hit and they were going to hit back. It was a natural military attitude and one that no one could quarrel with. Their only concern now was in seeing the affair brought to an end, not to inquire into the *ifs* and *whys* of it. They would be able to contemplate the battle-field when it was all over, with its splinter-scarred rocks, the yellow-green lyddite stains, and without doubt, they confidently expected, the body of their enemy, without having to answer the questions, 'Whose fault was it? Who started it? Could it have been avoided?' They were only doing their duty.

Kitto, Napoleonic in his strapped and buckled authority, draped with binoculars and compasses and revolver, the short crop in his hand, watched the first touch of light reach the peaks of Sheba and run down the slopes, and his eyes fastened on the two spire-like rocks where they had decided Sammy Schuter was hiding. He turned quickly, looking for Winter, thinking he might wish to watch, then he realised he had seen neither him nor the woman, Polly Bolt, since the previous night, and he wondered briefly where they were. Probably done a bunk, he thought casually. He'd heard some talk of a couple of horses going missing during the night and he wondered vaguely if Winter had ratted on them, and the woman had ratted on her gentleman friend up on Sheba and they had run away together.

Kitto's lip curled. There wasn't much to recommend either of them, he decided, both of them weak in morals and guts, neither of them measuring up to what Kitto regarded as a standard measure for decency. He shrugged and glanced up at Sheba again where he could see the black shapes of vultures hovering in the first streaks of light. Satisfied, he turned and moved to where Sergeant Hadman was standing by the pom-pom.

'I think we'll start now, Sergeant,' he said, nodding. 'Think you can drop me a few shells by those two spires?'

The sergeant nodded to the brightly-painted one-pound shells alongside him. 'Just been waiting the order, sir,' he said. 'That guy'll keep his head down all right when the hardware starts dropping round him. We'll have him outa there, toot sweet, you see.'

The crack of the gun made them jump, though they were all expecting it, from Kitto standing behind the weapon with Hoole, to Romanis and the men crouching among the rocks at the foot of Sheba, and the Kaffirs pushing the last of the equipment into the lorry.

They saw the first ranging shot burst viciously a few yards short of the two tall rocks, and the vultures who were hovering there wheeled and rose, floating easily among the topmost crags of the kopje. The sergeant turned to the gun crew and barked a short order, and the second shell burst directly on the rocks and the third just behind. They could see the livid greenish-yellow stain of the lyddite where they struck, marking the rocks in a garish streak, the oily cloud of smoke still drifting slowly like wraiths among the fissures, the flung fragments of stone whirling in erratic arcs over the smouldering grass which had been set alight by the explosions.

'Think that's found it, sir,' Hadman said. 'That's one for his nob, all right!'

'Keep them going,' Kitto said. 'Keep his head down.'

He lowered his glasses and walked deliberately out from behind the rocks where the gun was stationed, in full view from the top of Sheba.

'By Jesus, that's a cool 'un,' the sergeant said admiringly.

Kitto stood waiting for a second, then he called out: 'We'll try it now, Romanis,' he said.

He waved towards the armoured car and the Lewis gun began to rave towards the slopes, traversing the rocks, backwards and forwards along the line where they suspected their target lay. Bullets set the dust leaping everywhere, shredding the fleshy leaves of the cactus and sending the small stones flying.

Kitto watched for a while as the pom-pom shells flashed and sang among the granite spears and the Lewis bursts started little avalanches of dust, then he nodded towards Romanis and the men at the foot of the slope.

The movement forward was made slowly at first, uneasily, the men worming their way warily round the rocks, spread out on a wide front that would make shooting difficult, while the little gun dropped its shells tidily among the spires ahead of them every time they moved. Occasionally, one of the advancing troopers loosed off his rifle at an imagined target, but there was no reply, and as they gained confidence, they began to climb faster and faster until in the end, carried away by excitement, they were scrambling round the rocks, panting, cheering, indifferent to any possible danger.

Kitto saw the leaders reach a point just below the spires of rock, and they crowded together there for a moment, casting about like hounds after a scent. The slower climbers joined them, and one of them shouted and started waving, and a few of those who had gone beyond, stopped and turned back. Soon there was a whole group of them clustered together.

'Jesus Christ,' the sergeant said contemptuously from behind the gun, 'the sons-of-bitches'll never learn! They'll need to do better'n that if they come up against De Wet. Look at 'em, huddling together like a lot of sheep. If there was some guy with his wits about him, he could pick 'em all off without shifting his position. One shell'd bowl the lot over.'

The waving and shouting grew more general, and there was an urgency about Romanis' lanky figure as he swung his arms.

Kitto smiled. 'They've found him, Hoole,' he said, staring up at the waving men. 'You must have got him with your first shots, sergeant. Good shooting.'

'Thank you, sir.'

'I'd better go and identify him. You can limber up, now. We'll be moving off immediately.'

'Thank you, sir.'

They had all of them been so occupied with the shooting and the men scrambling up the hill, they had none of them seen the horseman who climbed out of the fold of ground behind their position. He wore the badge of Ackermann's troops, and his shaggy horse was as dust-caked as himself, its flanks raked into bloody streaks by his spurs. As Kitto started off up the first of the slopes in the direction of the waving men, the rider clattered past the cars, sawing at his mount's mouth, and swung round in a tight circle by the gun where he leapt from the saddle and confronted the sergeant.

'What in the name of God are you fooling about at here, man?' he demanded furiously.

The sergeant looked up at the thin-faced tired-eyed officer beside him and snapped to an instinctive salute.

'Where's Mr O'Hare?'

'Plummerton Sidings, sir,' Hadman said. 'They sent him in there yesterday with the other wounded.'

'Wounded? What in the name of Heaven do you mean? Who the hell are you fighting? What's going on up there?'

The sergeant gestured mutely towards Sheba but the officer bit off his reply.

'Didn't you get the message we sent last night? You should have been up with the column by now instead of acting the goat here. De Wet's out in force and hitting back and Ackermann wants his artillery up. God damn it, we lost him outside Waterbury last night, and that damn' gun might have saved the day.'

The sergeant stared up at Sheba helplessly.

'Who's in charge here, Sergeant?'

'Major Kitto, sir.'

'Kitto? So this is where the bloody old fool's been, is it? Still fighting his bloody Dhanzis, I suppose! Ackermann's been looking for him all over the place.'

The sergeant scratched his head and the officer glared at him.

'Did *he* get the message, Sergeant?'

The sergeant swore explosively. 'By God, sir, he musta! He musta got it last night. Someone came into camp. I saw him with me own two eyes. The old son-of-a-bitch musta had it all this time and didn't pass it on.'

The officer turned away. 'Never mind it now, Sergeant. We've work to do. They're still watching De Wet near Waterbury and he's finished if we get there in time. I'll attend to Mr Bloody Kitto later. Get moving, while I call the rest of the men in.'

Kitto paused as he reached the twin spires of rock, and turned just in time to see the horseman ride up to the gun and dismount. As he began his gesturing harangue with the

247

sergeant, Kitto guessed immediately that he was a messenger from the distant Ackermann in search of his missing gun.

Kitto frowned. His actions were going to take some explaining away under the circumstances, he knew, but he was aware of no uneasiness. In his own mind, he felt he had been right to do as he had done. No soldier worth his salt would quibble about his hitting out at someone who had hit at the army. The battle at Sheba would speak for itself. It was his excuse and it was his answer.

He stared down at the officer who was now climbing up the slopes after his men, noticing his infuriated face and the angry jerking of his legs. Then he shrugged and turned away to where Romanis was beckoning him.

The soldiers opened out to let him come through, and it was then he saw for the first time the body sprawled among the rocks, and realised that the battle at Sheba wasn't going to help him much after all, for the figure in the shabby shrunken suit was not Sammy Schuter, as he had confidently expected, but Francis Winter.

He lay on his side, as though embracing the ground, in that eager way that Kitto had seen so often with corpses, his left arm across him, clutching at the blackened wound in the right side of his chest. As Kitto approached, the flies which were crowding on a pool of drying blood rose, buzzing and loathsome. Then one of the troopers stepped forward with a thin blanket he had found higher up the slope.

'It's Winter,' Romanis said, and Kitto nodded, suddenly sickened.

Winter had defeated him in the end. As treacherous, as spineless and as morally useless as the boy for whom he had given his life, he had cheated all along on every moral ground he could think up and now, here, he had committed the ultimate act of perfidy, accusing him still from the shadows he'd gone to.

They'd blame the whole thing on him, Kitto decided resentfully – the tracking which had become a headlong chase, the death of Plummer, all the wounding and killing, the delaying of the gun when it was needed up north, everything, the sunset of Offy's empire even, which would certainly crumble now that it hadn't Offy's sure hands to hold it together. It was probably cracking already, like some toppling edifice. Already, they would know of his death in Johannesburg and Kimberley and Cape Town, and all the greedy financial vultures whom Kitto, in his bleak conception of honesty, hated, would come to pick up the pieces and see what they could get out of it.

When they'd finished, there would be precious little left, and nothing at all for Kitto, except a damaged reputation. His incredible awful luck had caught up with him again, he thought bitterly, that appalling luck which had dogged him ever since the day in Dhanziland thirty years before when he had become famous overnight. It never crossed his mind for a moment that courage alone had never been enough.

He squared his shoulders, sure of himself in his self-righteous sense of honour. There would be inquiries, he thought bitterly, and a lot of people to offer censures and reprimands, most of them people who didn't know soldiering and had never tried it. It was the old, old story all over again. If he'd been successful, nobody would have worried, and facts might even have been hushed up. Because he was unsuccessful, he would disappear into the limbo of the defeated, the soldier who hadn't managed to do what he'd set out to do. History always remembered the heroes and forgot the hard-working unknowns of Thermopylae and Trafalgar and Waterloo.

Kitto straightened up, the everlasting subaltern, arrogant, sure of himself, honest in his conception of duty, unafraid of the consequences and unashamed of his actions. He nodded at the man with the blanket and pointed with his crop.

'Better bring him down,' he said.

He looked round at Sheba, now bright and glaring in the full light of day, staring about him almost as though he were a conqueror. It was here on Sheba that the sun had set on Offy Plummer's empire as surely as if some vast plot to destroy it had been hatched among these rocky krantzes. And with it into the shadows had gone Winter and Offy and Kitto's laggard career. The sun had gone down on the lot of them.

He faced down the slope, his thin handsome face set and unafraid. Romanis and Hoole were watching him silently, knowing what he was thinking, but there was no indication of uneasiness about him as he flicked at his riding boots and set off to meet the angry-eyed officer who was climbing up to meet him.

The sun peered higher, flaming in crimson and gold behind the eastern folds of land and throwing dagger-like glints across the horizon, then it seemed to float abruptly above the curve of the earth and flooded the veld with a miraculous liquid amber, reaching down at last to the escarpment at the bottom of Sheba and touching everything with light.

John Harris

China Seas

In this action-packed adventure, Willie Sarth becomes a survivor. Forced to fight pirates on the East China Seas, wrestle for his life on the South China Seas and cross the Sea of Japan ravaged by typhus, Sarth is determined to come out alive. Dealing with human tragedy, war and revolution, Harris presents a novel which packs an awesome punch.

A Funny Place to Hold a War

Ginger Donnelly is on the trail of Nazi saboteurs in Sierra Leone. Whilst taking a midnight paddle, with a willing woman, in a canoe cajoled from a local fisherman, Donnelly sees an enormous seaplane thunder across the sky only to crash in a ball of brilliant flame. It seems like an accident... at least until a second plane explodes in a blistering shower along the same flight path.

JOHN HARRIS

LIVE FREE OR DIE!

Charles Walter Scully, cut off from his unit and running on empty, is trapped. It's 1944 and, though the Allied invasion of France has finally begun, for Scully the war isn't going well. That is, until he meets a French boy trying to get home to Paris. What begins is a hair-raising journey into the heart of France, an involvement with the French Liberation Front and one of the most monumental events of the war. Harris vividly portrays wartime France in a panorama of scenes that enthral and entertain the reader.

THE OLD TRADE OF KILLING

Harris' exciting adventure is set against the backdrop of the Western Desert and scene of the Eighth Army battles. The men who fought together in the Second World War return twenty years later in search of treasure. But twenty years can change a man. Young ideals have been replaced by greed. Comradeship has vanished along with innocence. And treachery and murder make for a breathtaking read.

JOHN HARRIS

THE SEA SHALL NOT HAVE THEM

This is John Harris' classic war novel of espionage in the most extreme of situations. An essential flight from France leaves the crew of RAF *Hudson* missing, and somewhere in the North Sea four men cling to a dinghy, praying for rescue before exposure kills them or the enemy finds them. One man is critically injured; another (a rocket expert) is carrying a briefcase stuffed with vital secrets. As time begins to run out each man yearns to evade capture. This story charts the daring and courage of these men, and the men who rescued them, in a breathtaking mission with the most awesome of consequences.

TAKE OR DESTROY!

Lieutenant-Colonel George Hockold must destroy Rommel's vast fuel reserves stored at the port of Qaba if the Eighth Army is to succeed in the Alamein offensive. Time is desperately running out, resources are scant and the commando unit Hockold must lead is a ragtag band of misfits scraped from the dregs of the British Army. They must attack Qaba. The orders? Take or destroy.

'One of the finest war novels of the year'
– *Evening News*

TITLES BY JOHN HARRIS AVAILABLE DIRECT
FROM HOUSE OF STRATUS

Quantity		£	$(US)	$(CAN)	€
☐	ARMY OF SHADOWS	6.99	12.95	19.95	13.50
☐	CHINA SEAS	6.99	12.95	19.95	13.50
☐	THE CLAWS OF MERCY	6.99	12.95	19.95	13.50
☐	CORPORAL COTTON'S LITTLE WAR	6.99	12.95	19.95	13.50
☐	THE CROSS OF LAZZARO	6.99	12.95	19.95	13.50
☐	FLAWED BANNER	6.99	12.95	19.95	13.50
☐	THE FOX FROM HIS LAIR	6.99	12.95	19.95	13.50
☐	A FUNNY PLACE TO HOLD A WAR	6.99	12.95	19.95	13.50
☐	GETAWAY	6.99	12.95	19.95	13.50
☐	HARKAWAY'S SIXTH COLUMN	6.99	12.95	19.95	13.50
☐	A KIND OF COURAGE	6.99	12.95	19.95	13.50
☐	LIVE FREE OR DIE!	6.99	12.95	19.95	13.50
☐	THE LONELY VOYAGE	6.99	12.95	19.95	13.50
☐	THE MERCENARIES	6.99	12.95	19.95	13.50
☐	NORTH STRIKE	6.99	12.95	19.95	13.50

ALL HOUSE OF STRATUS BOOKS ARE AVAILABLE FROM GOOD BOOKSHOPS
OR DIRECT FROM THE PUBLISHER:

Internet: www.houseofstratus.com including synopses and features.

Email: sales@houseofstratus.com
info@houseofstratus.com
(please quote author, title and credit card details.)

TITLES BY JOHN HARRIS AVAILABLE DIRECT
FROM HOUSE OF STRATUS

Quantity		£	$(US)	$(CAN)	€
	THE OLD TRADE OF KILLING	6.99	12.95	19.95	13.50
	PICTURE OF DEFEAT	6.99	12.95	19.95	13.50
	THE QUICK BOAT MEN	6.99	12.95	19.95	13.50
	RIDE OUT THE STORM	6.99	12.95	19.95	13.50
	RIGHT OF REPLY	6.99	12.95	19.95	13.50
	ROAD TO THE COAST	6.99	12.95	19.95	13.50
	THE SEA SHALL NOT HAVE THEM	6.99	12.95	19.95	13.50
	THE SLEEPING MOUNTAIN	6.99	12.95	19.95	13.50
	SMILING WILLIE AND THE TIGER	6.99	12.95	19.95	13.50
	SO FAR FROM GOD	6.99	12.95	19.95	13.50
	THE SPRING OF MALICE	6.99	12.95	19.95	13.50
	SWORDPOINT	6.99	12.95	19.95	13.50
	TAKE OR DESTROY!	6.99	12.95	19.95	13.50
	THE THIRTY DAYS WAR	6.99	12.95	19.95	13.50
	THE UNFORGIVING WIND	6.99	12.95	19.95	13.50
	UP FOR GRABS	6.99	12.95	19.95	13.50
	VARDY	6.99	12.95	19.95	13.50

ALL HOUSE OF STRATUS BOOKS ARE AVAILABLE FROM GOOD BOOKSHOPS
OR DIRECT FROM THE PUBLISHER:

Tel:	**Order Line** **0800 169 1780** (UK) **800 724 1100** (USA) **International** **+44 (0) 1845 527700** (UK) **+01 845 463 1100** (USA)
Fax:	**+44 (0) 1845 527711** (UK) **+01 845 463 0018** (USA) (please quote author, title and credit card details.)
Send to:	**House of Stratus Sales Department** **House of Stratus Inc.** **Thirsk Industrial Park** **2 Neptune Road** **York Road, Thirsk** **Poughkeepsie** **North Yorkshire, YO7 3BX** **NY 12601** **UK** **USA**

PAYMENT

Please tick currency you wish to use:

☐ £ (Sterling)   ☐ $ (US)   ☐ $ (CAN)   ☐ € (Euros)

Allow for shipping costs charged per order plus an amount per book as set out in the tables below:

CURRENCY/DESTINATION

	£(Sterling)	$(US)	$(CAN)	€(Euros)
Cost per order				
UK	1.50	2.25	3.50	2.50
Europe	3.00	4.50	6.75	5.00
North America	3.00	3.50	5.25	5.00
Rest of World	3.00	4.50	6.75	5.00
Additional cost per book				
UK	0.50	0.75	1.15	0.85
Europe	1.00	1.50	2.25	1.70
North America	1.00	1.00	1.50	1.70
Rest of World	1.50	2.25	3.50	3.00

PLEASE SEND CHEQUE OR INTERNATIONAL MONEY ORDER
payable to: HOUSE OF STRATUS LTD or HOUSE OF STRATUS INC. or card payment as indicated

STERLING EXAMPLE

Cost of book(s):...................... Example: 3 x books at £6.99 each: £20.97
Cost of order: .... Example: £1.50 (Delivery to UK address)
Additional cost per book:.............. Example: 3 x £0.50: £1.50
Order total including shipping:.......... Example: £23.97

VISA, MASTERCARD, SWITCH, AMEX:

☐☐☐☐☐☐☐☐☐☐☐☐☐☐☐☐☐☐

Issue number (Switch only):

☐☐☐

Start Date: Expiry Date:

☐☐/☐☐   ☐☐/☐☐

Signature: _____

NAME: _____

ADDRESS: _____

COUNTRY: _____

ZIP/POSTCODE: _____

Please allow 28 days for delivery. Despatch normally within 48 hours.

Prices subject to change without notice.
Please tick box if you do not wish to receive any additional information. ☐

House of Stratus publishes many other titles in this genre; please check our website (**www.houseofstratus.com**) for more details.